WIND

ALSO BY LEIGH ALLISON WILSON:

SHORT STORIES
FROM THE BOTTOM UP

WIND
STORIES

LEIGH ALLISON WILSON

WILLIAM MORROW
and Company, Inc.
New York

The author wishes to thank The Copernicus Foundation and the Iowa Writers' Workshop for the assistance provided by a James A. Michener Fellowship; gratitude goes as well to the New York State Council on the Arts for its assistance at a timely moment. Also, the author would like to thank Margaret Attenborough, Lane LeRoy, Robert O'Connor, Alan Filreis, Katie Estill, Elizabeth McKee, and, of course, Daniel Woodrell for their generous support during the writing of this book.

Library of Congress Cataloging-in-Publication Data

Wilson, Leigh Allison.
    Wind: stories / Leigh Allison Wilson.
        p.   cm.
    Contents: Massé—Where she was—Missing persons—Obscene callers—Women in the kingdom—Wind.
    ISBN 0-688-08111-8
    I. Title.
PS3573.I459W56   1989
813'.54—dc19
                                                            88-21659
                                                            CIP

Printed in the United States of America

First Edition

1 2 3 4 5 6 7 8 9 10

BOOK DESIGN BY RICHARD ORIOLO

For Jane Anne and Jane

CONTENTS

Between farewell and the absence of farewell,
The final mercy and the final loss,
The wind and the sudden falling of the wind.

–WALLACE STEVENS,
from "Like Decorations in a Nigger Cemetery"

WIND

MASSÉ

❦

The truth is it's not much of a city. When I moved in two years ago, all I knew about it was from a Chamber of Commerce brochure I got free at the courthouse: WELCOME, it said, TO THE BIG CITY IN THE LITTLE VALLEY BY THE LAKE. I had six suitcases in the back of my car and $350 and a good reason for leaving the place I'd left. For a woman like me, that's all people need to know. You start explaining things too much, you start giving heartfelt reasons for this and for that, and then nothing becomes clear and people don't trust you and you start looking at your life from bad angles. I like things clear. But the truth is it's not much of a city, not much of a valley, and you have to drive five miles to get to the lake. These are simple facts.

In the brochure they said the population was twenty thousand, but it is really closer to sixteen or seventeen. One problem is that most of the Chamber of Commerce live outside town, in big houses on the lake, and so maybe they don't come into the city much, to get the accurate head count. One thing I'm good at is counting. On Sunday nights at the local P&C grocery, the average customer head count is twenty-six; on weekdays it is fifty-four after five o'clock. I can tell you the price of leaded gas at ten different stations, the price of unleaded at seven of them. Anytime you get good at something, it's because of a habit; counting things is just a habit with me. Last week I counted twelve geese heading for Canada in two perfect lines, a perfect V, and twelve is enough to prove that spring is coming. You can sometimes live a good life figuring angles and counting things, if you're in the habit of it.

What I've done for the last two years is, I drive a UPS truck during the day and I play pool at night. I have had some trouble lately, but not because of the UPS or the pool. You might think that these are things that women don't do—drive trucks for a living, that is, and play pool—but I do them, and so you probably just don't know enough women. Take into account enough numbers, anything is possible. Phineas says that the opposite is true, that given enough numbers nothing is possible, but he is a bartender who doesn't like crowds. Very little he says makes any sense. I've been seeing him off and on for the past six months, mostly off.

I met him, as I said, about six months ago, when all the trouble started. It was November, but a clear day, and the wind was gusting to forty miles per hour. I know because I listen to the radio in my truck. Every street I drove down that day had hats in the air, like a parade, from all the wind. This is what you could call an economically depressed town, which means that everybody in it is depressed about money, so I remember that November day's weather in particular. It was the only time I have ever seen anything like a celebration on the streets, all those hats in the air and everybody running after them, their faces as red and distorted as those of any winning crowd on television. I do not own a television, but all the bars have them. There are thirty-three bars in this city, and only nine have regulation pool tables. This is just a fact of life.

That day I was behind in my deliveries, although mostly I am punctual to a fault. I have a map of the city inlaid like a tattoo in my mind—where the easy right-hand turns are, where the short lights are, where the children play in the streets and thus become obstacles. I had to memorize the map in the Chamber of Commerce brochure to get the job, but anyone can tell you that maps like that are useless to a good driver. Maps are flat; cities are not. Obstacles are everywhere, but the good driver knows where they are and how to avoid them. Picture the city as a big pool table, right after the break in eight ball. Your opponent's balls surround you, like seven stop signs all over the table. You must deliver the goods in a timely fashion. Knowing the correct angles is everything. The simple truth is I know all the angles in this town. But that day I was behind in my deliveries and Danny, the dispatcher, kept coming over the radio, kidding around.

"You're late, you're late," he said. "Frankly, I'm appalled. Frankly, your ass is in a slingshot." He was in his silly-serious mood, jazzing around with the radio, bored to death with his job. He used to be a big shot on some high school football team in the city, but that was years ago, and although he is still a huge, bruised-looking man, the only big shots in his life now come from bars. He drinks too much is my meaning, but in a town like this that goes without saying.

"It's the wind," I told him, clicking the mike. "It's the wind and about fifty zillion hats. I'm not kidding, there's exactly a hundred fifty hats out here today."

"Ignore 'em," he said. "Run 'em down," he said. His voice came out high and crackly, as though any minute he might burst into weird, witchlike laughter. Radios do this to everybody's voice.

"What's the matter with you?" I asked, but I could tell that he'd already signed off, was already kidding around with another truck, his big body hunched over the radio back at the office, surrounded by boxes and handcarts and no windows anywhere. Danny's life is highly unclear. Once I tried to teach him pool, to show him a few straightforward things about the game. He handled the cue stick the way lips handle a toothpick, all muscle and no control, then he tried a crazy massé shot that was all wrong for the situation and ended up tearing the felt of the table. Finesse and control are the names of the game in pool, but he would have none of it. They kicked him out of the bar. I ran the table twelve straight games after he left and picked up about seventy dollars—a very good night for me.

I made my last delivery at about four o'clock, the wind buffeting the truck every yard of the way. Usually I am punctual, but the fact is the elements are an important factor in any driving job. That day the wind was a factor. For another thing, there is always the customer factor. If your customer is in a hurry, he just grabs a pen or pencil and lets it rip; you get an unclear address and end up wasting precious minutes. My advice is, always use a typewriter. That way there is nothing personal to get in the way of the timely execution of your business. Chaos is no man's friend; clarity is everything.

I parked the truck in the lot at four-thirty, tied up some

loose ends inside the office, then went outside to my car. It is a '73 navy Impala with a lot of true grit. Most people picture a good car and they think of bright color or sleek line or some other spiffy feature. This is all wrong. The best part of a good car, what makes it a good car, is its guts: pistons that never miss a beat; a carburetor so finely tuned it is like a genius chemist, mixing air and gasoline as if from beakers; a transmission that works smoothly, the gears meshing like lovers. This Impala has guts; even Phineas says so. I drove home and on the way counted smokestacks, eight of them, all rising above town in the shape of cigars stuck on end. Then something strange happened.

I was driving past the pet shop where I buy fish, only six blocks from my apartment. Up ahead the street was empty as an old Western set except for a few newspapers, seized by the wind, that tented up in the air, then fell and lay flat on the pavement. Along the sidewalks on both sides telephone poles stretched way into a distance I couldn't quite see. Maybe being late that day had me all worked up. I don't know. But I began to imagine bank shots with my car. I began to figure out at exactly what angle I would have to hit a telephone pole in order to bank the car across the street and into the pole on the other side. Then I began to do it with buildings— double banks into doorways, caroms off two fireplugs and into a brick wall, a massé around a parked car and into the plate glass of the corner drugstore. By the time I parked at my apartment, the knuckles of my hands were pale on the wheel.

Overhead, slightly distorted by the windshield, I could see Mrs. McDaniels, my landlady, leaning over the second-floor railing of my apartment building, her eyes magnified by bifocals and staring straight down, it seemed, onto my knuck-les. I put my hands in my lap and stared back at her. She is a businesslady, never misses a trick; she calls all of us tenants her "clientele," just as if she were the madam of a whore-house. The apartment building looks like one of those ten-dollar-a-night motels—two stories with lines of doors opening onto a common walkway that has a wrought-iron railing down the length of it. But Mrs. McDaniels runs a tight ship, no monkey business.

"Have you tried goldfish?" she called down when I got out of the car. "My sister says she has goldfish you couldn't kill with a hammer."

"I think so, I don't know," I called back. My hands were shaking so much I had to put them in the trouser pockets of my uniform, fisting them up in there. When I got up to the second floor, I began it again, this time with Mrs. McDaniels —I figured I'd have to put a lot of left English on my body in order to graze Mrs. McDaniels and whisk her toward the right, into the doorway of my apartment. I brought out a fist with my keys in it.

"You're late," she said, her eyes large and shrewd as a bear's. "Are you drunk or what?"

I quit listing sideways, then jiggled the keys. "No," I told her. "Just a dizzy spell. It's from sitting down all day. All the blood goes to my butt or something."

"Goldfish," she said, sniffing the air around me until, apparently satisfied, she moved to the side so I could get to my door. "Well?" she asked, and she asked it again, "Well?" For a moment I thought Mrs. McDaniels wanted to shake my hand, then I noticed the Baggie of water between her fingers. In it two goldfish held themselves as rigid and motionless as dead things. And they might as well have been, because I knew right then that they were doomed.

"I don't know," I told her, opening the door with one arm so that she could go inside ahead of me. "I think I tried goldfish first thing."

Once inside the room Mrs. McDaniels began to war with herself. She prides herself on being someone who is easygoing and friendly with her tenants, but when she gets inside your apartment, she can't help herself. Those eyes behind the glasses glaze over with suspicion, search for holes in the plaster, gashes in the parquet. My apartment is one large room, with a kitchenette and a bathroom off it, a couch, a card table, three chairs, a bed, a dresser, and a fish tank. She went directly over to the couch, studying my new poster of Minnesota Fats.

"You're fixing the place up," she said suspiciously.

"I used the special glue, Mrs. McDaniels. It doesn't peel the paint."

"Oh!" she cried. "I don't mind at all, not at all. Not *me.*" I could see that good humor and business were tearing Mrs. McDaniels apart, but finally business won out and she pulled a top corner of the poster away from the wall. It came away cleanly, just as the advertisement for the glue had predicted, though after that the corner bent over and didn't stay stuck anymore. "Silly me," she cried gaily. She was in high spirits now. "I really like that poster."

For a year and a half I had lived in the apartment without anything on the walls. Every time Mrs. McDaniels came inside, she'd say, "You live like a transient, just like a transient." And I always said, "I like things neat." And I did. But this Minnesota Fats poster caught my eye. In it Fats is crouched over the cue ball, looking into the side pocket, which is where the camera is. You don't see the side pocket, you just see Fats looking squint-eyed at you, looking at you as if he knew a pretty good trick or two. And he does. The poster cost me two-fifty but was worth every penny.

"I think I tried goldfish about a year ago," I told her. "They didn't last."

"You never know," she said. "I think these guys are winners." She held up the Baggie and studied the fish for flaws. I did not bother to look at them; I knew. They were already as good as dead.

When I first moved in, the fish tank had been the only piece of furniture in the room, if you can call a fish tank furniture. The tenant before me had skipped out on his rent but had left the tank as a kind of so-long gesture. Inside there was even a fish, still alive, roaming from one end of the tank to the other. It was rat-colored, about three inches long, with yellow freckles all over its sides—an ugly, sour-looking fish. I called it The Rockfish. After a month or so, I got to thinking maybe it was lonely, maybe loneliness had made it go ugly and sour, and so I went down to the pet store for some companions to put into the tank. The guy there gave me two angelfish —two pert, brightly colored fish that he said got along famously with each other and with just about anybody else. I put them in with The Rockfish and waited for something to happen. The next day I thought to look in the tank, but there was no sign of the angelfish, not a trace, just The Rockfish patrolling all the corners. After that I tried every kind of fish in the pet store—guppies, gobies, glassfish, neons, swordtails, even a catfish bigger than The Rockfish. They all just vanished, as if the tank had pockets. Mrs. McDaniels became obsessed when I told her about it. From then on nothing would do but that we find a fish good enough to go the distance in the tank. We didn't know whether The Rockfish was a male or a female or some sort of neuter, but we tried everything again: hes, shes, its, they all disappeared. Soon I wished I had never told Mrs. McDaniels anything about it, because I could tell she was beginning to associate me with the fish. She started dropping hints about what a man could do for a woman around the house, about how a woman like me could use a good man to straighten out her life. I just told her I already had all the angles figured, thank you, and that a good man wasn't hard to find if you were looking for one, which I wasn't.

"Listen," said Mrs. McDaniels, shaking the Baggie. "My sister says these guys don't know the meaning of death. They're right from her own tank. She should know."

"She should," I said, "but frankly, Mrs. McDaniels, I think they're dead meat."

"When are you settling down?" she asked absently. She was bent over the tank, flicking the glass in front of The Rockfish, her glasses pressed right up against it. I wondered then, because it seemed strange, whether Mrs. McDaniels's eyes, magnified by the glasses and the glass of the tank, whether her eyes might look huge as billiard balls to The Rockfish. No mistake, it had to be a strange sight from that angle. "Here's hoping," she said. Then she dumped the gold-fish in. They floated for a few seconds, eye to eye with The Rockfish, but then they seemed to glance at each other and, before you could blink, the both of them shot down the length of the tank and huddled behind a piece of pink coral, sucking the glass in the corner for all they were worth.

"They know," I said. "One look and they knew."

"Look at the bright side," she said. "Nothing's happened yet."

"Not yet. But nothing ever happens when you're looking. It waits till you're at work or shopping or daydreaming or something—that's when it all happens."

"A big girl like you," she said, giving me the once-over, "ought to be married is what you ought to be."

"Thanks for the fish, Mrs. McDaniels." I showed her to the door.

"Listen. Keep me posted. My sister says they're tough buggers, says they can eat nails."

"I'll keep you posted," I said, then I shut the door. For some reason, I began to snicker like crazy as soon as Mrs. McDaniels left. I went over to the tank, snickering, but The Rockfish only hung in the middle, sedate and ugly as sin. The two goldfish were still sucking away in the corner. I had to lie down on the bed to keep from snickering. For a few minutes I thought maybe I was having a heart attack. There were these pins and needles in my arms and legs, this pain in my chest, but then it all went away after a while. I lay like a stick on the bed, trying to get some sleep, counting my breaths to relax a little. Maybe being late had me worked up. Usually I got through work at two in the afternoon, home by two-thirty, but that day I was all off. I couldn't relax and I kept thinking about how I couldn't, which of course just made things worse and aggravated me and gave me the feeling I was in a fix for good. I got to thinking, then, that my life was going to take a turn for the bad, that somehow I would be off-balance and out of step for the rest of whatever was coming. Across the room I could see the unclear, rat-colored shape of The Rockfish swimming the length of the tank, banking off the far walls, then swimming back again at the same latitude, back and forth, patrolling. And I wondered, to keep from snickering, to ward off the heart attack, I wondered if it knew I was watching. Did it know I kept count of things going on in the tank? Did it know I had all its angles figured, its habits memorized? Did it think I'd almost masséd my car around a fireplug and into a telephone pole? Did it think I was a friend?

I slept like a dead man, because I didn't wake up until around ten-thirty that night, my neck twisted at an odd, painful angle. The only light in the room came from the phosphorescent green glow of the fish tank. Mrs. McDaniels must have switched the tank light on earlier, because I almost never did. It gave me the creeps, as if the tank were the window onto some obscene green world where the tiniest ripple had profound ramifications, the kind of world you always suspect might happen to you suddenly, like kingdom come, if you lost all your habits. You lose your habits, and then you can kiss everything you've gotten good at goodbye.

I got out of bed, but things were still off somehow; the feeling of things gone wrong was like a fur on my tongue. Usually I got home at two-thirty, ate something, then slept until about ten o'clock, when business at the pool tables got going good. But that day I'd overslept and was late to begin with, and I knew as if I'd been through it before—which I hadn't—that trouble was just beginning. All I did was grab my keys and I was out of the apartment, almost sprinting to my car. Outside the wind grabbed hold, but I tucked my chin against it until I was inside the car, gripping the wheel and breathing hard. I figured by hurrying I could get a jump on whatever might come next, though when trouble comes, mistake number one is hurrying. I knew that, but I hurried just the same.

On the way to the bar I kept my mind on driving, no funny business. There are nine bars in this town with regulation pool tables, and I always go to a different one each night, until I have to start over again. That night I was due for a bar called The Office, which is a nice enough place if you can stand seeing typewriters and other office equipment hanging on the walls. Oddly enough, it is a favorite hangout for secretaries during cocktail hours. They seem to like the idea of getting drunk surrounded by the paraphernalia of their daily lives. At night, though, the clientele switches over to factory workers and middle-level management types—supervisors, foremen—and you can pick up a nice piece of change. All the way to The Office I kept myself rigid as a fence post. Only one thing happened. I was passing the button factory, a big yellow building with two smokestacks that went at it all the time, burning bad buttons maybe. It struck me, as I passed, that those smokestacks looked a lot like pool cues aimed right for the sky—that's all I thought, which was strange, but nothing to knock you off-balance. Nothing like banking your car off buildings. I'd even begun to think I could relax a little by the time I got to the bar.

Because The Office is situated among gas stations and retail stores, it gave off the only light on the block except for occasional streetlamps. The plate glass in front glowed yellow like a small sunset surrounded by nothing at all and out in the middle of nowhere, the kind of sunset people plan dream vacations around, and a sure recipe for disappointment. For a moment I thought better of the whole thing, almost turned around and went home, but the fact of the matter was, I knew that if I did all was lost, because once you gave in you kept on giving in. A good habit is as easily lost and forgotten as hope for a better shake in things. So I went on into the bar.

As soon as I got inside I thought it would be all right. The two tables were busy, mostly guys in blue workshirts rolled up to the elbows, holding the cues like shotguns. It was promising because anyone in town recognized the blue work-shirts. They came from the nuclear power plant up on the lake, the one that might or might not ever get built, which meant they had money and didn't much mind throwing it away on a fifty-fifty possibility. I had played a foreman from the power plant once, a year before, and during the course of the game he explained that even though the job was dan-gerous half the time, the money they got was the real health hazard. "More of our men die from drunk driving," he said, "than from touching the wrong wire," and he said it in a proud, bareknuckled sort of way. He was an electrical engi-neer from East Tennessee, where he said anything that hap-pened had to happen big or else nobody noticed it from one valley to the next. I took him for twenty dollars, then he got unfriendly. But that's the way with those guys: They see a woman playing pool and they automatically assume a fifty-fifty chance, usually more. Then they get unfriendly when they see you've got a good habit. They just don't know enough women. Numbers count.

In The Office, to get to the pool tables you have to finesse your way through about twenty tables full of people who have had too much to drink. Cigarettes, flitting through the air on the tail end of a good story, are obstacles, and so are wayward elbows and legs. One sure sign that you're drunk is if you're in somebody's way. But I got through that part.

I made a beeline for Bernie, who was chalking his cue at the second table, the good table, the one with a roll you could figure.

"You are tardy," he said in his formal way, still chalking his cue. Sometime during his life, Bernie had been a school-teacher: astronomy. On certain nights he'd take you outside and point out the constellations, his old nicotine-stained fingers pointing toward the stars. He knew his stuff. And he knew pool, too, except for a tendency to grow passionate at the least provocation, a tendency that combined with old age and Jack Daniel's was ruining his game. Given a population of sixteen or seventeen thousand, Bernie was the only rival I had in town. But we never played together, sometimes never saw each other for weeks; we just appreciated the habits we'd both gotten into.

"You are tardy," he repeated, giving me a dark look. "And the stars are out tonight." He meant that people were spending money like nobody's business.

"I think it's the wind," I told him. "I think there's something funny in the wind."

"Ha!" Bernie cried. He put down the chalk and picked up his cigarette, puffing on it. Then, in a cloud of smoke, he wheeled around to the table, brought up his cue, and nailed the eight ball on a bank into the side pocket, easy as you please. It threw his opponent all off. His opponent had on a blue workshirt that was either too small for him on purpose or else was the biggest size they had: His muscles showed through the material as though he were wearing no shirt at all. On the table only one ball was left, sitting right in front of a corner pocket, and by the look on the guy's face you could tell he'd figured he had the old man on the run, the game sewn up. What he didn't know was that Bernie's opponents in eight ball always had only one ball left on the table. But the guy was a good sport and paid his ten dollars without muscling around or banging his cue on the floor. Sometimes with your big guys chaos is their only response to losing. It is just a fact of life.

"That is that," Bernie said, putting the ten into his wallet. "The table is all yours."

"Where you going?" Bernie always stayed at the tables until about midnight, and if he was around, I just watched and took pointers, waiting for him to get tired and go home before I got busy. Usually I took over where he left off. "It's only eleven," I said, "and you say the stars are out."

"I have a granddaughter coming in on the midnight train." He made a face that meant he was tickled pink, the corners of his mouth stretched and stained with a half-million cigarettes. "All pink and yellow, like a little doll. She can point out Venus on the horizon with her eyes shut. A beautiful girl. You should meet her."

"Maybe I will."

"Seven years old and she knows the difference between Arcturus and Taurus. For Christmas last year, do you know what she told her mother she wanted? Guess what she wanted."

"A pool cue," I said, which was exactly what I would have asked for.

"No, you are insane. A telescope! She said she wanted to get close to the sky, close enough to touch it. She's no bigger than a flea and she asks for a telescope!" Bernie slapped his palms together, then sidled closer. "Between us, she is a genius, has to be. My granddaughter, a genius."

"You must be proud of her," I said. All of a sudden I wanted Bernie out of the bar. His very breath smelled like trouble. Then I noticed his shot glass of Jack Daniel's was missing from the stool he usually kept it on; he was sober as a judge. I wanted Bernie gone.

"Oh, she is going places, I can feel it. I can *feel* it!" He slapped his palms together again, bouncing on his feet a little, then he swung toward the men in the workshirts and opened his arms enough to include me in the sweep of them. "Gentlemen, I leave you with this young lady as my proxy. Do not be fooled by her gender." He looked at me appraisingly. "Do not be fooled by the uniform. She can handle herself."

"Thanks, Bernie," I said, but I didn't look at him then, and I didn't look at him when he left. Instead I looked at all the guys in blue workshirts. At first they each one had an expression of irritation and rebellion: They didn't like the idea of me usurping command of the table just because the winner knew me. And I didn't blame them, except that the next expression on each of their faces was a familiar one.

"All right, George, you're up," one of them said. "Take her and then let's us get serious," he said, which was exactly what I had expected from their expressions. I could read these guys like a brochure. Any other night I would have grinned and aw-shucksed around, leading them on a little bit. I might have even offered to wait my turn, humbling myself to the point of idiocy, until they said, "No, you go on, honey," gallantry making idiots of them, too. That night, though, something was wrong with me. For one thing, the whole day had been all wrong. For another, seeing Bernie sober and giddy as a billy goat really threw me. I hadn't known he had a granddaughter or a daughter or even a wife. I'd never seen him sober. Something about it all set me going again. I imagined flinging myself headlong into the knot of blue workshirts, sending them all flying to the far corners of The Office, like a good break.

"OK, little lady," said the one named George, winking and grinning to his friends. "Let's see how you deliver." He could not contain himself. "Did you hear that? Did you hear what I just said? I said, I asked her, 'Let's see how you deliver.'"

They all snorted, stamping their cues on the end of their boots, and I regretted not changing out of my uniform. It was a bad sign because I'd never worn it to the bars before, just one result of hurrying trouble. You never knew when somebody might take a wild hair and try to mess up your job, somebody with a poor attitude toward losing and a bad disposition and a need for spreading chaos. I felt dizzy for a minute, as though I'd been submerged in water and couldn't make the transition.

"Winners break," George said. Now he was all business, ready to get the game over with so he could play with his friends. He strutted around, flexing his workshirt. Most nights, when I had the break, I would try to sink a couple, then leave the cue ball in a safe position, ducking my chin and smirking shamefacedly, as though I'd miscalculated. The point is, never let the guys waiting in line see that your game in no way depends on luck; it scares them if you do, shrinks their pockets like a cold shower, so to speak. But that night I was crazy, must have been. George went into an elaborate explanation of how he had to go to the bathroom but would be back before his turn, how I'd never even know he was gone. I said, "Five bucks." He rolled his eyes comically, performing for his friends, then said it was all right by him. "You're the boss, Chuck," he said. I don't know what got into me. Before George was out of sight, I broke and sank two stripes. Then I hammered in the rest of them, taking maybe three seconds between each shot. By the time old George could zip up his pants, I'd cleared the table.

"Fucking-A," said one of George's friends.

"Whoa," another one said. "Holy whoa."

It was a dream, that whole game was a dream. I had read somewhere that a sure sign of madness was when life took on a dreamlike quality, when you started manipulating what you saw as easily as you manipulate dreams. Those pins and needles came back into my feet, prickly as icicles. George came back, too. I figured the night was over. They would all get pissed off and quit playing and begin to attend to their beers. But—surprise—they ate it up, practically started a brawl over who was up next. It wasn't anything you could have predicted. I guess it pumped them up with adrenaline, or else with a kind of competitive meanness, because for the rest of the night they banged the balls with a vengeance. They were none too polite, and that's a fact. Whatever happened during those games happened in a dream. A wad of five-dollar bills began to show through the back pocket of my uniform trousers. The guys in blue workshirts were like a buzzing of hornets around me, their faces getting drunker and redder every hour.

Near closing time, around two in the morning, George came back for a last game. I'd been watching him play on the other table, and even with the handicap of a dozen beers he could run five or six balls at a time, which is not embarrassing for bar pool. But there was real hatred on George's face, sitting there like a signpost. All those beers had loosened his features until his eyebrows met in a single, straight-edged line, the kind of eyebrows the Devil would have if he had eyebrows. Some men just can't get drunk without getting evil, too. I suggested we call it a day, but George would have none of it. He swaggered around, foulmouthed, until I said all right just to shut him up.

"Fucking dyke," he said, loud enough for me to hear. I kept racking the balls. He was the one who was supposed to rack them, but now I didn't trust him to rack them tightly.

"I said," he said, a little louder, "fucking *dyke* in a uniform." He was drunk—and I should have known better—though, as I've said, that day was the beginning of trouble. One rule of pool is never get emotional. You get emotional and first thing you know, your angles are off, your game is a highly unclear business.

"Asshole," I told him. "Fucking *asshole* in a uniform." My hands shook so much I gripped my cue as if it were George's neck. I am not a grisly or violent person, but there you go.

"Just play, for God's sake," said one of his friends. They were all grouped around the table, their faces as alike and featureless as the balls in front of them. I imagined that their eyes were the tips of cues, blue, sharp, nothing you wanted pointed in your direction.

"Radiation mutant," I said. "Rockfish." Then I broke. Sure enough, emotion had its effect. None of the balls fell.

"Fifty bucks, you pervert," George said, rippling those eyebrows at me. "No, make it a hundred." All that beer was working up some weird, purplish coloration into his cheeks.

They say that during important moments time goes by more slowly, elongates somehow just when you need it most. It is a falsehood. Time goes slowly when you're utterly miserable, or when you might be about to die, and both are situations any sane person would want to go by quickly. When you really need it, time isn't there for you. I wanted to study the table for a while, get myself under control and ready. I wanted to go outside and have somebody point out the constellations, show me the difference between Taurus and Arcturus. I wanted somebody to give me a fish that didn't die in the tank. I wanted somebody, anybody, to tell me that I was living a good life, that my habits were excellent, that I was going places.

"This is all she wrote, Chuck," George said, leaning over the table like a surgeon. It looked grim, not because the spread was all in George's favor—which it was—but because I had gotten emotional. Nothing was clear anymore, not the angles, not the spin, nothing. My cue stick might just as well have been a smokestack.

"Shit!" George cried, and he slammed a beefy hand against his beefy thigh.

He'd run the table except for the eight ball, leaving me with some tricky shots—stop signs all over the table. By now everyone in The Office stood around the table, watching, belching, not saying a word. I thought about what Minnesota Fats would do, how Fats would handle the situation, but all I saw was that corner of the poster, unstuck and curled ominously over Fats's head. I wondered what would happen if I picked up each of my balls and placed them gently in the pockets, like eggs into Easter baskets. Crazy, I must have been crazy.

The first couple of shots were easy, then it got harder. I banked one ball the length of the table, a miraculous shot, though it left the cue ball in an iffy position. I made the next one anyway. After each shot I had to heft the stick in my hand, get the feel of it all over again, as if I were in George's league, an amateur on a hot streak. Finally the game came down to one shot. I had one ball left, tucked about an inch and a half up the rail from the corner pocket, an easy kiss except that the eight ball rested directly in the line of the shot. There was no way I could bank the cue ball and make it.

"All she wrote," George said, "all she by God *wrote!*"

I hefted my cue stick for a massé, the only thing left to do.

"Oh, no," cried George. "No, you don't. You might get away with that shit in lesbo pool, but not here. You're not doing it here. No, sir. No way."

"Who says?" I asked him, standing up from the table. I was sweating a lot, I could feel it on my ribs. "Anything goes is my feeling."

"Bar rules." George appealed to his friends. "Right? No massé in bar rules. Right? Am I right?"

"Phineas!" somebody called. "Phineas! No massé on the tables, right?"

Phineas came out around the bar, rubbing his hands on an apron that covered him from the neck to the knees. He had short, black, curly hair and wore round wire-rimmed glasses, the kind of glasses that make people look liberal and intelligent somehow. He looked clean and trim in his white apron, surrounded by all those sweaty blue workshirts. For a minute he just stood there, rubbing his hands, sizing up the table.

"What's the stake?" he asked philosophically.

"Hundred!" George said. He was practically screaming. Phineas puckered his mouth.

"Well," he said, drawing the sound out. Maybe he was buying time. Maybe he was leading them on. Or maybe he was a bartender who didn't like crowds and didn't like crowds asking for his opinion—which is exactly what he is. "Any-thing goes," he said. "Anything goes for a hundred bucks is my opinion."

"I'll remember this," George said, snarling, his purple face shaded to green. "You prick, I'll remember this."

"Fine," said Phineas, almost jovially. He folded his arms across that white apron and looked at me. He might have winked, but more likely he was just squinting, sizing me up.

"Massé on the ten into the corner," I said stiffly, for-mally, the way Bernie would have done. Anybody will tell you, a massé is ridiculous. You have no real cue ball control, no real control period. You have to bring your stick into an almost vertical position, then come down solidly on one side of the cue ball, which then—if you do it right—arcs around the obstacle ball and heads for the place you have in mind. It is an emotional shot, no control, mostly luck. And anytime you get yourself into the position of taking an emotional shot, all is pretty much lost. I hefted the cue stick again, hiked it up like an Apache spearing fish. Then I let it rip. The cue ball arced beautifully, went around the eight ball with a lot of backspin, then did just what it was supposed to do—kissed the ten on the rail. The trouble was, it didn't kiss the ten hard enough. The ball whimpered along the rail about an inch, then stopped short of the pocket. A breath would have knocked it in, but apparently nobody was breathing.

"That's all she wrote," I told Phineas. He just smiled, looking liberal and intelligent behind his glasses.

The upshot was, George won the game. I'd left the cue ball in a perfect position for making the eight in the side pocket. Any idiot could have made that shot, and George was no idiot, just a drunken jerk. He even got friendly when I paid him his money, wanted to take me home, his breath hot and sour as old beer. But then Phineas stepped in, cool as you please, and said that *he* was going home with me. Between the two there was no choice: I told Phineas to meet me out front at my car. "A '73 navy Impala," I told him. It was not that unusual, even though the day had me off-balance. I'd had a couple of guys over to my apartment before, after the bars closed, the kind of thing where in the morning you find yourself clenching the pillows, hoping they don't use your toothbrush or something. Even if I did see those guys again, their faces would mean no more to me than the faces of former opponents in a pool game.

The wind had died, nothing moved when I went out to the car. On the way to my apartment Phineas told me about how he hated crowds, how there was nothing possible with those kinds of numbers. I told him numbers counted, but he didn't argue the point. Then he told me how nice my car was. "True grit," I said. "Nothing spiffy; just good guts." He put his hand on my thigh. We rode like that for a long time. When we passed the button factory, I told him about the smokestacks looking like pool cues. Then, for some reason, I told him about driving my car into telephone poles, banking it off buildings.

"You shouldn't get all out of control over a game," he said. After that I didn't tell him anything else, pretended I was concentrating on his hand against my thigh.

Inside my apartment I didn't turn on the lights. The green glow of the fish tank let me see all I wanted to see, maybe more. Phineas, of course, went right for the tank, which was what everybody did when they came into my apartment.

"How come you only have two fish?" he wanted to know.

"That one there, with the yellow freckles. It kills everything I put in there. Wait see. In the morning that other one won't be there. It's a shark," I said.

"No kidding," he said, peering in at The Rockfish. "Really? A shark?"

"No. It's just an it. A killer it."

Phineas straightened up. "What's your name?"

"Janice," I said.

"At least in this town it's Janice," I said, revealing myself a little, although I wasn't about to go into heartfelt reasons for this and that. It didn't matter because then he kissed me, hard, standing there in front of the fish tank. In a minute or so, he broke away.

"You can play your ass off in pool, Janice," he said. He began to unbutton his shirt. It was flannel, which matched his glasses somehow; the apron he'd left back at the bar. I took off the trousers of my uniform, then he kissed me again, his hands down low.

"You look real nice," he said. "Out of uniform, as it were." He laughed, and I laughed, too, in a strange kind of way.

After that I was on the couch with him on top of me. He got busy. I put my hands on his back, but he did all the work. The whole time I was thinking, my head to one side, staring into the fish tank. I was thinking that maybe I would leave town. Maybe I would pack up my car and move and get around my trouble that way. I could leave the fish tank, skip out on the rent, just like the guy before me had done. Let The Rockfish chew its own gristle, I thought, let Mrs. McDaniels drop hints to somebody else. The Rockfish was patrolling the tank, whipping beside the lone goldfish like terror on the move, and the goldfish sucked madly on the glass in the corner, behind the pink coral, wriggling whenever The Rock-fish swept by. It struck me as the saddest thing I'd ever seen. Then I began it again, with Phineas this time. I imagined he was performing a massé on me, several massés, coming down hard on one side and then the other, one emotional shot after another, only I wasn't going anywhere. I must have snorted, because Phineas worked harder all of a sudden.

"Feel it?" he said, or asked, whispering, and I could tell that he'd come to a crucial moment. "Can you feel it?" And I said, "Yes." I said, "Yes, yes, I can feel it," but I couldn't. I shifted slightly to make things easier, but I couldn't feel a thing, not a thing—nothing.

WHERE SHE WAS

∽

Late in May my father drove us north in a new car, a tan station wagon with green carpet that smelled like rubber. Before that we'd had a very old used '54 Chevy, and before that we hadn't even had a car. My father kept the air conditioner on most of the way from East Tennessee to Lake Ontario. We all wore sweaters, but my mother wore two. Outside the car it was green and inside it was green and everything smelled like rubber. That's what I remember.

I turned ten on the trip up. My father stopped at the Pennsylvania State Fair on my birthday, about halfway to where we were going. Only the two of us actually went to the fair, because my mother had gotten a cold after the first day in the air conditioning; she lay down in the motel room with complimentary Kleenexes in little piles around her on the bedspread. I remember about the Kleenexes because they looked like the mountains we'd just left in Tennessee, only all covered in snow. The bedspread was a light green, "puke green," my mother called it. The motel room didn't have any air conditioning.

"You all go on to the fair and have a good time," she said, her eyes closed tightly. "Don't think twice about me."

And we didn't, or at least I didn't. First my father and I just looked at everything. There were places with farm animals that you could pet, there were pottery exhibits and basket-weaving exhibits, and there was even a place where they gave you a glass of milk straight from the cow. It tasted warm and sweet, solid somehow, the way milk at the bottom of a cereal bowl does. At one end of a big building, a kind of barn, they had an exhibit named after the motto of the fair: AMERICA, it said, WHERE SHE WAS, WHERE SHE IS, WHERE SHE'S GOING. I don't remember much about it, except that my father got really excited and wanted to buy me something they were selling in the stalls.

"It's the land of opportunity, Susan," he told me, slapping his palms. His face was very red. "The land of goddamn opportunity."

I didn't want him to buy me anything. All that day he'd wanted to buy me something, but every time he asked me he'd pull out his wallet and look inside, as though the money there contained a secret message. I already knew that money was dangerous, that both my mother and my father could turn sour and silent at the slightest mention of it. Sometimes the problem was spending money, sometimes it was not spending it, but usually it was spending it. I told him I didn't want anything.

"Yes, you do," he said, loudly, and I couldn't tell whether he was excited or angry, his face was so red. "You do, yes, sir, you do. You want something to take back and show your mother. Anything, buy anything, anything at all." He kept showing me the wallet with his money in it.

In the end he bought me a necklace made out of plastic beads, connected to a plastic medallion that said WHERE SHE WAS in big letters beside an Indian's head. The Indian was squinting ferociously, and had to look through the words to see anything. My father and the man in the stall bickered over how much change should come back from the dollar. After that I only remember the Ferris wheel—it was as big as the town I'd grown up in, huge, and it scared me to death. It swooped me up for long moments, then, on the way back down, I could see my father waving to me from a great distance. He waved, then he disappeared, then there he was again. It seemed to me that he was waving goodbye each time, waving as seriously and violently as if I were going away for good at every turn of the wheel. It embarrassed me, seeing him so small and waving goodbye, and I didn't wave back. I was too afraid. At the motel he made me show my mother the necklace with the medallion. She laughed.

"It's perfect," she cried, laughing. "Shit, it's so *perfect!*" And she laughed until her nose began to run.

By the time we reached Lake Ontario the air conditioner had broken down. My father wouldn't let us roll open the windows, so we'd taken off the sweaters and were sweating when we got there. "People notice things like air conditioning," he'd told us when we complained. Everything was new to us, the car, the place, the traveling. My father had been a foreman for meter readers and linemen at an electric company, but he lost the job over a management problem. The chairman of the board wanted the linemen to install a utility pole in his backyard, to keep away burglars, but my father wouldn't let his men do it for free. They fired him and got somebody who *would* do it for free. My father had been very proud of himself, but my mother thought it was silly and childish and secretly believed he'd done it just to get out of Tennessee. "He's going nowhere," I overheard her telling a neighbor, her elbows propped on the kitchen table, her hair glistening and gold in the sunlight. "He's going directly nowhere." I didn't have an opinion, except that the part about the burglars frightened me. I imagined men without faces shooting each other underneath utility poles. My father sent out hundreds of letters, all over the country, explaining his moral position and showing what a good foreman he had been, but the only response he got was from Oswego, New York, where they said they could use a good man like him. Then we sold the Chevy, bought the new car, and moved. That trip everything was green as a new dollar bill.

The neighborhood we moved into was on the side of town that had a lot of boarded-up factories. From our porch you could see smokestacks without any smoke and windows broken with BB guns. Most of the houses needed paint, the paint on them blistered and peeling like skin, but inside they were roomy and had big windows and, as my father said, all that sunlight was free. My friend Raymond lived four houses down, in a house just like ours, except his parents owned theirs and we were just renting. "We're just renting," I told Raymond, echoing my father, "because we have to put *feelers* into the town," and Raymond nodded the way he usually did, understanding completely.

There were plenty of kids on the block, some my own age, but Raymond and I hit it off. He was fourteen and very tall and a little slow. I only say he was slow because it is the truth. Two days after we moved in, my mother and I walked to the corner store. Raymond and his father, Mr. Scofield, were shopping and Mr. Scofield was saying, "You can eat it when we get home," because Raymond had a handful of grapes that he was tucking, one by one, under his tongue. I liked that; it was something I'd always wanted to do, eat grapes right there in the middle of a store. I went up to him and asked if I could have one and he gave me the whole bunch, smiling down hard at me. Then my mother and Mr. Scofield introduced themselves, the both of them smiling hard, too.

Mr. Scofield was a black man with slashes of green and yellow and red paint on his hands and arms. He had on shorts and a sport shirt that matched and wore a kind of beret with a short brim that shaded his eyes from the glare of the store's fluorescent lights. His eyes looked darker than his skin, the way eyes look behind sunglasses, and there were even darker circles under them. Afterward my mother told me he was an artist, a painter, and somehow I got the idea that she meant he put the slashes of paint on his arms on purpose, that what he did for a living meant doing something strange and exhausting to himself. She kept saying, "How intriguing, how fascinating," and she kept tucking a strand of golden hair behind her ears. I remember that—how she kept tucking back her hair in the middle of the canned-goods section. She looked very beautiful.

Raymond didn't have any paint on his arms, but he was dark, like old newspaper clippings, and I appreciated, right from the start, the way he seemed to understand everything you told him without committing himself to anything. I told him we lived up the street from him, and he nodded. I told him I was afraid of burglars and rapists and anybody with a gun, and he nodded. When Raymond nodded his head you could never tell whether he meant he was in complete agreement, or whether he meant he understood but wasn't taking a position—I mean, you never knew whether he was for you or against you, but he seemed to understand. The only thing he didn't nod at was when I said that money was dangerous, that it was the root of all evil. He just looked at me then, his eyes staring at the pocket a grape made in my cheek. I had been quoting my mother.

That business in the store was only the beginning of everything. Raymond and I started doing things together every day from then on. We neither of us had many friends; we neither of us had *any* friends. He couldn't run very fast, or play any kind of game that required split-second decisions, but he had what my father called good sense. Good sense meant that the person was your friend, and Raymond was that. He had a blue parrot named Benito who rode on his shoulder and said, "Stop it! Stop it!" in just the tone of voice his mother used most of the time. Mrs. Scofield wouldn't let Raymond play over at our house because she was afraid something might happen. She was as pasty and dumpy and white as the bread she was always making. You could never make noise in her house because the bread was always rising, and you could never be quiet because she was so busy with the bread she was afraid you might be doing something destructive. "Children are always destructive," she'd say, "and the role of their mothers is to make them *con*structive." She was a pain in the ass, though I liked Raymond.

"My mother," Raymond said, "is a very troubled woman."

I wondered, at the time, how anybody who made bread

all the time could be troubled, but I nodded my head, to show I understood. Actually, she was a pain in the ass.

"Evil," said Raymond, "lurks at the corners of everybody's life."

I just nodded my head at that, too. It sounded a lot like his father, but I didn't say anything. Raymond had good sense; he was my friend.

One day, in the middle of June, my father took the two of us to see the electric company. Mrs. Scofield wanted to try a new recipe so she said all right, but she made my father promise to keep an eye on Raymond. Mr. Scofield was busy out back in the garage he called a studio, and my mother—well, I don't know what she was doing. I know she said all right, too. It was a cloudy day and the lake was as smooth and silver as a sheet of aluminum. Raymond had on his Yankee baseball cap, I had on my Indian medallion, and my father had on his blue uniform. Over the breast pocket it had HOGAN written in large script, and underneath that it said NIAGARA-MOHAWK POWER in smaller block letters. Our last name was Manley, though.

"I tell you what," my father said on the way over. He was in a good mood, and he'd had the air conditioner fixed. It hummed like wings in the background. I was in the rear seat, so I had a good view of the backs of their heads. My father had a new crew cut, his hair sticking up brown, almost orange, and bristly. Raymond's head was a few inches taller, and he had what you could call a crew cut, except that his hair was so wiry and curly it just sort of rounded the shape of his head. You could see that even underneath the cap.

"I tell you what, this is the last frontier, a goddamn new world," my father said. "You can't go any farther in this country than the Great Lake of Ontario, I swear to God." I was used to my father's expansive moods, but I worried that Raymond might think the wrong thing. He didn't; he just nodded his head seriously, taking it all in.

"Nothing but foreign country past that lake," my father said, "nothing but the tip end of America. Honest to God, the very end of America!" And, truly, that day the lake did look like the beginning of something. Along the shore the water didn't seem to move at all; in the distance was nothing but flat, silver lake water butting up against an immense, even whiteness. Besides carrying the parrot, Benito, Raymond could draw pictures. He was very good at it. He always used his father's canvases, huge squares of silver-white empty space that scared you with the thought of having to fill them up. The lake that day looked a lot like one of those canvases.

"Silver means a cloudy day," said Raymond, and he seemed to be reading my mind. "Gold," he said, "means a sunny one. In between you've got your green."

"You've just said a mouthful," my father cried, hitting the steering wheel with his palms. "Son, it don't get any better than this right here. We are Americans." Raymond nodded his head.

We drove along the lake for about a mile and a half, then we got to the electric company. The only way you could tell it was an electric company was by looking at the stack of pine poles they had in the back lot. Other than that, it might have been a used-car dealership. There were about twenty beat-up Chevy trucks parked around the building, some of them packed with loops of thick wires, some of them with empty spools the size of kitchen tables arranged in the beds. The building was low and made out of scuffed yellow bricks, the sort of bricks you would expect an electric company to be made out of. Behind the building was the parking lot, and beyond that was the lake, and beyond that, invisible as an empress, was Canada.

"It would take about a week to cross that lake in a boat," I said. "It would take exactly a week to get to Canada from here."

"You could do it, Susan," my father said, "you could do it, but what's the point when you got all *this* right here?" He lifted his hands from the wheel, opening them up as if he expected an embrace. The car veered to the right a little, then he grabbed hold of the wheel again. "No, sir. No, sir! We're on the edge of things right here. I'm telling you, the tip end of America is where it's at."

We went into the building the back way, past a bunch of guys in blue uniforms who lounged at the entrance and made a point of not looking at us. My father said, "How's it going, boys?" but they all just looked past us, maybe staring at the lake. It smelled like gasoline inside there, I remember, that and ammonia. The floors were highly polished brown tile and there seemed to be acres of it, which put me in mind of roller skates. I imagined whipping myself from one end of the building to the other, doing figure eights, or moving backward so quickly my eyes streamed from the wind I'd created, moving free as you please.

"Roller skates," I told Raymond. "You could fly in here."

"I don't know how," said Raymond and he pulled his shoulder blades together, not shrugging so much as he seemed to be dismissing the thought. He didn't know what to make of it, since he hadn't done it. I could tell that. "I saw

49

a jet airplane take off once. SHOOM!" He shoved his hand in the air, his mouth a round, tight circle, and I laughed.

I have a Polaroid of Raymond, taken on my front porch earlier that day, before we went to the electric company. Benito is riding on the shoulder of his windbreaker, staring at him, and Raymond's looking past Benito, at something too far away to be in the picture. He isn't smiling. Behind his right ear a smokestack rises up in the distance, dark against the sky. I am beside him in my pedal pushers, wearing my medallion, and I'm smiling. In the background there's the fuzzy, fat figure of Mrs. Scofield and she looks very pale. At the bottom of the picture is the shape of my father's thumb, a mistake, dark against the porch steps. My mother and Mr. Scofield are not in the picture. There is no way of knowing where Raymond is looking.

"Sixty thousand people," my father said, "over twenty thousand families, and our baby supplies all the electricity. We're talking the mighty wattage here."

He showed us all around the place. There were big transformers, and expensive copper wires that got stolen every time you turned around, and a police dog named Howie they kept on the premises to keep an eye on things. The police dog was a German shepherd who rolled on his back and looked helpless as soon as you said his name. He barked ferociously at Raymond at first, but Raymond went right over and grabbed his ears and said, "You old gray dog, you old black-and-gray old dog," and then everything turned out all right.

"Old Howie," my father said, his cheeks pink with emotion, "old Howie don't like *tall* people, and Raymond, you're one *tall* son of a gun." Raymond put his hands on the dog's stomach.

"Those men at the back door are taller than me," he

muttered, rubbing hard against the fur. Then he stood up. "That thing," he said, meaning Howie, "that thing was bar-kin' at my *face.*"

"That's right, Raymond," my father said, and this time his cheeks were red. "Old Howie don't like new faces, never did." He clapped Raymond on the back of his windbreaker. "Wouldn't be a police dog, would he, if he *liked* new faces."

"Huh," said Raymond.

After that we all three saw some offices and a couple of bathrooms. All those places had the smell of ammonia and gasoline coming out of them, but I couldn't see anything that should smell like that, nothing but tile and scuffed yellow bricks. When we'd looked at everything there was to see, we ended up in the break room. My father bought us both orange Nehis, then we lounged around for a little while. It was a nice room, plenty of light. Along one wall were soda ma-chines, popcorn machines, even a machine that told you what your weight was and your future would be. My father gave me a penny, but Raymond pulled a penny out of his own pocket and said, "I got my own copper." He said it in a weird way, his face pulled together somehow, so I started paying atten-tion. There were three or four guys in blue uniforms hanging around the break room, but I didn't notice them until Ray-mond said that. In the far corner two guys were playing Ping-Pong on a piece of painted plywood, sending the ball from one end to the other, the ball looking incredibly white against the dark green of the board. Every once in a while somebody said, "Dammit," and then the ball scooted along the floor somewhere.

I got onto the machine first. I put the penny in, waited a minute, then found out my weight. It was a little on the light side, though I figured you couldn't count on a machine that weighed so many heavy people to weight a skinny kid like me accurately. I figured I was too small to count on my money's worth.

"What's your fortune, Susan?" my father asked. He was standing over by the soda machines, keeping an eye on the Ping-Pong game, and keeping an eye on us, too. Mrs. Scofield had nothing to worry about. More than half of his orange Nehi was gone, and his hair shone as orange as the bottle from the light coming in. I noticed he was shorter than the soda machines, by about six inches.

" 'Prepare to learn a lesson,' " I said, reading the card. I got down off the machine.

"It means you better get ready for school in August," my father said, then he finished his Nehi. "It means these New Yorkers are a century ahead of Tennessee. You better hit the books, Sue, I'm telling you, hit the books." Then he leaned against the machine, holding his bottle bottom end up, holding it in distaste, like the empty thing it was. "Your turn, Raymond. Put the Coke down or it'll give you the wrong future."

Raymond set his orange soda on the arm of one of the easy chairs around there. He took off his windbreaker. I'd heard his mother make him promise not to take it off, but he took it off. I liked that. I just liked Raymond. In my mind I kept hearing Benito say, "Stop it! Stop it!" but Raymond wasn't kidding around. He even took off the Yankee cap. If we'd been alone in the room, I believe he would have taken off everything, just to get the accurate future. That's the way he was.

He was standing on the machine when some guy in a brown suit yelled for my father. I didn't appreciate the way he yelled for him, yapping like a terrier. And his expression made him look exactly like a terrier, too, his face short-tempered and pointed and furred at the nose by a mustache. He yelled, "Manley! *Man* ley!" and my father said, "Yes, sir!" and set down his Nehi bottle immediately. I didn't appreciate the "sir" part either. It embarrassed me, my father saying that to a guy in a brown suit who looked like a terrier. *Sir,* I thought he should have said, *you are a pain in the ass. Sir,* I wanted him to say, *this is my daughter and her friend Raymond and we are Americans.* I wanted him to say anything except what he did say.

"It's probably something important," I told Raymond, embarrassed. The guy had taken him inside a room with glass walls, and you could tell he was still yelling, even though not a sound came out. My father was about four inches shorter than the guy in the brown suit. "It's probably some kind of *management* difficulty," I said, echoing my father. Any time there was trouble at work, I'd learned, it had to do with a management difficulty.

Raymond paused on the machine; he hadn't put the penny in yet, though I could see it between his fingers. *"Huh!"* he said, and there it was—that weird tone of voice. It made me pay attention again, so I looked around at the guys playing Ping-Pong. They were leaning against the table now, holding the paddles, looking at the room with glass walls and snickering about something.

"What it is," I said, turning my back on the Ping-Pong table, "is probably that some important power line fell down. Those lines come down all the time." I tried to sound intelligent, forthright, like a newscaster on the radio, somebody who made all the unreasonable things in the world sound reasonable, but Raymond had changed somehow. He didn't understand. "It's either power lines," I said, "or else it's a wattage emergency. That's what I think it is, a wattage emergency." I had no idea what a wattage emergency was, but I figured I could lie, if Raymond was going to act that way.

"God, Susan!" he said. He jammed the penny into the machine. The whole machine started shaking. He didn't even wait to see what his weight was, he just grabbed the fortune ticket and got down off the machine. For a while the machine kept rattling and shaking. It either did that, or I was upset and only imagined that it was shaking. I don't remember about the machine.

"Maybe the dog died," I said, trying to be funny. I was upset, but I thought it might turn out all right if I was funny. "Maybe old Howie kicked off. Heart attack. Chasing burglars."

"*God,*" said Raymond. "What it is, is he's getting his *ass* chewed off in there!" He was agitated, I could tell, because he kept trying to put on his windbreaker with the fortune in his hand. It got in the way of the sleeve. "*White* people," he said and shook his head back and forth, doing that almost quickly, for Raymond. Nothing he did was really ever done that quickly, except that right then everything was speeded up. I know I was speeded up; I lost my head.

"Well," I said, "well! At least I know how to roller-skate. At least my father hasn't got *paint* on his arms. At least *I* am an American and not something *in between*!"

As soon as I said it, I knew it was the wrong thing. Sometimes you say things that your brain automatically memorizes, like a machine, and you know you'll never forget whatever it was. That was exactly the right thing to say if you were a pain in the ass. As soon as I said it, I started pretending to myself that I'd meant something else. I kept putting the words in a different order, putting the emphasis of the words in different places; my mind worked at high speed, going backward. But I knew what I'd meant and Raymond knew what I'd meant and that's what I remember.

I said I was sorry. "Just leave my dad out of it," I said. "It's nothing in the world but a management difficulty."

Raymond said something I couldn't hear, then he just looked at me, the way he'd looked at me when I'd said money was the root of all evil. I didn't want to hang around the break room of the electric company anymore. I was tired of all that. I didn't want to roller-skate on the tiles, or have another orange Nehi, or see any more copper wires. I was thinking that, if where we were on Lake Ontario was already the tip end of America, then there was no place left for me to go. I began to toy with the idea that maybe I would go ahead and grow up to be a loser. Maybe I would grow up and go directly nowhere. I was tired of being an American; it was too much like lying all the time.

When my father came back, Raymond had on his windbreaker and his baseball cap and looked ready to go. I was ready to go, too. His face, my father's I mean, was very red, not the cheeks but his whole face. Even his neck was red. "All right, then," he said, smacking his hands together. "What next? You all want some ice cream? Some popcorn? We got it all in here."

"I think maybe we're ready to go home," I said.

"What? Already? What about the pole yard?" He looked at me, then at Raymond. "Listen, tell you what, I think I could arrange a ride on the linemen's truck. What say I pull a few strings and we take a ride?"

"I really think we ought to go home. I think I'm tired, Daddy."

"Sure," he said. "No problem. My time is your time."

Raymond and my father headed for the back door, but I hung back. I pretended I had to tie my shoe. Instead I went over to the easy chair and picked up Raymond's fortune ticket. He'd either forgotten about it, or else he didn't want it anymore. There was no telling which it was. Raymond's fortune said: "Prepare to learn a lesson."

After that trip to the electric company, things changed. Everything changed. I still went over to Raymond's house, but not as often. Things were different, funny, soured somehow. We taught Benito how to say "SHOOM!" like a jet airplane, though the bird kept saying "SHOO!" and we got tired of fooling with it. It seemed like we'd outgrown jet airplanes. My father wanted to take the two of us to see fireworks on the Fourth of July, at the electric company, but Raymond said no, he had all the color he needed in his paint box. For a while I blamed myself for the way things turned out, then I blamed the way the world was. Then, because it was the best I could do, I pulled my shoulders together, the way Raymond had done about the roller skating, and pretended to dismiss the whole thing: I didn't know what to make of it. It seemed like we'd outgrown each other. We were troubled people. Evil lurked at our corners. That's the way I thought he saw it, too.

At the end of July my mother and Mr. Scofield disappeared. That's all there was to it. One day they were where they were supposed to be; the next day they weren't. I wasn't surprised because I had seen my mother in the grocery store, tucking her hair behind her ears and saying, "How intriguing." I was upset, but I wasn't surprised. My mother was very beautiful and Mr. Scofield was a painter. My father cried for a few days, made some phone calls, then he gave it up. He made do, I mean, which was what he'd always done. He never did find out where she was.

A week later, in the beginning of August, Mrs. Scofield and Raymond moved to Rhode Island, where Mrs. Scofield had a sister. I didn't say goodbye when he left; I don't think Mrs. Scofield would have let me if I'd wanted to. I did watch them get into the car and drive away, though. Benito was sitting on his shoulder, so he must have been slumping a little. I could imagine the bird whispering its vocabulary into his ear. His head was turned to one side, dark in the shadows, turned toward the window of the car. I don't believe he was smiling. They were already pulling away, moving pretty fast, and so there was no way of knowing where Raymond was looking.

Late in August school started. My father stood on the porch and waved goodbye. The school was close by, so I walked, though I was nervous and walked slowly. The neighborhood we lived in, besides having factories, had huge elm trees along the sidewalks, and everything was green with the leaves of elms. I walked backward for a ways, watching my father wave goodbye between the trees. He waved, then he disappeared, then there he was again, looking smaller each time and still waving goodbye. It embarrassed me and I didn't wave back. Beyond our porch and our house, beyond Raymond's old house, past the whole neighborhood, I could see the lake: a patch of deep, awful blue that met the curvature of the world, all of it framed by leaves. I walked backward until it seemed my father, and the houses, and the lake, and even the curvature of the world disappeared in green. I walked backward until my eyes teared from the movement— until everything I recognized turned as green as the elms and then vanished abruptly at the tip end of America.

MISSING PERSONS

ॐ

Susan sits in the dark corner of the porch on a lawn chair, swinging her legs, making faces at Aileen, the woman who wants to become her stepmother. Aileen is talking, which is just about the only thing she knows how to do as far as Susan is concerned. Susan doesn't want a stepmother, especially Aileen, but she is eleven and realizes that hers is an age with very little bargaining power. One thing she can do is sit in the dark and make faces while Aileen talks about movie and TV stars. They are her favorite topic, particularly ones with diseases or drug habits, and every time she comes over Aileen brings a bunch of creepy magazines about movie stars and perverts. Sometimes Susan has nightmares that involve three-headed babies, and ninety-year-old mothers of twins, and pregnant five-year-olds, things she reads in the magazines Aileen brings over.

"Honey," Aileen is saying, "just let you or me get ourselves hooked on cocaine and heroin, let us crawl on our knees begging to the Betty Ford Center, and will they let us in? No. Uh-*uh*, no way. Miss Betty only dries out the best. We could shoot ourselves up right on the front steps and tough luck to us. And do you know why? I do, let me tell you. It's because we can't get on the TV and tell how come it is we feel so much better now that we're not dope fiends. Honey, everything is PR nowadays, but everything."

Susan quits making faces, letting Aileen's voice skitter past as if it were the sound of crickets. She wishes her father would hurry up and come back with the chicken wings, even though Aileen talks as much when he's there as when he's gone. The difference is that instead of saying "honey" all the time, she says "darling." Her mother never said things like that. Her mother ran off over a year ago with a painter, and although Susan can remember many things about her, for some reason she can't remember her face. She remembers the sweet smell of the soap she used and her long blond hair and her slender, pale legs, but to fill in a face she has to look through Aileen's magazines for the face of a star. There aren't any pictures of her mother in the house, at least to her knowledge, and she's looked everywhere. In her dreams her mother appears often, her face blurred and unclear, like the print of a thumb. She feels that if she can only make the face come clear in her dreams, then at that moment her mother will come back. At that moment Aileen will disappear like the nightmares she's been having.

"Darling," Aileen cries and Susan sees her father coming down the dark sidewalk, winded from his walk up the hill. "Susan and I have been just chatting away, chat-chat-chatting away."

"Then you two just keep right on at it," her father says, breathing hard. "Don't let me interrupt a thing."

Tonight her father went to the Wing Wagon, where they serve Buffalo-style hot wings, her favorite. He carries the bag of wings under one arm and in the other a half gallon of diet Pepsi. The Pepsi is for Aileen, who's always dieting, to set an example, she says. She works as exercise coordinator for the YWCA. Susan saw her at work one afternoon, flailing her arms and jogging in place in front of a dozen fat women who looked like they were in great pain. Aileen was wearing pink leotards, which hid the network of purplish veins that run up and down her legs. At the time Susan wondered whether anybody had ever dropped dead in one of the exercise classes. Now she wonders whether Aileen has a weak heart, because of the veins.

"Smell that clover," her father says, pausing at the bottom of the porch, holding still as if he were listening for something. "Sweet as butter."

"You're going to have to get in there with hand clippers to get it all," Aileen says. "The mower can't reach around the side of the porch."

"Don't I know it. I'll do it this weekend. You can make iced tea and bring it round whenever it looks like I might faint from the heat."

"Oh, go on with you," Aileen says, "I'm the fainter in this family. Before I got in such good shape, I used to faint once a month, like clockwork. I might be in the shower or on the sidewalk or sitting still, didn't matter, over I went like a ton of bricks. It's a valve in my brain that acts up."

"You told us that," Susan says. "You already told us all that before." She is irked by the *this family* business, the way

Aileen has insinuated herself into their lives until by now she can talk about family and yardwork and valves that act up, just as though she had a right to do it.

"Did I? Did I?" asks Aileen, her hand pressed between her breasts. She's imitating someone Susan has seen on TV, the mocking tone, the flutter of eyelashes, the slight Brooklyn accent—all of it straight from a Monday night sitcom. "Excoose me. I'd hate to bore somebody. I'd hate to bore somebody that never says the same thing twice. I'll shut my mouth."

"Fat chance," Susan mutters, but then her father comes blustering up the porch steps, waving the bag of wings like a matador. He puts the Pepsi down on the wicker table, then he puts the wings beside Aileen.

"Did you get hot?" Susan asks.

"He better not've," Aileen says sullenly.

"Ladies," her father says grandly, pulling two baskets from inside the bag. "We've got your hot"—and he gives her one basket—"we've got your mild"—and he gives Aileen the other basket—"and we've got your in between." He leaves the third basket where it is, inside the bag. "Let me get some glasses from the kitchen. Who wants ice?"

"Aileen does," says Susan. Aileen always takes ice in her drinks, a fact that irritates Susan. She says, "Aileen the Ice Queen."

When her father goes inside, Aileen turns around in her seat, leans her face close, and says, "You better just cool your britches, little miss. I'll tell you one durn thing. Life is all about taking what comes your way. Not another thing but taking what comes. And, honey, I have come your way. So you better just cool your britches and fasten your little seat belt. For one thing, I was raised to be polite in my family."

Susan sticks out her tongue until her face hurts, but Aileen is already digging around in her wing basket. She knows that making faces is childish and doesn't change a thing, but nothing else she might say or do would change anything either. At least she feels better with her tongue sticking out at her, as if Aileen's head were something she could bite into and spit out like a seed. Upstairs in her bedroom Susan has a calendar with one day in May marked in black crayon. That's the day they met Aileen, Saturday, the thirtieth of May.

After her mother ran off, her father began to take her places every weekend. Somebody had told him that that was what you were supposed to do with kids when their mothers ran off, if you didn't want them to grow up to be delinquents. He had explained all this to her very seriously, acting as though the two of them had their work cut out for them, to keep away delinquency. Susan had never thought about it before, had never wanted to take a drink or smoke a cigarette or steal contraceptives from the drugstore—whatever it was that delinquents did—but the seriousness of those weekends made her feel that all those things were just around the corner, waiting to snatch her up one Saturday morning when she least expected it. She might wake up one day with an irresistible urge to have a marijuana cigarette and some heroin. But usually her weekends were so full she didn't have much time to explore any urges. They went to auctions, just to watch, and they went to movies, skating rinks, swimming pools, beaches on Lake Ontario. The Saturday they met Aileen they went to the Oswego Speedway, to watch the super-modifieds.

It was just outside town, so they'd walked over. The day was unusually hot, and the tar of the road felt soft underneath her sneakers, like bubble gum. She asked her father whether tar was something you could eat if you had to. He said no, it was nothing but chemicals; then she said that Cheetos were nothing but chemicals, too—she'd heard it on the radio show *Let's Talk About You.* He began to explain the difference between edible chemicals and inedible chemicals, though by then the heat had carried her attention away. Everywhere she looked the heat rose up, shimmering like the effects of a time warp. She'd read about time warps in a comic book, places where one minute you could be walking toward the speedway and the next minute you would be beside a pond with dinosaurs angling their long necks toward cattails. Time sort of shivered into pieces until you could end up almost anywhere. She wondered whether time warps could be controlled, like a car maybe, so that you ended up on the exact date you wanted—July a year ago, for instance, the day before she woke up and her mother was long gone with Mr. Scofield. In the distance the super-modifieds revved their engines, a murmuring sound that the heat might have made if it had had the mouth to do it.

"So basically," her father said, "you've got your petroleum chemicals and then you've got everything else. You can't eat the petroleum chemicals. The other stuff, they can make taste like anything from cheese to bananas. I tell you what, Susan, we're living in the Age of Miracles—believe it, the Age of Miracles. This is an age where a man on the moon can eat a hunk of cheese no cow ever made. Think about it! Substitute cheese! We're talking miracles here."

Susan thought that miracles were no good if you couldn't even ride through a time warp. It was no good being able to eat chemicals if what had happened to you would always stay the same, and what might happen to you would always be changing and unknown. The real miracle, she felt, would be if you could get somebody else to live through all that; if you could get a substitute life liver the way they got substitute teachers and made fake cheese. Then she might be able to sleep at night without all the ugliness of things going on in the dark.

Inside the speedway the roar of the super-modifieds was louder than bombs being dropped. At first she clapped her hands over her ears, feeling desperate and surrounded by the sound. Then she backed up against a stand of bleachers while her father pantomimed for her to come on, waving the tickets, his mouth working against the roar of the cars. By the time he pulled her on the arm, though, she was all right again, her ears managing to tune out most of the commotion, the way skin gets used to cold water. They sat in the D section, across from where the checkered flag got waved; her father had seat 15 and she had seat 16 and, wearing a pink pantsuit, Aileen had 14. The sun shone off the pantsuit so that you couldn't miss her sitting there, no more than you could miss a thunderbolt striking the seat beside you.

The first thing Aileen did was lean over toward her father, pointing at the program with a puzzled expression. When she leaned, the fabric of her pink top rubbed up against her father's red T-shirt. Susan couldn't hear what she said, or what her father answered, but after that neither of them watched the race. Every once in a while Susan tugged on her father's sleeve and asked a question, any question she could think of to ask—What's a super-modified? How many races are there? How many laps in a race?—until finally her father borrowed Aileen's program, giving it to her with a look that meant she better sit still and no funny business. From what she could see, Aileen did most of the talking, although for long moments she could feel her father's arm shake, which meant he was talking, too. She knew what he was saying, what he always said to women who showed the least bit of interest: how his wife had left him for another man, how he reckoned he was divorced though it was no fault of his own, that he was just a simple man doing his best, how he spent as much time as he could with his daughter so that she wouldn't be a tramp like so many kids these days. Aileen kept shaking her head, squinching up her eyes and biting at her pink lipstick, making her face look so concerned and sensitive it was straight out of daytime TV. Susan rolled her eyes, hidden behind her father's shoulder. When the first race finally ended, she could hear Aileen's voice as clearly as if she were on the telephone with her.

"Honey, I ain't kidding," Aileen said into the sudden silence. This was when she still called both of them "honey," before her father became "darling." "I don't come here to root for this car or that car or this driver, that driver. No kidding, I come here to root for an accident. Not another thing but an accident. If you were to take a poll right now, ninety-nine percent of these people came for the same reason, if they were honest with themselves, which they wouldn't be. I'm not the best person in the world, but I *am* honest with myself and proud of it!" She lifted her chin at a daring angle, as if to mean that the people in section D could come and burn her at the stake before she'd be dishonest with herself. Susan wanted to say, *You are a sick old pain in the ass is what you are,* but her father said, "I know what you mean!" with so much admiration in his tone, she knew that something bad was just beginning.

66

"Time warp," she said and both of them looked at her. "This is my daughter, Susan."

"Well, how-de-do to you. And how old are you, hon?"

"Seven," she said without hesitation. Aileen looked at her, then at her father.

"What a big girl," said Aileen, politely.

"She's eleven. What's the matter with you, Susan? Turned eleven last week."

"Eleven!" Aileen cried. "Gosh, a girl that old needs a mother's care. I feel so sorry for you." She laid a hand on her father's arm, clicking her tongue. "When I was eleven I was a big ball of fire. My mother swears she didn't know whether to raise me or shoot me. One big rolling ball of fire."

"Oh, she's a handful," her father said and laughed, shifting his weight uncomfortably.

"I'm an honest person," said Aileen, "so let me be frank. There's no way a single man like you should have to raise a kid all by himself. It's cruel. It's unhumane. If I was a single man, you couldn't make me do it with a hammer and that's the honest truth."

"What about a jackhammer?" Susan asked.

"Susan!" her father cried.

"I was only being funny," she said. "I was trying to be funny."

"You get any more funny and I'll fix it so you'll have to do it standing up. You understand me?"

"I like discipline in families," Aileen said vaguely, looking satisfied about things.

"Where's *your* husband?" Susan asked.

"Susan!" her father cried again, but she could tell the question interested him. He stared out across the speedway, as though a trance had come over him.

"It's all right, kids are always curious." She shot Susan a look of complicity, or of gratitude—whichever it was, it was irritating. She felt that somehow she'd given Aileen an advantage over her. "I had a husband one time, a good one. Dead as he can be, now. Maybe you heard about that accident in Bean Station, Tennessee?"

Her father shook his head no. "But I grew up in and around there," he said excitedly. "That's where I'm *from.*"

"Then you must've heard about it. It was on all the news, even CBS and ABC. He was a trucker, the trucker driving that semi that went barreling into the side of a Greyhound bus. You *must*'ve heard about it. It was a *conflagration,*" she said in a church whisper.

"A what?" Susan asked.

"It burned him right down to the fillings in his teeth," she said crisply. "Fifty people dead inside a minute, and he was probably the first one to go. I cried like a baby for three straight weeks, with my mother buying Kleenex by the cartload. Couldn't keep anything on my stomach but what it seemed like ashes. You know, *his* ashes. I'm not lying, I was ready for the funny farm."

"That's just terrible," said her father. "I never heard such a tragic story." He seemed ready to cry. Instead he picked up one of Aileen's hands and patted it, then quickly released it. He didn't seem to know where to look after that, and Susan felt sorry for him, sorry and embarrassed at the same time. The telling of her story had made Aileen as giddy as a drunk person.

"I was twenty-one years old. I was a widow before I was a woman. But listen, time heals everything, I can promise you that. Time is the great healer. It all happened so long ago it seems like it happened to another person."

"That's good news," her father said. "It's nice you trying to make me feel better." He was opening and shutting his fist, watching himself do it.

"How long?" asked Susan. "Exactly how many years did it take before you were healed? Did you wake up one day and it was over? How long was it?"

"Susan," he warned.

"Curious as a cat," Aileen teased, putting a hand on her father's arm. "I believe you've raised yourself a little reporter. I'll tell you this. It wasn't a month and it wasn't three months. It's something you don't put a number on. What happened was, one night I went out bowling with my sister and brother-in-law and some fellow my sister works with. I'd been down and out and it was driving my sister crazy, so she dragged me to the bowling alley. I threw one gutter ball after another, couldn't concentrate. Then, it was the strangest thing, I happened to look down a few alleys and there they were. Little people."

"You mean kids?" asked her father.

"She means midgets," Susan said.

"How did you know?" Aileen asked. "I never told this story before."

"Saw the TV show."

"What TV show?"

"Never mind all that," her father said. "What happened?"

"Dwarfs or midgets, either one. They like to be called little people. I asked 'em. Isn't that cute? One of them looked just like a little old owl with his feathers ruffled on top. There was two of them going at it hell for leather, with kiddie balls no bigger than a dog's head. Well I watched and I watched, and my sister says a great big smile spread over my face. She says my face lit up like a spotlight was turned on. All I know is, when I left that bowling alley I wasn't a widow anymore."

"That's some story," he said. "What do you reckon it was about them that did you that way?"

"I can't a bit more tell you that than the man in the moon. Maureen—that's my sister—she says seeing them made me realize that I wasn't the only one in this world with trouble on my head. Personally, I don't know what it was."

"Well," said her father. "Well."

"Life is a big mystery," Aileen said, "the whole ball of wax."

"It's the Age of Miracles," Susan said, and Aileen looked at her, squinting her eyes as if to square something in her mind.

"That was chemicals I was talking about," her father said and stood up. "I think all this calls for some hot dogs. What do you ladies say to some hot dogs?"

"I wouldn't mind a diet Coke with some ice in it," Aileen said. "The ice fills me up so I won't eat so much. The figure's important in my line of work."

When her father left, Aileen had turned around and stared at her for a while. "Do you mind me telling you something?" she had asked. "Do you mind me telling you something you need?"

"What?"

"Excuse me for being frank, but you need to get yourself a training bra." Aileen looked her up and down. "Yes, sir, you're getting to be a big girl, if you know what I mean."

At that moment the second race began and the roar of the super-modifieds filled the air so suddenly and completely that Susan, for a moment, thought the sky had fallen in.

* * *

After they eat the wings, they go inside and Aileen turns on the TV to watch *Simon & Simon*. Aileen puts up with the blond one because he's cute, but she thinks he's prissy; the one she likes is the dark one, with the mustache. Susan doesn't like either one of them and wants to watch *Cheers*, but ever since Aileen started spending nights, the TV has become a symbol for all the changes going on so quickly around the house. Even the inside of the refrigerator looks different. Where there used to be only a loaf of bread, some ham, and a carton of eggs, now there's so much stuff that stalks of celery or plastic bottles of diet blue cheese dressing fall out on the floor whenever she opens the door. Things like dish towels and the back of the easy chair and the bathroom sink have begun to take on Aileen's smell. It is not at all like the smell of her mother. There is something fake about Aileen's smell. Chemicals, Susan thinks.

"He sits around on the set reading *The New Yorker*," Aileen says. "*The New Yorker*, of all things," she says in mock horror. "They say he's the same way on the set as he is in the show—blond and brainy and picky about what he eats."

"Just like me," says her father, ducking his head and grinning.

The Simons are looking for a missing person in a nudist colony. They don't have a picture or anything, but somehow you have the feeling they'll know him when they see him. They keep running into a woman at the colony who seems to have some information but turns out to be just another nudist with nothing to hide. The Simon with the mustache is ashamed to take off his clothes. The blond one is all business and sheds his clothes without a second thought. Bushes keep getting in the way of seeing anything, and all the women are shown from the neck up. In the end it so happens that the missing person was never even near the nudist colony. Susan can't figure out why they ever went there. She wonders whether nudists have to be brainy and picky eaters; then she wonders whether Aileen sleeps without clothes on in her father's bed. Her father used to sleep in pajamas with half moons printed all over them, but considering all the changes going on, there's no telling if he still does.

"That was a good one," Aileen says. "I hate it when they run around office buildings in suits, talking with English accents."

"I guess you like your men naked," says her father and laughs, smirking and embarrassed and delighted with himself.

"Oh hush, you," Aileen says, slapping at the air since her father is across the coffee table in his easy chair. One of her tricks, if her father is close enough, is to pretend to slap at him, then casually leave her hand on him somewhere, usually against his thigh. Aileen is full of tricks. Susan wonders if she learned them all from her husband, the dead trucker, or if she picks them up in the magazines she reads. The trucker fascinates her, even though he's dead and can't come back and take Aileen away. She wonders how he'd like the idea of Aileen being healed of him and dating a perfect stranger. He probably looked exactly like the Simon with the mustache, the one Aileen likes so much, only he was probably not ashamed to get naked. With a little shock, Susan realizes that the trucker couldn't get any more naked than being burned to a crisp.

When *Knots Landing* comes on, she feels sleepy. All the shows with plots that go from one week to the next make her feel that way. They bore her, and since she's half asleep during them, she can never keep up with what's happening in the story. She suspects that Aileen watches them on purpose, just to make her go to bed that much sooner.

"If they don't find those twins today," Aileen says, squaring her jaw, "I'm going to personally hire a private detective and find 'em myself. I can't take much more suspense."

"It's only make-believe," her father says. "Don't get all worked up."

"I'm not *worked up*, darling. It just breaks my heart, is all."

It seems to Susan that all the shows on TV have something to do with missing persons. At any given moment, on one of the four channels they get, there are at least two persons gone from where they are supposed to be. Her father calls it a national crisis; she has seen him study the pictures of missing children on the backs of milk cartons, concentrating so hard he might have been expecting one of them to show up on their front porch one day. The saddest thing about it all, he says, is that most of them are old by now and their pictures might look nothing like them. You could be sitting on a bus beside a missing person and never know the difference. She wonders whether the parents of missing children end up adopting someone, to fill in the gaps; whether all the stepfathers and stepmothers and stepchildren in the world are really just fillers for missing persons. It seems to her that, any minute, her mother's face will come clear, if she can only figure out how they make the cheese substitutes. When her head drops suddenly, Susan straightens up and looks around, catches Aileen making eyes at her father.

"Somebody is ready for bed," Aileen says.

"You're worn out, Susan," says her father. "Get on up to bed."

"I'm awake," she says, sitting up very straight. "I'm awake."

"You want a piggyback?" he asks. She shakes her head no. She is too old for that kind of thing. Ever since Aileen showed up, she's felt too old for almost everything. Last week her father left a package on her bed, then practically ran out of the room. Inside was a training bra, a white one, with instructions on how to wear it so it didn't rub you the wrong way. She placed it in the bottom drawer of her dresser, still wrapped up, and neither one of them has mentioned it again. "Sleep well, then," he says.

"Don't let the bedbugs bite," says Aileen.

At the top of the stairs Susan pauses and hears Aileen say, "What *is* a bedbug anyway?" Then, just as she expected, she hears her father get up out of the easy chair and go over to sit beside Aileen on the couch. He rarely sits beside Aileen when she is around, and Susan is grateful for at least that much consideration.

"You really want to know?" she hears him ask, and then floating up the stairs come Aileen's muffled squeals.

She is in a very white place, for a very important reason. She isn't sure what it is, but she has the feeling she'll know it when she sees it. All of a sudden she realizes that Simon and Simon have led her there, except that they are midgets; they are exactly the size they seem to be on the TV, about six inches tall. She keeps thinking she better be careful or else she'll step on one of them. In one corner of the place is her father's stepladder, the one he uses to change burned-out light bulbs. She can't figure out what it's doing there. There is yellow paint splattered all over the rungs, a real mess. She has a rag in her hand, so she decides to clean up the ladder some, since there is nothing more important to do yet. She cleans one rung at a time, but when she gets to the top there's a neck and a head attached to it. She doesn't recognize the face, and the sight of it scares her to death. She bats at it with the rag. Then she understands that this is not a white place at all—it is a red and orange and yellow place, a conflagration. She is burning right down to the fillings in her teeth.

"It's all right," somebody says, "it's all right, honey."

"Momma!" Susan cries when it dawns on her who the person in front of her is. "Momma!"

"It's Aileen, hon. You just calm down. You've had a bad dream is all, a real bad dream."

"Who is it? Just *who* is it?"

"It's Aileen, it's just old Aileen." Aileen's face looms over her. She places a hand on her forehead. "You aren't feverish. I don't think you're sick. Was it bad? It sounded real bad."

Aileen has on a powder-blue nightgown with lace at the neck. Over that she wears her father's tattered maroon robe with the belt tied in a knot. When she steps back a little, Susan can see the blue veins swarming her legs like vines up a trellis.

"If you want to tell me about it, I'll listen. I mean, sometimes it's better to get it off your chest, you know, let the bad things out and the good things in. Or something."

"Where's Daddy?"

"He's asleep. You want for me to go get him? I'll go get him, all right? You want some water? Some Pepsi?"

Susan has seen Aileen act a lot of different ways, but she has never seen her be kind. Seeing Aileen be kind is the worst thing of all, almost unbearable. "Leave my daddy out of it!" she cries, squirming against the sheets. "Whatever it is, you just leave my daddy and me out of it!"

"You keep acting this way," Aileen says, "and you're gonna get an ulcer."

Susan leaps out of bed, runs around Aileen into the hall, then runs down the steps as fast as she can go. She knows that she is being crazy, but she has read in one of Aileen's magazines that 67 percent of the world's population is certifiably insane, and that thought is comforting. In the living room she thinks about hiding in the closet, then decides that it would be the first place they'd look. She runs out the front door, down the porch steps onto the walkway, where she stands for a while, wondering what is next. When the living room lights go on, she ducks and crawls around the side of the porch, huddling up in the tall, warm clover. In a minute Aileen and her father come out on the porch.

"I shouldn't have said a word about ulcers," Aileen whispers. "That's what set her off."

"She's just upset," answers her father.

"You suppose she's run off? I was trying to be nice. I could pull out my tongue for saying that about the ulcers."

"She's around here somewhere," he says. "She's probably run right around to the back door and's sound asleep in her bed already. Anyway, she's got good sense."

"I used to dream about this old weaselly guy in a white trench coat. He was always following me around, making weird faces. I wonder what her flavor is. I bet it's those hot wings. You shouldn't let her eat all those things. It's the wings if it's anything."

"It's her goddamned mother," her father says bitterly.

"Listen, you," Aileen says. "People always get used to things. No matter what. Kids are people, too. One day she'll get herself a boyfriend and all these bad dreams'll turn into cheerleading outfits and sun roofs. I know what I'm talking about. You think this is bad, wait till she really gets going. You won't be able to chain her home."

"Maybe she needs to get out of here for a while. Hey! Maybe we could drive down to Tennessee, the three of us, and see my family down there." Her father's voice is excited, and Susan can imagine his face turning red, the way it does whenever he gets an idea. "She could see her grandparents, and I could show you around the place. You've never seen the mountains."

"I bet your folks would love that," Aileen says. "You already told me that the only reason they stopped liking Nixon was because he cussed on those tapes. I mean, they'd have me put in jail for being a loose woman."

"That," says her father, "is a problem we can fix up real soon."

From her corner Susan can see their shadows spill onto the walkway, elongated by the light from the living room and broken up by the porch steps. They are so close together the shadows look like one person, someone with a large head and padded shoulders. Anybody driving by would see a couple kissing on their porch steps in the middle of the night, and they would think it was touching or perverted or depressing, depending on how they felt right then. Susan wishes she were driving by. If she were, she would look at them and wonder whether they were really happy, whether they were really meant for each other, whether they were only kissing because their lives were full of conflagration and missing persons. She wonders whether her father would give her a whipping, if he happened to look over the porch railing and see her hiding in the weeds. But she is too old for that, she decides. They are so close together no light comes between them, not the slightest glimmer. She imagines that they are saying goodbye, like two stars in a movie, kissing because it is the last time on earth they will have anything to do with each other. Then, because she is tired into her bones, she leans sideways, into the soapy smell of the clover and the promise of sweet dreams.

OBSCENE CALLERS

§

That day, the day I'm thinking about, I was sitting at my breakfast table alone. It was a bright Saturday morning in summer and I had some things to account for to myself. For one thing, I'd already been in that town three years. And, to be honest, "town" is stretching the meaning of the word: It had about twenty thousand people and about two bars per person and there was a lake nearby full of fish you couldn't eat without poisoning yourself. That isn't a town in my book. For another thing, my husband, Bucky, had run off two months before with this woman from around there. I won't reveal her name, but she had fake blond hair, wore her blue jeans like hands grabbing her butt, was no more than twenty-five, and was looking for trouble. And that's exactly what she got in Bucky Gilman. The only other thing I had to account for was that I turned forty that day. Nothing much, except that forty was precisely two years past half my life expectancy, and not a pretty idea. These are thoughts that bright days and breakfast tables bring home to a person.

Bucky had made the breakfast table, which was one reason you couldn't touch the top of it without spilling your coffee. It was so unsteady I had to keep folding junk mail under the legs to even things up, though no matter what I did, the table turned out unsteady. It was a meaningful table. I'd been married to Bucky for ten years, nine of them pure torture and one of them worse. I was sitting at his table, thinking all these things and wondering what was next. I thought maybe I'd pack up the apartment and go someplace a little different, go to a real town, for instance, where good things could happen to a person for a change. Wishful thinking, though forty is an age where balancing the good and the bad makes a lot of sense. I had a job up at the speedway in the ticket booths, decent work except it closed during the winter and there was no way you could look at it as a place where I explored my personal career potential, like they say in the ladies' magazines. My personal career potential was zip at the speedway, although it paid the rent and that's the bottom line those magazines don't mention. You read that stuff for too long and you start thinking everybody in America is two steps ahead of you and you don't have a prayer. But, like I said, it paid the rent. No one can hate that.

I'd just about decided to call in sick to work, it being my birthday, when the phone rang. I figured it was Granby at the speedway calling to ask me to work an extra shift, which would figure since I'd gotten used to getting just exactly what I didn't want. For a second I thought about not answering, but the fact was, I couldn't be sick and not home both. So I answered it; I said, "Yes, what is it you want?" I've never been one for the Good-morning-Gilman-residence bit, just another bone of contention between Bucky and me. That one with the fake hair and the tight blue jeans would be perfect for it is all I can say, if he ever marries her, which he won't.

There was silence on the other end of the connection, so I said "What is it?" again and waited. Then the guy on the line started murmuring, a kind of low, awful rumble that made me think whoever it was, was sick or something. And I was right. It took me a while to figure out where the chips were falling, but I finally did.

"Then cut it off and use it for a doorstop, you shithead," I yelled, then I slammed down the phone, hard. There's no need to tell what he said, though it was language I don't appreciate from anybody, not nobody, especially not some sick old bastard like this guy was. I don't mind saying it scared me a little bit. Maybe it scared me a lot. I got to thinking about how I was forty now and not as quick as I used to be, about how anybody and his brother could crash into my apartment and beat me senseless with a broomstick, or worse. I got to thinking I was there in the apartment all alone and that wasn't a good place to be. I wanted to wring Bucky's neck. I wanted to wring the phone's neck, though when I looked at it, it already looked wrung, the cord twisted crazily around the receiver like a rat's tail. It was upsetting, and the more I thought about it, the more upset I got. I sat back down at the breakfast table, put my elbows on it, but when it rocked toward me I jumped, just as if somebody had tapped me on the shoulder. I was a little upset and that's a fact.

The way I see it, you're at the mercy of anybody who phones you, just one reason you don't have to be polite about it. But an obscene phone call is different. When you're in a bad spot, it means something worse is just around the corner.

All of a sudden those ten years with Bucky looked like decent ones. My mother always said the assholes you know are better than the ones you don't; she knew a thing or two, except she's dead now. I thought maybe I'd get up and lock my door, then I thought that was stupid: Any maniac knew how to break down a door. I wondered if this obscene maniac knew where I lived. The table top kept rocking back and forth and I couldn't tell whether it was because of me or whether it was Bucky's crazy construction—there was no telling where the fault lay, except the table kept rocking. I was almost in tears, just from not knowing anything.

He walked by the window when I was feeling that way. I looked out the window, then the table rocked forward and I thought, *There's the only man on earth I know didn't make that call.* It was a simple thought, but it had the beauty of being true and made me feel as though I had company coming over, as though things might get better and forty was a hell of a lot better than dead. I leaned over and rapped the window with my knuckles. He stopped on the sidewalk, looking around, his lunch pail swinging back and forth on its handle. I gave another good rap or two, then he saw where I was. His square face was full of confusion, but it was friendly confusion, the way a smart dog looks at you when you talk baby-talk to it. I waved my hand at him in a festive way. He waved back, still looking confused, the bottom of his lunch pail glinting in the sun, then he turned around and moved on down the sidewalk. I watched him go, thinking he looked pretty good, real good, like a guy who could get rid of trouble faster than he could get into it. There aren't but a handful of men who look like that, and that's God's truth.

* * *

The best part was, I knew who he was and where he lived. He lived in the apartment building next door to mine, he worked for the nuclear power plant up on the lake—doing nobody knew what, like everybody else who worked there— and his name was Grover. Grover Littlefield. I knew all this because of a fishing pole. One day in May I'd answered my doorbell and a parcel post man stood on the walkway, holding on to a long, thin box. This was about three weeks after Bucky had run off, so when I saw the guy my heart gave a little leap; I figured if Bucky was still ordering things to the apartment, he might come back, might be on some kind of lark that he knew all along would soon go bad. But fat chance, nothing turns out. What did turn out was that the parcel post man had come to the wrong apartment building.

"You got a Grover Littlefield here?" the guy wanted to know.

"Hell," I said, "I don't even have a husband here." I wasn't in the mood to be cheery. The guy just looked at me, scratching his head. It seems like every parcel post man in the world has an itch under his hat. They're always scratching.

"Says here there's a Littlefield," he said and showed me the address slip to prove himself, though I didn't look at it. "One-oh-eight and that's this."

"*This*," I told him, "hasn't got any Littlefields."

That irritated him, I could tell, but he didn't say anything about it, must have seen my face, which felt like it was coming unstuck and falling onto the concrete of the walkway. Bucky was an asshole, no doubt about it, except I didn't know anything better than wanting him to come back.

"Look, ma'am," the guy said and quit scratching, put the box out in front of me like a present. "All I know is I've got a name and an address and a fishing rod right here and they all of them have to shake hands by the end of the day. One-oh-eight is what I've got. It's from a Littlefield in Georgia," he said hopefully, as though that might clear things up.

"Georgia," I said. "God Almighty. Let me look at the address." He handed it over and I looked at it. Right away I knew it was the wrong building, though something about the writing caught my eye. Grover Littlefield and I lived cater-corner on Ontario Street and the Littlefield in Georgia had drawn a tiny picture of Lake Ontario beside that part of the address. He'd also drawn a picture of a fishing pole that stretched out across about half of his picture of the lake. There was even a drawing of a little cornfield beside the name. "Cute," I said. "Southern Indians with fishing poles. I swear to God. Littlefield. That sound Indian to you?"

"Frankly," he said, "it could say Jacksquat and I'd have to deliver it."

I told him where he needed to go, almost invited him in for coffee, I was feeling that low, but he was so grateful for the right address I knew he was in a hurry to get his job done. Sometimes I got that way myself at the ticket booths at the speedway: stiff and efficient as all get out. Even sorry jobs have a certain amount of personal career potential, I guess, though there are better things in life.

A few days later I was walking down a sidewalk in town when I heard a screech of tires so close I thought I was a goner. It was that parcel post man, leaning out of the door of his truck.

"You scared me to death," I called, not so much mad as relieved, considering how many drunk drivers there were around there. You wouldn't believe how dangerous it was to walk down the sidewalks in that town after five o'clock. It was high noon all the time, after five o'clock.

"You were right," he called out.

"Right about what?" I walked over to his truck, taking my time even though some horns had started honking. I'll accommodate myself to anybody who stops traffic for me.

"He *is* an Indian, or at least partway. He took that box with the fishing rod, looked at the address, and just laughed. Just laughed and laughed. I've never seen a happier guy. Over an old fishing pole. I saw him take it out. It was *old.*"

"That's nice," I said, wondering what the point was and watching a car swerve around the truck toward the intersection.

"That's *him,*" he said, all excited, and I looked where he was looking. "That's why I stopped. It was too perfect, seeing you and him at the same time. I'm telling you, that's *him.*" Parcel post men are strange, but they're good with faces, I'll give them that. Maybe this one was just grateful to me for setting him straight that time. I looked at Grover Littlefield. He was half a block away, stopping at shop windows and staring at things. He was tall, as tall as most of the shop windows. He was tanned, too, except you could tell it wasn't a tan that came from the sun but from something almost as old as that. And he was handsome, the way some furniture is handsome, chiseled out somehow. He was around thirty years old, an age I knew well, having been through it before.

"Well," I said, "that's one good-looking partway Indian."

"Get this," the guy said. "He works for the nuke plant. An Indian at a nuke plant. It beats all."

"It does. It beats all." I gave a mean look to some guy in a Pontiac behind the truck who kept leaning on his horn.

"I'll bet he isn't married," he said. "I'll bet you he isn't even *engaged.*"

"Nice to see you," I told him, backing away, embarrassed all of a sudden. "Thanks," I said. Then the parcel post man switched gears in the truck, made the tires squeal, and I never saw him again.

All of this went through my head while I rapped on the window. Grover Littlefield had just happened to walk by, though I saw it was a good omen. Anything is a good omen when you need it to be. Right then this plan unfolded like a clean sheet in my mind, just as if it had been waiting there for years to snap itself open.

I called Granby at work and said I was sick, said I was too sick to come to work that day. I made my voice sound pitiful. "*Female* trouble," he said in a nasty way, which was the only way he could be. The walls of his office at the speedway had posters of naked women spread out awkwardly over the hoods of super-modifieds, and anytime you went in there, he made sure he stood in front of one of them while he talked to you. Whenever I thought about Granby I saw his ferrety face with the breasts of some poster woman sticking up behind his head like fat devil's horns. "I'll get Maureen to come in," he said, "but your ass better be behind the counter tomorrow. I've got a speedway to run, not a goddamn whorehouse. I'm hiring *men* from now on, that's all, no fucking *females.*" Maureen was his wife, a big-boned woman who, at least once to my knowledge, had knocked Granby cold in an altercation involving some missing receipts. He'd been in the hospital for two days. His grease-monkey friends brought him posters of naked women and cars by the fistful, like flowers, until the nurses on his floor at the hospital threatened to go on strike if all that stuff didn't get taken out of there. I told him fine, OK, I'd be there tomorrow. Then I hung up and got busy.

The cake was the hardest part. I kept opening the oven every five minutes to see what was happening, couldn't leave it alone, so of course the cake fell. What I did was, I baked another one, only this time I tried to make it fall, which is harder to do for some reason, though I did it. When I stacked the two on top of each other, they looked just about right, and with icing all over it, the whole thing looked exactly right. The chocolate was as peaked and dimpled as the face of the moon, a fine-looking cake.

I took some time dressing. At first I put on some clingy polyester pants and a nice print shirt, but they were too dressy and made me look like I was forty, which was ten years older than I felt I deserved to be. Finally I decided on jeans with a cotton smock, red leather sandals on my feet. I'd kept my figure pretty well. If I held my breath, I was about the size I'd been at twenty-five. Whatever happened when I wasn't holding my breath, the smock would cover up.

Around five-thirty I went over. My sandals made sucking sounds on the hot pavement, the cake smelled of butter and chocolate and weighed about ten pounds. I felt proud of the cake, kept hefting it in my hands. Way down the street, squared by the municipal buildings, I could see a piece of Lake Ontario, green at the bottom of the square and going to blue where it met the sky, crisscrossed all over by telephone wires. Seeing the lake made me think it might not be such a bad town, when you discounted everything else about the place.

Grover Littlefield's apartment was on the ground floor, next to the street, just like mine was. In fact, our apartment buildings were identical, all the doors opening up onto the parking lot, all the windows made so that you couldn't open them, the buildings slapped together in about three months during the boom that had come when the nuclear plants started construction. There were three of them around there, which has to be some kind of crazy record. All I could think was, *The power plants had better be built with more sense than these apartment buildings, or else everybody around here is a goner.* Bucky once said that nothing on earth was safer than nuclear power, which was a crock and I told him so. "I can think of ten different things that are safe," I said. "Nuclear power ain't one of them and another one ain't *you*." I already knew he might be fooling around. I wondered where he was right then, what he'd do if he saw me holding a cake in front of Grover Littlefield's apartment, holding that thing and my breath, too. It was a sight I'd have paid admission to see.

I stood in front of his door for a while, figuring out how to knock with the cake in my hands. Finally I just set it down beside the door. Out in the parking lot a seagull made what sounded like a series of hacking coughs, and I suddenly realized I didn't know what the hell I was doing there or why I was doing it or what might come next. I knocked twice on the door, fast, before something worse came over me, then I picked up the cake and stood there, smiling for all I was worth.

Grover Littlefield opened the door wide, a big smile on his face, too, though it turned into something else when he saw me, a sort of smile with its breath knocked out. He looked at the cake, then back inside his apartment, as if there might be people with party hats about to jump out from behind the furniture. He had on a black T-shirt that said GO FOR IT and jeans that looked so worn they were almost white, but his face, framed in the doorway, was something that made me hold my breath without thinking about it. My God, it was a good face. It was a face that might have done push-ups, strong and hard and smooth, a face that told you it looked that way because whatever was behind it was in just as good shape. I don't mind saying I loved him at that moment. I don't mind saying that at all.

"Do I know you?" he asked, pulling the neck of his T-shirt with one finger. He stared at the cake, then back at me.

"Oh, no," I said and gave a little laugh. It was a snort, not a laugh, but I couldn't help myself. "I'm just a social caller. I mean, I'm just visiting. Since I knew I was coming, I baked a cake." I snorted again, then held up the cake for him to see it better. "It's my birthday and everything."

"Jerry!" he called out, laughing hard all of a sudden. "Jerry, where are you, you son of a bitch!" He leaned past my shoulder and looked around, his laughter a nice sound, like the hooves of horses pounding grass. There wasn't anything out there, nothing but the walkway and the parking lot and maybe some seagulls. "Jerry?" he asked, straightening up. He quit laughing.

"Honest to God," I said, "I'm just visiting. I saw you outside my window this morning. Remember? I knocked on my window and you turned around and waved. Remember?"

"I guess so." For a while he pulled on the neckline of his T-shirt, as if his breathing had something wrong with it. His eyes were exactly the color of the chocolate icing. I could still smell all that butter as well as something even richer, which might have been him. "You say I waved?" he asked.

"Sure you waved. You stood on the sidewalk and waved. I'm a hundred percent sure on that—you waved. Listen, could I set this cake down? It weighs as much as a two-year-old."

"I guess so," he said, though he didn't move, expecting, I guess, for me to set it down right there on the doorstep.

Instead I said, "Great!" and moved around him into the apartment. It was a bold move, at least it was for me, one that had my heart pausing for so long I felt maybe I'd left it outside in the parking lot. You might think your heart always pounds like a jackhammer in big moments, but you'd be wrong.

"Nice place," I said, which was a lie. I had to throw some clothes on the floor to set the cake down on the coffee table. "Listen," I said, "my name's Dale," which was the sorry truth and my mother's fault. "I'm real glad to know you. I mean, it was real nice of you to wave and everything." He was standing in the doorway, this time with his back to the outside, standing there and looking like he had some things on his mind.

"Can I sit down on this couch?" I asked, trying to stir up his attention a little.

"OK," he said, and I did, right then. "But let me get this straight. Are you trying to sell this cake or give it to me or, just what all is this business with the cake?" He came into the living room, then stood over the cake, putting it square between us like an argument.

"It's a present, you know, a sort of calling card. Like a bunch of flowers, like a casserole, like a— Frankly, I don't know what the hell it's like. It's a cake. I'm giving you a cake."

"Oh," he said, as though that was all he needed to know. "Grover, Grover Littlefield. Pleased to meet you." He stood behind the cake, holding a thumb toward his chest as if he were pointing himself out in a crowd. "I never had a cake give me before."

"That's all right," I said, giving him a smile. "I never baked one before."

"Well, Dale." He squatted in front of the cake, the way

he might have squatted in front of a stream full of fish out in the woods. "It smells real good. That's always a good sign."

"It's the butter. That and the chocolate. We're talking cardiac alley right down the middle of that cake, but I figure, what I figure is, you can't cut yourself off from all the pleasures in life. I had a friend that wouldn't eat anything but celery and carrots. Day after day it was celery and carrots. I'm telling you, she was one unhappy woman."

"That's right," he said and grinned, pointing to his T-shirt. "That's my philosophy on life in a nutshell." He held the grin for a while longer. He was the smoothest man I'd ever seen—not a hair you could see anywhere except on top of his head, where it was as dark and thick as a mink stole. Bucky had been hairy just about everywhere, hairy as a pink-bottomed baboon.

"I appreciate the cake there, Dale. What do you want me to do with the plate when I'm finished?" He stood up, as though he were already finished with something.

"Keep it, it's just an old five-and-dime thing. But say," I said, maybe a little too quickly, "why don't we have us a piece right now? I haven't tasted it myself."

"I'd love to do that. I sure would, Dale, sit here and eat a piece of cake and all that. But I've got a fishing trip lined up this evening. Jerry, my friend Jerry and me, we've got a trip all planned. There's walleyes with our names on them out there. Or I would. I sure would."

"Oh," I said, thinking fast. "That's exactly why I came over. It's an amazing coincidence, but that's one big reason I came over." I told him about the parcel post man and the fishing pole, at least the parts I wanted him to know. Then, for some reason, I got creative. I told him about how my

father—I kept calling him Daddy in front of Grover Littlefield—how my daddy used to take me fishing every Sunday
of the spring and summer. I told him about how my daddy
would stand on the bank of a lake for hours, telling me about
the fish we neither of us could see and only caught once in
a while. There were fish, I said he'd said, that looked like
hammers and screwdrivers down there, whole toolboxes of
fish. I went on and on about what my daddy had said. It was
a pack of lies, though it *could* have been true, and should have
been. The only thing my father had done with me, that I
could remember, was play checkers every once in a while, but
he threw the board on the floor every time he lost. It was as
family oriented as he got, which was pretty good for the kind
of man he was. Some men just don't know how to act with
a kid.

"So the upshot is," I told Grover Littlefield, "I'd like to
go fishing sometime and I figured you were somebody I could
do it with. I'll bet you there're some walleyed bastards out
there with my name on them, too." I was trying to sound like
one of the guys, so he'd know I could fit in and make do if
I had to. The truth was, I didn't know a walleye from a
waterbug; all I knew about fishing was that you had to throw
something in to get something out and that, come to think
of it, was exactly what I was doing on Grover Littlefield's
couch with a cake in front of me. "So what do you think? Do
you think old Jerry would go for it? Do you think I could try
my hand at this thing or not?"

"Jesus, Dale," he said. "I don't know about this. I don't
know about this at all." He stood there, scratching his head
just like the parcel post man, staring down on the cake as if
it were still the issue under discussion. He looked good doing

it, too, as good as a man can look when you're hoping for something from him. "Jesus," he said. "I don't know. Do you have a rod and everything?"

"No, I don't, I'm sorry to say. I lost it when I moved up here. Either that or I broke it, I don't remember which. Don't you have more than one? I figure, what with that pole you got in the mail and everything, I figure you've got more than one. Don't you? Don't you have more than one?" I had to stop myself after that, mostly because I wasn't breathing correctly when I said it all, I was talking so fast. The sad truth is, sometimes you find yourself being pathetic and all you can do is hope nobody else knows what you know, which is that you're being as pitiful as they come.

"Well," he said, his eyes on the cake, "I guess it's all right. I don't know what Jerry'll say, but I guess it's all right, being that you really want to and your dad being what he was. I guess so. Boy," he said, shaking his head, "I don't know about this. This is something."

"Great!" I said and stood up, staring at the cake since that's what he was doing. "Great! I'll run home and be right back. Should I get some cold cuts or some hamburger or anything? Pack a picnic or something? This is great. Maybe some charcoal and a grill? What?" I don't mind saying I felt crazy right then, crazy with something that was just about the opposite of always wondering what was next; that might have been the exact opposite of turning forty or having your husband leave you or having somebody give you an obscene phone call that made you wonder whether your doors were locked, your life was in order. I was crazy with it all. "You name it in the food department and I'll get it," I said.

"No," said Grover Littlefield. "We don't need a thing.

We fry up some of the fish we catch." He shook his head, looking at the cake, shaking his head like a pretty dog clearing flies. "I don't guess there's a thing we need from you."

They were standing by a beat-up Chevy pickup when I came back. I'd changed my shoes, thrown the sandals across the room and pulled on my sneakers as though my life depended on it. I figured the jeans and smock were just fine for a fishing trip, although I was moving so fast I don't know if I was figuring things out at all. It had taken maybe six minutes for me to sprint to my apartment, put on the sneakers, then sprint back again. I was gasping like a fish by the time I got up to them and probably looked a little walleyed, too. I didn't know but what they might leave me behind, if I made myself late.

Right from the start I didn't like Jerry's looks. It wasn't just wanting Grover Littlefield to myself, either, even though that might have crossed my mind. Being behind the ticket booths at the speedway had given me more people sense. I could tell some things. I could tell who was a tourist just passing through, who was a gambler willing to sell his fingers for a shot at some action, who was bloodthirsty and anxious to see at least three fatal accidents. I could tell after a while, that's all. And I could tell that Jerry wasn't quite right. He was overweight and had squinty eyes, like Granby's, squeezed together somehow from the sheer pressure of what could have been lust or greed or a thing even meaner. His hair was short and blond, cropped close like a government agent's, his scalp pink and weak-looking through the stubby hairs. Right from the beginning I didn't like the guy. But I told myself, and rightly so, *Get along with him and you'll get along with Grover*

Littlefield. Sometimes—all the time—you have to put up with the bad to get to the good. Even the wild animals know that.

"I seen you somewhere before," Jerry said as soon as I got to the pickup. He had one arm draped over the bed of the truck, his little eyes so hidden there was no telling where he was looking. "Where'd you pick her up?" he asked Grover, not moving an inch. "I've seen you somewhere."

"I work at the track," I told him, acting cheery and upbeat. "Maybe you saw me there. Seems like everybody and his brother goes to the speedway sometime or another."

"I got better things to do," said Jerry. "I got better things to do right now," he said, sighing through his nose, "though I guess I don't have no vote on the matter."

"So let's get ourselves in gear," cried Grover, hustling around the pickup, although he hustled right back, not having anything to do on the other side. "Let's get this show on the road."

"Shit," Jerry said. "For shit's sake." Then he sighed again, as though he had the weight of the world on his shoulders and was weary from it. To be honest, I wanted to kick him right in one of his fat old legs. I'm not a hurtful person, but some people test you more than others.

"We're on our way," Grover said loudly, when Jerry moved around toward the driver's side. He was being positive about things, and I appreciated it.

Before I got into the truck I looked over the bed of it, mostly to see what it was that fishermen took on fishing trips. There was a pea-green tarp, folded into a square. There were four fishing poles lined up side by side and alongside them was a blackened grill next to some charcoal in a little box. Near the cab were two cases of beer that looked like enough alcohol to fill an entire fishing stream. But I've already mentioned what the town was like after five o'clock. Other than that, there were two metal carrying cases that looked like toolboxes but were probably full of fishing doodads, worms or hooks or fake mosquitoes or something. It was only when I saw the two toolboxes that I started worrying maybe I'd be an idiot when it came to fishing. It was six-thirty and still light and would stay light till about nine-thirty—a lot of time for ignorance to make a spectacle of itself.

"Walleyes, here I come," I said, trying to beat down the way I felt.

"Wonderful," said Jerry and he started the engine. "Just wonderful."

I was between him and Grover Littlefield in the cab of the truck. We all kept our legs together, even Jerry, who was driving the truck, so there were spaces between us on the plastic seat cover, like checkers on a checkerboard. I played a game with myself with rules that said if my left knee touched Jerry's right knee, I'd die then and there. But the other game I played was with Grover Littlefield, was that if my right knee touched his left knee, I'd die, too, but in a much better way. There was a shotgun on hooks across the windows behind our heads, and that made everything seem more fateful somehow.

"So where do we go to get the walleyes?" I asked. "I can taste those babies right now." We'd already turned onto a country road I didn't recognize, and so what I really wanted to know was, *Where are we going?* I was trying to sound like a big-shot fisherman, somebody who knew walleyes and wall-eye ways, somebody to be afraid of and admire and be good to all rolled into one. But what I really wanted to know was, *Where are we?*

"Grover," said Jerry, his fat red face like a tomato aimed

down the road, "Grover, I'd appreciate it if you'd get her to sit still and be quiet for the rest of the trip. I'd appreciate that. And hand me one of those beers while you're at it. All this talk's worked up a thirst in me."

Grover slid open one of the windows behind our heads, then leaned out, tearing at the paper around a case of beer. After a while he turned around, holding three beers that clinked in his hands from the movement.

"That's more like it," Jerry said and opened his with the bottle caught between his big thighs. "I can take just about anything with a beer in my hand."

"That down there is what I'd call an extra hand," Grover said, giggling in an embarrassed kind of way. "I'd call you a three-fisted drinker."

"You know it, buddy. You got it. I just hope the little lady don't get too excited from the revelation of it all." He took a quick swig of the beer, driving with one hand as though there were something smart involved in being able to do it. I'll admit right now I couldn't stand him. I couldn't stand the sight or the sound or the smell of him. The only thing that kept me from saying so was Grover Littlefield, who seemed to be in a trance, staring at the trees going by his window.

"Yes, sir, Grover boy," Jerry said, "I just hope our little expert here don't lose her concentration."

I was all turned around and lost by the time we got where we were going. Jerry had made some unpredictable left- and right-hand turns until we ended up on a dirt road with high grass growing up between the tire tracks. The air had turned more humid. The smell of water hung inside the cab like something ripe about to fall down on our heads. Through the windshield I could see a line of trees that went in both directions as far as the eye could make them out. Behind those trees were the flickering lights of a brown, slow-moving river. We'd all had three beers, which put us about forty-five minutes and thirty miles away from where we'd started. I was in a better mood by then, what with the beers and the smell of water and the fact that Jerry had kept his mouth shut for most of the drive. I've seen decent men turn mean with alcohol in them, and I've seen assholes turn nice as pie from the same thing, and I thought maybe Jerry fit into that last group.

We got out of the truck. Although the sun was low, it wasn't that low, still cleared the tops of the nearest line of trees. You could hear the leaves moving together, the water rubbing against the shore, and, every once in a while, the splash-thunk of a fish downstream. And on top of everything was the thick, humid, gamy smell of the river.

"Are there wild animals around here?" I asked, but the two of them were bringing stuff from the truck and setting it down under some pines. They opened the tarp, then laid it on a flat space on the pine needles, about twenty yards from the riverbank. Grover carried the two cases of beer, one on top of the other, his arms stretched and smooth and brown against the paper. I felt a ripple of something, seeing that. He put them on the tarp. After that Jerry took the grill and the box of charcoal down toward the river, toward where there was a burned place in the grass near the bank. Wherever we were, you could tell they'd been there before.

"Nice little place you found," I told Grover.

"It's Jerry that found it. All I do is go where he points me. I'd never have found it on my own."

"Oh," I said, "I think you just don't know yourself. I think you could've found a place just as nice on your own."

"Well," he said, "well, you'd be wrong to think that way. I don't know shit about the woods up here." He smiled when he said it, as though not knowing shit were something he was secretly proud of. "Let me get you your pole and some tackle." He went over to the truck where Jerry was already leaning the poles against the bed, fiddling with each one before he set it down. It made me nervous, that he seemed to know exactly what he was doing when he fiddled with them.

"She's not using none of my jigs," Jerry said. "She can have some bait but none of my jigs."

"That's all right," said Grover. "I got plenty."

I moved up behind them and said, "We didn't have jigs where I come from," just in case I was supposed to know what they were. "We didn't have walleyes either." Saying all that, I thought I had the bases covered. One thing I did know about being ignorant was: Tell the truth as much as you can, but stop short of sounding like an idiot in trouble.

"Well what *did* you have where you come from?" Jerry asked.

"Oh," I said, "all kinds of things." I tried to think of the names of fishes. "All manner of fish," I said. "Except walleyes."

"Here," Grover said and handed me a pole. "Let's go down to the bank and let you test the action. You like your action light?" The way he said it, I knew it was a test question.

"You bet," I said. "Nothing but light action for me." From the look on his face, I could tell I'd gotten the answer right; I felt dizzy for a second, just from being 100 percent on the money for a change. "It's light action or nothing as far as I'm concerned."

"You'll like this pole then." He touched the pole right above where my hand held on to it. "It's a good old pole. My brother gave it to me."

"I know," I said. "That's one thing I know and like about today."

When we got down to the water I noticed how big the river was. From a distance it might have been a large stream, but when you got right next to it the perspective changed, opened up somehow until the light of the sun going down, and the flow of the brown current, and the almost invisible movement of the trees overhead—until all of that made the river look as large and mysterious and deep as what your future life would always be like. It was only a thought I had, standing there on the bank, trying to account for what I felt and what I saw both. Nature has a way of making you think about things, whether you want to or not.

"What is this river?" I asked Grover. "Just what is this river?"

"I don't know. It's a river. It's just a river." He laughed a little. "I don't know, it's a cake, it's just a cake," he said and I laughed, too, feeling cheery all of a sudden. When I looked out there again, it really was just a river and not all that big, either.

"OK. Cast her on out there and see how you like her."

I hefted the pole in my hand, feeling the awkwardness of the thing. Down toward the end the hook and line had been doubled back and hooked inside one of the metal circles that held the line close to the pole. I unhooked it, which seemed to be the thing to do, then let it hang at the end of the pole. A few inches up the line from the hook was a shiny metal piece.

"It gets their attention," Grover said, fingering the piece. "Even if they're not hungry, these babies stir 'em up. It's a jig. That's a jig, if you want to know. All right. Let her rip." He moved over a little ways.

There's no need to go into detail. I cast twice and both times the line caught in the trees with the hook hanging down like a noose over the river. There's nothing in the world lonelier-looking than a hook hanging in midair, nothing except maybe a woman just turned forty trying to fish, and doing it badly.

"I guess you don't have no trees where you come from neither," Jerry said behind me. It was irritating, that he'd snuck up behind me and couldn't help but mouth off.

"As a matter of fact," I shouted, turning on him, "as a matter of true fact, I always did my fishing in a boat. Out in the water. Out in the water where the *fish* are. Out in the water where I'm close to what I'm aiming to get. That's what we did where *I* come from."

"A real fighter," he said and grinned, his eyes squinted up till they disappeared. "A true sport. C'mon, Grover, let's us move upstream some. You take one of the cases. I got your gear here." After Grover went away, Jerry held out a Styrofoam cup. "Here's your bait. Watch out for the worms, they bite. Like to have taken my finger off one time."

He looked so serious I said, "Thanks." Then I said, "But where are you going? What's going on?"

"We need somebody to stay and watch the gear. All right? Seeing as how you're such an expert and everything, I figured you wouldn't mind fishing down here by yourself. I mean, I know how privacy is meaningful when people fish. OK? Fine."

"But," I said, "but . . ." I looked around, but all I saw was the tarp and the grill and the little box of charcoal. It didn't exactly need an armed guard to defend it, I could see that.

"We'll be back as soon as it gets dark," Grover said, coming back with the case of beer. "We'll be back before you know it." Then the two of them headed off upstream, and then there wasn't a thing to see except the leaves of trees, the muddy river, and the hook hanging down in midair like a question nobody had paid attention to.

The sun had sunk low enough to make the river turn bright yellow down the middle by the time I got my line out of the tree. After I reeled it in I stood for a minute, staring at the water over the tip of my pole. It wasn't muddy any-more, just bright and yellow. Occasionally I heard the splash of a fish, though I never saw one; the glare was too much—or else I was a fool for something and didn't know it. That glare might have been a million fish, all of them huddling together, their scales flashing the sun, and I wouldn't have known the difference. All of it put me in mind of the beer in the case on the tarp, so I went up under the pines, grabbed the case by a flap, then pulled it all the way down to the bank. I opened a bottle and put the cap back into the box. For a while after that I just drank the beer, then after that I drank another one. Then it seemed to be time to do something else.

I'd leaned the pole against a tree, right beside the cup with the worms in it. The worms were thick and long in there, writhing in and out of a thimbleful of dirt. They didn't look like they had teeth; they didn't look like they had heads; but I was careful. I had to open up another beer to Dutch my courage, which should have told me to stop what I was doing then and there, except I couldn't stand the thought of Jerry's fat face saying he guessed we didn't have fish where I came from either. And worse, the thought of Grover's face, disappointed in me maybe, his good feeling for me gone forever because I couldn't catch a fish, because I was a liar and forty and pitiful. When I pushed the middle of a worm onto the hook it corkscrewed itself around the shaft, grabbing on like a furious hug. Both ends of the worm were as blind and helpless as the tips of fingers.

"That's terrible," I said and looked behind me, as though somebody else had said it. "God Almighty," I said loudly, then turned back to the river.

This time I cast beyond the trees, right into the river where the current immediately began to take the line downstream. All I did was stand there and watch it and hold the pole, even when the line stretched out to a 90-degree angle. As long as the hook didn't bite into the bank downstream, I figured I was fishing. I stood there like that for a long time, at least for two beers' worth of standing, although after a while I sat down on the case of beer. I didn't know anymore how many beers I'd had—which is just exactly too many— but I began to think, sitting there on the case. I began to think about fish, the walleyes and the other things down under the water. I could picture them swimming through the brown haze, the glare of the sun overhead like a sky on fire, swimming through all that because they knew what they were doing. They belonged there and knew what they were doing, and I didn't. I wondered whether Bucky belonged wherever he'd gone, whether he'd come back, the way I'd read that salmon did, except then they died. Thinking about Bucky coming back and dying was almost a peaceful way to look at it.

"Come back and die, you old bastard, you," I said out loud, but not in a hateful way. Sometimes a curse is a way of showing affection or hope about things. "Or else don't," I said, "and stay with Miss Tight-ass and see what happens. I might have other fish to fry, by God." I was a conversational fool right then. It must have been the beer, I think, that and the nature everywhere.

Then I felt a pressure on the line, which scared me to death. Of a sudden the last thing in the world I wanted to do was catch a fish. I jerked the pole, started reeling in the line as fast as I could, reeling it in so quickly I could tell it was all right, that I hadn't hooked anything. When the hook came up the worm was gone. It had been a sorry sight from the beginning, so I was glad to see it gone. Nothing curled up the way it had been is a pleasant thing to see. I leaned the pole back against the tree and left it there.

Upstream I saw a beer bottle floating down and I knew it was Jerry's, Jerry being a pig and an asshole. Another one came by, too, and that was Jerry throwing Grover's bottle in. I thought about all those fish under there looking up at the bottles, wondering what the devil they were, friends or enemies. It made me sick to my stomach, though that might have been the beer. I was a little dizzy and sick. I went up to where the tarp was spread out on the pine needles, lay down, and stretched out. For a minute everything swarmed around, but it quit that after a time. It might have been a few minutes or a few hours; I don't know how long it was, except when I woke up it was dark and my head hurt and I could hear them coming through the woods.

I lay still to keep my head from hurting. They were laughing about something when they came, Jerry's voice snorting and hawking, Grover's voice strange—high-pitched, gigglish, like a girl's somehow. It wasn't the same pleasant laugh I'd heard him make back in town, so I knew they were drunk as skunks on the beer. I rose up on my elbows to see better, wincing as I did it. They had fish, at least four of them that I could see hanging from Jerry's hand; all Grover had was a six-pack in one hand the poles in the other. It was dark and they were just dark shadows against the even darker trees.

"Where's the little lady?" Jerry called out. "Where's that little Dale Evans fishing champion? Shit, she didn't even start the charcoal. I told you, I told you she wouldn't have." I stayed put, just watched Jerry's big fat shadow crouch over the grill. "Grover, you start this up. I'll clean the fish. I'll clean *my* fish, you worthless son of a bitch. You got no talent, I swear, two fucking no-talents and me smack in the middle." Grover giggled, crouching over the grill now.

When the charcoal lit up, I could see Jerry squatting over a fish with a knife in his hand and blood everywhere. He'd taken off his shirt, showing a fat stomach that hung like two huge bloody lips over his belt buckle. He was none too steady, kept clutching the fish to his stomach, grabbing it up, and pulling stuff out of it. The charcoal settled into an orange glow that made the needles over my head look like a blue wave crashing down.

"I'm more of a goddamn Indian than you are," Jerry said and stood up with half a fish in one hand and the knife in the other. I could see his silhouette flexing its arm muscles at the river. The river was invisible, though. "I'm a goddamn savage is what I am." He turned toward where I was and I could see the blood and fish scales all over the front of him. I wished that the light from the grill would go out. I wished the sun would come up and then it would all be over.

"Where's the little lady?" he called, stumbling up toward the tarp. "I see you," he said. "I see you, you fucking liar. Fishing, my ass."

"Keep away from me," I said when he got close. "You keep away from me."

He stood at the edge of the tarp, swaying, squinting down at me with the light from the grill glowing off the back of his head. Then he dropped the knife and the fish and his face grimaced in a terrible way. "You don't know for shit about fishing. You don't know for shit about *me*. Grover, he's a puppy. He's a damn ass-backward puppy." I could see Grover come weaving up from the grill, still giggling, giggling as though there were a mosquito in his throat.

"You come near me and I'll kill you," I said. "I'll kill you. Grover? Grover?"

"Grover, Grover," Jerry said in a voice he thought was mine, but wasn't. "I know you. I seen you somewhere before. I seen you and you're up to a different kind of fishing. I know you. I know you. Honey," he said, "honey, I'm your friend."

I flipped over and got on my knees, scrambled up the tarp with my head pounding, but Jerry was quicker and grabbed hold of my ankle. I kicked at him, then he pulled me down and I punched his chest, but my fist just grazed off all that blood as if I were wiping him off.

"I'll kill you, you fat asshole, I'll kill you!" I shouted, but I could hear Grover giggling off to the side and I could smell Jerry and then I could feel Jerry and it was no use. It was no use. It seemed like it was Jerry doing it all, then it seemed like it was Grover, and then it seemed like it might have been

Bucky or Granby at the racetrack or the obscene phone caller or my father with checkers in his hands. It seemed like I was underwater with beer bottles everywhere. Then I started throwing up and it was over.

For a long time I didn't move. I could hear the two of them talking down by the grill. They sounded exactly like two men on a fishing trip talking about things men talk about on fishing trips. I turned on my side, curled myself up, then lay still. I lay so still I thought I could feel the river moving underneath me. I lay still so long I wondered about myself. Off above the trees I recognized stars, all of them flung out across a million billion miles of nothing, but I recognized them. They looked like candles on a cake, a cake as big and sad as dying one day would be. I wondered if I'd done something to deserve all this. I wondered what it was that had brought me to this. I could see the stars and feel the river moving under me and I wondered, to keep myself still, I wondered, *Did I do something wrong?*

WOMEN IN
THE KINGDOM

∽

Every once in a while they still come by, wearing smiles as stiff as the brims of hats, but I never let them in anymore. If I see them coming up the walk, I hide in the bathroom till they go away. Amy, the woman I share a house with, says I should talk to them, says I should settle things once and for all; I say, what on earth good will it do? They'll come by and keep coming by until I move out of this town, or until I die, or until something snaps in their brains and they forget me. Amy is sick and tired of them. I'm just sick to death of all of it, and tired, too.

It's almost spring here and Amy says I should get out more, take an interest in things, maybe pick up a hobby. Yesterday was my birthday—I was twenty-eight, if it matters, which it doesn't—so Amy bought me a bunch of wood and carpentry tools: gadgets that drill holes or smooth edges or nail the wood straight, things like that. I said, "This is great.

This is nice. What are two women like us going to do with all this?" She said, "Make something nice for ourselves, for one goddamn thing," and then she got mad and said some other things. She's on the back porch now, making a table and still being good and mad at me. I'm sitting on the couch, looking out the front picture window, waiting for them to drive up through the melted snow so I can go hide in the bathroom. They usually come on Sundays, sometimes on Saturdays, but the bottom line is, I know they can come at any time.

Three months ago it all started just like that—I was sitting on the couch, looking through the picture window, then there they were. This was before Amy moved into the house, before I really knew anybody in town, still the thick of winter with snow falling like a fog outside the window. Earlier that day I'd taken a walk down by the lake, nothing you'd plan, just a walk. I had been thinking. I'd been thinking about how I'd come to this new town because a woman named Arnette had betrayed me for a divorced man, had left me as easily as you leave a movie, or a church, or some other place that is supposed to be familiar and comfortable, but is easy to leave. I wasn't being morbid or gloomy, though; I was just thinking. Arnette left me, I left town. I would meet somebody else, then she would leave me or we would agree to leave each other, because there was *this man.* Then it would begin again. That's what happens. And that's exactly what Arnette had said, she'd said, "Honey, honey, I've met *this man.*" Women leave you, and what it means, who is responsible, why it happens, all of that grows uncertain as time passes, all of it fades, until what you have to remember are vague moments strung together as tenuously as tissue paper. Husbands, fathers—these are not vague or tenuous. The thought I carried with me that day was: *Women come and go, and* these men *are always out there, they're out there waiting for women— single men, divorced men, men.* I may have been a little depressed or lonesome at the time I took the walk, because I don't think that kind of thing much. Maybe I missed Arnette. Maybe I missed the town I'd lived in for five years. Or maybe I secretly wished I could meet some man and settle down into certainty, though I doubt it.

Down at the lake it was something else. It was cold, but that didn't matter. It was windy, too, but that didn't matter either. All I saw were huge castles in a fog of snow, hundreds of them, thousands, lined up along the shore like spun sugar, all of them made of ice. Waves from the lake had made them, except I wasn't thinking about that. I was thinking about how it would be to live in a castle made of ice that looked as white and blue as spun sugar; how it would be to lie down inside there with all of it glittering around you, huge and glittering and you're inside there lying down. And right then I thought that kings must know that feeling, families of kings and queens and princes, all those people at home in a beautiful kingdom of ice. I don't know why, but I almost cried from a good feeling that felt a lot like being scared out of my wits. After a while they began to look like ice, just ice, no castles, so then I turned around and went home through the snowstorm.

Inside the house I got myself some coffee, sat down on the couch, and lit a cigarette to relax a little. Everybody says that walks are supposed to calm you down, but unless you're blind, you can't help seeing something along the way that sets you off. That ice set me off. I thought maybe I was dying.

There were these shooting pains in my arms. For another thing, the room began to look very dark, not gloomy exactly, but dark. I turned on all the lights, but then I started feeling cold, colder than I had on the lake. Something was screwy, although the thermometer inside the house said 75, so there was nothing for it but to sit still and try to think of other things. I've noticed that sitting around just thinking is a sure way to feel very cold in winter. That's when they pulled up in their brown Pontiac.

At first they looked like they might be lost. One woman got out on the side of the car closest to me, another got out on the opposite side, then each of them pointed in a different direction down the street. Both had on old, worn overcoats, the kind of thing you get at the Salvation Army for five bucks. I felt bad for them, that they were lost in the snow and had to wear those coats through it all. I worked at a department store, had been for a week, loading little boxes of shoes mostly, but I kept an eye on the fashions in the women's section, knew one kind of material from another, and those two women had coats that couldn't have been any warmer than cotton pajamas. I felt bad about it. The Pontiac had rusted out from the back door all the way to the muffler, blue exhaust mingling with the snow, all of which didn't speak well for their being able to find their way out of whatever they'd gotten themselves into. Anytime people have a car like that, other things are falling apart around them, too. I knew that from personal experience. After a minute or so, I got up from the couch and went to the window, to get a better view.

By then they'd taken their bearings, stood next to the car and conferred about something, their breath coming out in white patches. The view wasn't all that great because of the snow, but I could see a third one, sitting in the front seat of the car. At that distance it might have been a big dog sitting there, though when he pressed his face against the car window I could tell it was a kid, a big-eared kid with a red face. I stepped back from the window with a little shock, because I knew I looked just like him: my face pressed against the picture window and red from the cold I'd been feeling. Sometimes you recognize yourself in the strangest ways, and it's always something of a shock, too.

The two women came on up the walk. A half inch of snow had accumulated on the shoulders of their coats, on the tops of their heads. One of them had reddish-brown hair and the other had black and neither of them had on a hat, which was what anybody with any sense would have worn in that weather. Anybody with any sense wouldn't have been *out* in that weather, though I myself had been guilty of that. It all matched up with the coats and the rusted-out car and the fact that they didn't have any hats on. I felt bad and hoped I could tell them something that would get them where they wanted to be. To be honest, I'd been in that position not long before: I'd been in town just a while, maybe five days was all, no job, no house, no nothing. I met Amy in the post office where I'd gone to get a look at the want ads they kept posted there. In ten minutes I had an angle on my job at the department store and a phone number for the man who rents this house and a crush on the woman who told it all to me and all of a sudden things weren't as confusing as they might have been. Amy works at the same store I do—check-out, women's lingerie section. I knew what it meant to be pointed in the right direction, even though half the time the right direction turns out to be a dead end later on down the line. I know that well enough; everyone does.

The one with the red hair knocked on the door. I went into the kitchen and then came right back out again, just in case they were looking through the little window in the door. I didn't want them to think I'd been witnessing their trouble. I could hear them talking, then I opened the door wide, then I opened the screen door and held it open for them. They were both smiling so hard I thought maybe they'd gotten hysterical out there lost in the snow, maybe they'd gotten so upset they didn't know anymore what kind of expression to wear on their faces. It was an odd sight, seeing those two stand there and smile so hard. The one with black hair was young and nice-looking, but the one with the red looked about sixty, looked like she'd seen some different times and not many of them good ones. She was the one who spoke first and that was another odd thing—she managed to talk and smile both, at the same time, the wrinkles of her skin stretched like confusion all over her face.

"How are you?" she asked pertly, just as though she were the one who'd opened the door for me.

"Fine," I said. "Just fine."

"That's good," she said and nodded twice, real hard. Some snow came off the top of her head and settled on the doorstep, but the two of them blocked most of the snow whipping around outside. I was shivering, though.

"Why don't you two come inside for a minute? It's no kind of day to lose your bearings and that's a fact."

They came inside and I shut the door, although before I did I looked out and saw the kid again, sitting there in the front seat of the Pontiac. He was staring out the side window, not moving an inch, as if there were a mystery going on in front of him and he planned to get to the bottom of it. I was with him on that, knew just exactly how he felt. And to be sure, the snow came down hard enough to form a kind of smoky screen between him and where we were, as though whatever mystery was going on was a barrier and a problem for us both.

"Is he all right out there? It's awfully cold," I said.

"Hugo?" asked the black-haired one. She had a sweet face. She had a nice voice, too, or might have had if all that smiling hadn't tensed it up somehow. "Hugo always waits in the car. He's a good boy. Besides," she said, "we left the heater on for him."

"Well," said the one with red hair, "you have a very nice home. You're a lucky person." She looked around, but the smile wavered a little, as though there might be something she resented about my luck.

"Thanks," I said. "I don't own it or anything. I rent, I mean."

"You're *still* a lucky person," she said, and then I began to worry some. Up close they didn't seem all that lost. They didn't seem lost at all. They just stood in the middle of the living room, dripping onto the shabby carpet, looking at me. It was what you could call an awkward moment. Then I thought maybe they were going to try to sell me something; all the signs were there—that business about being a lucky person was one step from being even a luckier person if I'd just buy this or that. Working in the department store with Amy had made me aware of that kind of trick.

"I don't have the money to buy anything," I said, suddenly embarrassed for some reason. The one with the black hair and the sweet face had a pained look, although the redhead didn't miss a beat. You could tell that she was the go-getter of the team. It was embarrassing because of the difference between those two, that and the fact that there was a difference between what I had thought I might do for them and what I might have gotten myself into. Embarrassment is a thing that crops up when you're expecting something else, the way relationships begin, the way relationships end, or else like the way car accidents begin and end.

"Are you afraid of nuclear war?" asked the redhead.

They were hovering around the couch now, looking as miserable and as wet as two beagles come in from the rain, their teeth showing in what was either a smile or a pant. I knew it was a trick question; I knew pretty much who those women were by then. Once, when I was with Arnette, two guys from the Mormons had come by our apartment. They'd looked like a couple of penguins. I don't mean to be critical, but that's how they looked: dark coats, dark ties, dark hair, white shirts—and neither of them could come up with something different from what the other one had said. They were definitely a team of men. They kept asking me, "Are you happy with your family life? Are you satisfied with the way things are going?" At the time I was and said so. At the time I was satisfied that no divorced men figured in my life in any way, and I felt happy that these two Mormon men in particular could never hurt me in a million years. I looked at Arnette and said, "My family life couldn't be happier," then I grinned at her in a meaningful way, but she was looking at their pants. Both of them had their trousers' legs tied back with string, so they could ride their bicycles without messing up the gears. I looked over and decided I liked that; it was the only thing they did that seemed practical. But they were intelligent men, even though they repeated each other, and I listened to them for quite a while before I made them go away. After they'd left, Arnette said, "I can't believe you let those bozos stay so long." I don't know what I said after that. And I'm only telling the part about Arnette as an example of how tenuously moments can be connected.

"Have a seat," I told the redhead. I pointed at the couch, which looked shabby and uninviting under all the lights. "Both of you, have a seat." I thought about offering them a cup of coffee, but with religious people you never knew when something you did every day might turn out to be evil. "Milk?" I asked. "*Hot* milk or what?"

"Oh, no," said the one with black hair, the one I liked. "We can't stay long."

"Tell me something," said the redhead. She was on the couch, leaning back, her coat pressed up against the cushions, shabby pressed up against shabby. "Tell me, are you afraid of the nuclear holocaust?" She squinted her eyes impatiently, as though she might answer the question herself if I didn't hurry up about it.

"Sometimes," I said. "Not today though. I forgot to be afraid of it today." I laughed a little, hoping to loosen up the atmosphere, which had gotten fairly tense. The strange thing was, I liked it. I liked standing there and talking to those two women while their Salvation Army coats warmed up and gave off steam as faint as radiation above the couch. I must have been lonesome, that or depressed, as I've mentioned before. When you move around a lot, like I have, you get used to enjoying the company of whoever comes your way. My feeling is that even complete strangers have some truth and direction in them, if you listen long enough. Name just about any topic of conversation and there will be something you can use in your life from listening to it. I know what I'm talking about: I've heard many things from many people, and not all of it uplifting, but there are useful items in even the most bizarre opinions. Arnette always said that most people are bozos and idiots, but on the other hand, look at her, she's married and pregnant. Bizarre opinions were never her strong point. I liked these two. All of a sudden I felt as though something important might happen.

"Listen," I said, "why don't you two tell me about being afraid of the nuclear holocaust? Listen, don't get me wrong, but why don't you just tell me what it is you're getting at? We'll discuss it. We'll get to the bottom of it." I sat down in the easy chair next to the couch, to show I was ready for anything. And I was.

"Nuclear war is nothing," said the redhead, "nothing compared to the coming of Jehovah God's Kingdom of heaven on earth."

"That's right," said the one with black hair, her head moving around. "That's pretty close to exactly right."

"Do you ladies have names?" I asked. "Before we really get going, I thought maybe we could introduce ourselves. I'll bet you're mother and daughter. Am I right on that? Am I right?"

The redhead shifted her coat testily and said, "We're all of us sisters in the Kingdom."

"Oh," I said, a little disappointed. Then it occurred to me that the redhead had been insulted, that maybe she wasn't as old as she looked, although she'd certainly been through some tough times if she was less than sixty. Tough times can tear anything down, I know. "All I mean is, I know how important family is. Doing things with family. I don't know, husbands and wives and children and everything, doing things—family. I thought maybe you two were family, is all." The truth was, I didn't know squat about family. There had been Arnette. And before that, Sharon. And before that, Kathy. Before that my mother had run off when I was thirteen

and I'd waited for her to come back for two years, then my
father had gone somewhere and so I'd been on my own since
forever, it seemed like. Family had meant no more to the
people in my life than a piss in the wind. I don't usually
appreciate bad language, though it has its uses, and that's
what family was.

"At least tell me your names," I said.

The redhead sighed and looked at her friend, who
looked at me and said, "I'm Mary Magdalene." She said it
kindly, as if I were sick in bed. "But everybody calls me
Maggie. Even Hugo." She smiled then, and this time it was
a real one. Her face lit up and looked as sweet as a saint's. You
could see that family meant something to *her*, anyway. "This
is Mary Ellen," she said and touched the redhead's coat
lightly with her hand, though Mary Ellen shrugged it off.

"That's amazing, Maggie," I told her. "My name is Mary
Alice—three Marys in one room. That's an amazing coincidence." It wasn't really my name, but it seemed like a good
lie, the kind of lie that breaks the ice just when you need it
broken most. Sometimes that's all it takes to get the ball
rolling, although I could tell that Mary Ellen still hadn't
gotten into the spirit of the thing.

"You have a husband or anything?" she wanted to
know, peering apprehensively toward the back of the house,
as if she expected to see a naked man come out any minute.

"That's a good question, Mary Ellen. No, I don't. Never
had one. Never will. No husbands here anywhere. What
about you ladies, either of you married?" I was warmed up
now, the whole room had warmed up, and everything seemed
brighter, homier somehow. The only cold spot in the room,
if you could call it that, would have been the place where
Mary Ellen sat. She was all business and you could see that

chitchat made her crazy. Maggie, though, Maggie was sweet and polite as she could be.

"I have my Hugo," Maggie said. "My husband's gone now." She said it almost with relief, and that made me try to picture the guy. All I could imagine was a big-eared fellow with no smile and a stiff back, dead as a doornail and deserving it. He'd probably beaten her unmercifully, in between prayer meetings.

"He's probably in heaven right now, happy as a clam," I said, trying to draw her out some.

"He's in Albany," said Mary Ellen with a mean look. "He was an atheist. A scarlet-colored wild beast that was full of blasphemous names and that had seven heads and ten horns. Revelation, chapter seventeen."

"Well." I looked at Maggie, then at her. "Well. That was certainly colorful." I pictured the guy again, but this time I saw a big-eared, scrawny fellow driving a car hell-for-leather out of town, toward Albany, toward women less colorful than Mary Ellen. He was even panting in my picture, looking in the rearview mirror at her. In fact, I thought, he was probably the guy Arnette had married, for all I knew.

"He couldn't adjust to my Kingdom interests," Maggie said. "He had some bad habits and, I'm sorry to say, some bad ideas, and he wanted Hugo and me at home all the time and—"

"And he will be flung into the abyss before the Millennial Reign of Jesus Christ." Mary Ellen leaned toward me. "And where will *you* be when the present wicked system of things ends? Where will *you* be when Jehovah's Kingdom turns the earth into a paradise?"

"I don't know," I said. "I move around a lot." I'd had just about enough of old Mary Ellen. To break the mood I got up and went to the picture window, stared out through the snow to see what Hugo was up to. The car windows had fogged up around the edges from the heater, but I could see him leaning back against the front seat. He'd taken off his coat, had it tucked up under his chin. Comfortable is how he looked, as though he'd had practice getting that way under difficult circumstances. "What about you, Mary Ellen, are you married?" I came back to the chair and sat down.

"I am," she said. I waited for more to go on, but she was finished.

"And does he have Kingdom interests, too?"

"He does."

"I don't mean to pry, but could you tell me something? Say that paradise comes. Say that Jehovah's Kingdom comes, life everlasting in paradise on earth and everything. Tell me, could you stand being married to him that long? This is hypothetical, I know, but could you?"

I was interested. I knew I was ignorant, too. Anytime a conversation headed toward the topic of eternity—or two weeks in the future, for that matter—my mind went blank. Amy says I have a blind mind's eye when it comes to planning, and she's right. Half the time, I'd just as soon stay ignorant. Besides, Amy had a boyfriend who was sober till maybe nine o'clock in the morning, so I wouldn't call her an expert on planning anyway. But Mary Ellen had me interested, irritated but interested. I kept seeing her and her husband buck naked in paradise, billions of buck-naked husbands and wives, the sins of everybody around them burned off like a second skin, all of them as miserable and unequal to the new occasion as they could be. They'd be waiting, all anxiety, for somebody like me. Maggie, on the other hand, I could see in that sort of paradise; she definitely fit the description of somebody whose future has been as good as guaranteed from the word "go." Anybody who looked and acted like she did deserved something good and usually got a lot of nothing. If the apocalypse came, the change wouldn't be anything disruptive to a woman like her. It put me in mind of the ice castles down by the lake, each a place fit for queens to lie down in, each a place like a perfect family, a kingdom so delicate and beautiful it had to be doomed. I just admired her from as close as I could get, which was the easy chair.

"I'm sorry," I told Mary Ellen when the silence dragged on. "I don't mean to pry. Everybody says I'm a curious person, at least they would if they knew me. You don't have to tell me about your husband in paradise if you don't want to. Really, I can be a maniac in the curiosity department."

"Now, *honey*," Maggie said, patting Mary Ellen; then it dawned on me that the woman was crying. I hadn't noticed before because she looked exactly the same, sitting there on the couch, except that now tears came down and slid through the wrinkles on her cheek. She didn't look very emotional about it, might have just gotten something in her eyes—it was a strange sight and I felt bad for being irritated with her and her husband in paradise.

"God, I'm sorry. I mean, I'm really sorry. I could kill myself for saying that about her husband and the Kingdom and stuff. Honestly, I—"

"Hush now," Maggie said, looking past Mary Ellen at me, and I did. I started thinking, then, that maybe I had it all wrong, maybe Mary Ellen was the one with the husband who beat her unmercifully. It would certainly sour a person on the idea of eternity, having that to look forward to. After a while, since I didn't know what else to do, I got up to check on Hugo again. Outside the snow was all over everything and still coming down hard. Past my neighborhood I could see the dark, ugly-looking cloudbank that always hung over the lake during a storm. It might have been the Hand of Doom at work, edging toward shore; either that, or those two had made me more colorful in my thinking. At any rate, it gave me the creeps, as though something all wrong was just getting started. There were several inches of snow on top of the Pontiac, but I could still see through the windows and Hugo wasn't there. Then I looked up and down the street, as far as I could see, but Hugo wasn't there either.

"Hey," I said, still looking down the street, "Hugo's gone."

When they didn't say anything, I turned around and saw why. The two of them were on their knees in front of the couch, praying for all they were worth. Maggie had one arm around Mary Ellen, her free hand stuck palm-open in the air; it looked as if she were signaling *stop right there* from across the room. That was a little shock, not at all what I expected. Mary Ellen had gripped her hands in a knot, then tucked them under her chin, her coat in disarray around her thighs. The two of them looked exactly like a picture I'd seen on some religious brochure one time: YOUR FAMILY *CAN* AND *SHOULD* PLEASE GOD AT HOME, it had said underneath the picture. At the time the picture had struck me as a very sad sight indeed, the way the praying family on their knees in somebody's living room looked as though the Devil himself had them by the throats—they'd all looked scared to death, and that was how Mary Ellen looked, too.

Maggie opened her eyes and said, "Won't you join us?" It wasn't really a question, I could tell. She patted the floor in front of her in a way that meant she held me responsible for how Mary Ellen was acting, which I suppose I was, though I couldn't have predicted it. I regretted mentioning Mary Ellen's husband, then I regretted mentioning paradise, and then, when I thought about it deeply, I regretted just about everything I'd ever done in my life. Any way I looked at it, I was responsible for whatever had happened. Maybe Arnette *had* met a better person; maybe I *was* an asshole. There was no telling. There was no telling whether I was a jerk or women were jerks or men were jerks—no telling. All I knew was that I would wait for the women. I figured I could go ahead and spend a few minutes on my knees, if it would make everybody feel better about things. Call it simple courtesy if you have to call it something.

When you don't do it much, praying like that can be painful. Your knees ache, your ankles ache, your back gets twinges, and everything you see has a weird perspective, elongated and huge and distorted, the way a kid sees things. That's why people close their eyes. It wasn't something I could see myself getting used to and that's a fact. At first I tried to keep my mind on Mary Ellen, since I felt responsible for her being the unhappiest of us. I thought about her husband, the wifebeater, and prayed that somebody would catch him in the act and cut his hands off. It worried me, though, so next I prayed that if he wasn't a wifebeater, if I had it all wrong, then nobody would cut his hands off. I felt like that squared things up and took care of Mary Ellen. Actually, I was in the dark about Mary Ellen's problems. For a while after that I just concentrated on how much my knees hurt. Then, because I couldn't help myself, I got a little selfish. I got to praying—or hoping—that I wouldn't have to spend the rest of my life enjoying the company of women in a kingdom. I hoped I'd just lost my way for some reason and this town might turn out to be the right one for me after all. Real ice melted eventually and so, in a world of prayer and hope, might a real kingdom—families, marriages, kids, whatever it was that Arnette was aiming for—all of it might melt, disappear, I don't know what. It might all melt away and bring back to me what I had lost. That's what I hoped, what I prayed for. It came to me then that the troubles I had had nothing to do with my knees or my back aching, or with the awkwardness of being on the floor with women called Maggie and Mary Ellen, whose lives, when you got right down to it, were a complete mystery to me. I thought about Hugo and wondered whether he had ever gotten sick and tired of waiting out there in that car, as sick and tired of waiting for the right thing to happen as I had gotten just then, waiting out there for women to come back to you. There was no telling, but I wondered just the same. Once you get down on your knees and try to hope and pray—if you're not used to it—you get very dissatisfied about things. All you can imagine looks a lot like wishful thinking.

"I feel much better," said Mary Ellen, and she straightened out her coat. "That was just what I needed." She shook her head, stiffly, as if she'd downed a shot of whiskey and the feeling of it burned her throat, but not in a bad way. For a minute or so I pretended I wasn't finished praying—and, to tell the truth, I wasn't, if hope is anything like a prayer, which it is. I peeped at the two of them, pretended my eyes were closed, just to see whether they'd be impressed by my participation. And they weren't. Neither of them was looking at me; they were looking at each other. I was disappointed. They weren't very good at what they did if they didn't know a possible convert when they saw one. I felt outside of things somehow, and lonesome.

"*I feel much better now, too,*" I said loudly, even though I didn't. "Now what I want to know is, where's Hugo?"

They stood up together, Mary Ellen holding on to Maggie's arm, both of them looking ready to go. They'd been through the mill, though over what was a mystery to me, and their faces weren't smiling anymore—they'd given up on all that. I had a moment of panic, then, at the thought of being left in that living room with all the lights on and them not there. Even the couch looked sinister to me, now that they weren't sitting on it.

"Listen," I said, "what say I fix you two some supper and we find Hugo and all of us sit down to a nice meal? Sort of a family kind of thing, I don't know. I've got some frozen hamburger patties, take just a minute to whip them up. Or maybe you don't eat meat. Jeez, maybe you're vegetarians. But I've got vegetables, too. You name it, you can have it." I had to stop myself after that; being on my knees made everything sound a lot like begging.

"We've got to be going," Mary Ellen said and she moved toward the door. She'd had enough of me, which was plain, because she was already pulling at the door before I could stand up and get the circulation back in my legs.

"Hot chocolate?" I asked. "Milk? It's no trouble."

"You've been very kind," said Maggie, "but, really, we've spent way too long here already. I mean, we have a schedule and everything. Usually we don't even get in the door of places. This has been a real, a real, well—it's been different." She stood by the door and looked apologetic, her nice face tired and drained and, it seemed to me, on the edge of being fed up with something. I wondered whether that something was me or Mary Ellen, though by then I could see it didn't much matter: She was already heading into whatever the future had in store for her. She was already as good as gone, into the way things were supposed to be, into the realm of husbands and children and men and children, the realm of the Kingdom and paradise on earth and ice and God and whatever else those things meant, even if they, and He, meant trouble. She was a beautiful woman.

"Look," I said very quickly, "maybe we could get together again sometime. Go out for lunch maybe, see a movie."

"We don't pay to see filth," Mary Ellen said under her breath. She'd gotten the front door open but the screen door was giving her some trouble.

"Bowling? Pool? Anything like that?" I was agitated, must have been, because I don't play any of those things myself. "Or, say, maybe you people have meetings. Maybe we could get together after one of those meetings. What about that? What do you say to that?"

"Well, fine. *Good*," Maggie said. "Let me give you some brochures. We haven't really described our faith to you."

"I think you have. At least I caught some bits and pieces, here and there. I think I could make an educated guess about it. But sure, give me some brochures. Maybe we could get together and discuss it. Shoot the old bull on that topic."

"They're in the *car*," Mary Ellen said, as though the car were a foreign country. She was on the porch by now.

"I'll go with you out there," I said, but Mary Ellen was making her way through the snow, about eight inches of it, toward the car.

"She's just upset," Maggie told me.

"I'm sorry about it." Then, because I was agitated, I said, "Look, Maggie. Let's you and me get together and talk sometime. Just talk. We could take a walk, go down by the lake, tomorrow maybe. We'll talk about Kingdom interests. What say we get together and take a walk?"

"That's nice of you, but I can't, really I can't. Real Kingdom things take too much of my time. Honestly, I don't have the time to do *anything*. But thanks anyway."

"Sure," I said. "No problem." And anyway, I thought, I should have known better than to put the moves on a woman in Jehovah's Kingdom, Jehovah's or anyone else's.

Outside was pure silence. Even Mary Ellen, stomping to the car, didn't make a sound. I hadn't put on a coat but the snow had mostly quit coming down, just scattered flakes that hit my neck and felt warmer than the air. The last of the dark cloudbank had moved off over the lake toward Canada, so the sky was a huge, unbroken white fog all the way to the horizon. There was absolutely no difference between up and down, and the three of us walked right through the middle of it, hushed and looking very small. I was thinking that Maggie, at least, looked very small, even in her oversized Salvation Army coat. Even in that she looked sweet somehow. I was thinking all that when Mary Ellen opened the car door on the passenger side.

"Ah!" she said. It was a little sound, like a pebble hitting pondwater. "Ah! Ah!"

Maggie began to run and I followed right behind her. The way the sky swallowed up Mary Ellen's voice was an awful thing. About ten feet from the car Maggie slipped on the snow and fell down, her legs moving against the ice anyway, and that was an awful thing, too. I got her back upright, pulled her up by the arms, which was easy because she weighed nothing; either that was true or I had so much adrenaline I could have lifted her and her car as well. It isn't only men this happens to. But I have never felt that way since and probably never will, and that's a fact.

"Oh, my *God!*" Maggie cried. I knew then, without having to look, that it was Hugo and it was hopeless; I knew, without ever looking, that we were—in that one moment, in that one place—we were all of us doomed.

For a while nobody came, then they started back at it again about two weeks later. But Maggie and Mary Ellen never came back, though I waited. So far there have been twelve different ones, men in cheap raincoats who come in pairs and knock briskly on the door, like policemen. Two of them even went around the house, tapping on windows. The thought of all those men swarming the house scared me to death. I began to get agitated at work, kept dropping boxes of shoes and running into mannequins. That's when Amy decided to move in with me, figuring I could use a helping hand, although when you come right down to it, she'd just had enough of living with her boyfriend, the drunk. Apparently he's a madman after a couple of drinks. I am glad to have her here, even though I can't relax when she's not around and I can't relax much when she is around and I believe it might be better for everybody concerned if I went ahead and tried out another town, maybe looked up Arnette, discussed birth control or casseroles or married bliss or whatever it is she now discusses. I'd be willing to wait patiently for a more interesting topic to come around.

Amy comes into the living room holding the table she's made with the carpentry tools, but she sets it down in front of the picture window and so I have to tell her to move.

"I can't see outside," I say.

"You better relax," she says. "You'll be a loony tune in a month. What you need," she says very seriously, "is a hobby."

"I have a hobby. My hobby is waiting beside this window."

"You'll be crazy, I'm telling you. You already *are,* a little. I mean, those women aren't coming back. You're crazy not to face it. I mean, *crazy.*"

She feels sorry for saying that, I can tell, because she comes over to the couch and starts kneading the muscles of my neck. For a petite person who works in the lingerie section of a department store, she has strong hands. I've seen the look on people's faces when she shakes hands with them. She is not a bad person, is probably even a good one, but I will never get involved with her. She has that ex-boyfriend and I know, as surely as if it were something legal, that as soon as I got involved with her, she would go back to him. "Honey," she would say, "honey, but I've got *this man.*" I lean back a little, but not too far—not so far that I can't see out the window. The muscles relax in my neck, then she moves to my shoulders. All of the muscles relax; they can't help it with hands like those at work against them. I think, *This is nice, this is great,* but it's not. It gets to the point that I have to close my eyes, and then there it is, right outside my window, even though it's spring here, and thawing. I can see it. You're lying down in a fog as blue as exhaustion, waiting. All around you is a glitter with no top and no bottom and no direction and you're still waiting. It's nothing you planned for yourself, that there are only women in your life, but you'll wait for them for some reason. You'll wait and wait. You'll wait until you're lonesome and scared—you'll wait until the world ends, and keep waiting, waiting for those women in the kingdom.

"What is it?" Amy asks, her hands gripping my shoulders. "Just what's wrong? Just what on earth is wrong?"

And I say, because that's what I'm thinking and because I think it is true, I say, "It's paradise."

WIND

ᔕ

I

That terrible spring, the spring I turned fifteen, was a season of storms in East Tennessee. Every day for weeks the sky hung as indifferent and thick as cigar smoke. The sun simply disappeared. And it was hot, muggy hot, a mean-tempered heat that worked at you from the inside out, like a fever, and you felt you couldn't move or think or even breathe. Around five o'clock in the afternoon the electrical storms would come and we'd all sigh—the whole town would sigh, I think—and then we'd take a breath of that crackling, galvanic air, sucking it in as though we'd only just that moment come alive. Then the storms hit, crazy violent storms, tree-twisting storms that seemed a blessing compared to the awful stillness that came before them. It was a terrible spring, everyone said so, a terrible, frightening spring: We felt the beginning of the end of the world would come like that. Or maybe I'm the only one who felt that way.

Late that spring my mother and sister and I moved out of town. For fifteen years I'd lived in the same town, the same house, the same room, but that spring we left it all. It was a sudden thing, like the storms. One week we were where we'd always been, becalmed; the next week we were electrified, galvanized into action that changed everything. I remember about that afternoon, the day we moved. I remember my sister with a huge cardboard box, fooling around in the yard, kidding around, staggering inside it against the hot, still air, only her arms and legs showing. It seemed logical to me at the time that all our belongings, our things, my sister, my mother, everything would just get inside a box and walk out of town toward the new place, a bunch of packing cases with legs going God knew where. Nothing could have been stranger or stranger-looking than the fact that we were moving at all.

I stood on the rise in front of our house and watched it all. I was supposed to be doing something, I don't remember what, but my mother was so busy with the moving van men she didn't notice. "My *God*," she'd yell out, "those are *breakable* items!" She'd worked herself into a frenzy, and had managed to do the same to the moving men, so they were all down below me fussing and dropping things. The men had hangdog expressions, the faces of men resigned to doing things all wrong, but my mother was exultant, in her element, frenzied with the thought of having these men and a job for them to do and all of it paid for already. Above their heads the sky was an immense, even slate-gray that looked ready to stay that way till the end of time, but it was early afternoon and the hour of the storms hadn't come yet. To my right and left the mountains stretched out like the curves of women's hips, as far as I could see, the green of them turned blue because of the clouds. I knew those mountains, knew them as though they were my own body, and had known them for fifteen years. There's no reason to suppose that the first fifteen years of a life are any less discerning or meaningful than the second fifteen, or the third, or even the last; I knew all about them, loved them. I'd walked all over them, had searched out tiny things on them while I was still a tiny thing myself—no matter. They were home and I was leaving and down below my mother bickered with complete strangers.

"Harriet," my mother cried, gesturing at me with a blue-green notepad. "Goddammit, Harriet!"

She didn't mean anything. She was worked up. What she meant was that she was tired and happy and just wanted my sister and me to rush around, looking busy. She was beautiful, too, standing there in the muggy heat, some of her dark hair pulled from the barrette and sticking to her face like the fragile strokes of an ink drawing. She couldn't bear the thought of us fooling around when the moment was so ripe for something important to seem to be happening. Something important *was* happening, but that it should seem to be was even more important. I knew that. I went down and got my sister out of the cardboard box and told her we should go in and vacuum the floors of the house. We were a messy family, so it really did need doing. We were none of us tidy, at least not in appearance, which is exactly where tidiness counts in the world.

Inside the house my sister said, "When we get to New York, I bet you I'm going to be a cheerleader my first year. I bet you I know more routines and stuff than anybody up there. I bet you I'm very advanced."

"Sure," I said. We were cleaning the living room, sucking up all kinds of things with the vacuum, finding little toys and papers we hadn't seen since we were six or seven. "Ann," I said, "you're probably advanced as they come."

"I bet you I'm very popular. I heard they think blond hair is sexy up there. I mean, they're backward like that, is what I heard."

"What do you know about sexy?" I asked her over the whoosh of the vacuum. My sister was thirteen and was blond, and frankly, a little stupid. I've never liked people who bad-mouth their families, but the fact was, my sister lacked a few things back then. Maybe everybody who's thirteen is stupid in some way, but she was my sister and pretty and I believed her to be almost a half-wit. I was plain and had dark curly hair and had never had a chance even to think about cheerleading. You have to be a certain kind of person to want so much good for somebody else, and then to believe in it with all your heart. For one thing, in our hometown you had to be blond to be a cheerleader. For another thing, you had to be able to flip yourself around and you had to be cheerful all the time and you had to have so many friends you could almost fill a meeting hall with them. My sister could do all of those things; in my opinion, she could do all of those things and more, except think straight.

"What do you mean, sexy?" I asked her.

"Jesus, Harriet," she said. "You're so *backward*."

I turned off the vacuum cleaner. "I'm not backward," I said. "I want to know what you mean by saying 'sexy.' I just want to know what it is you mean."

"I know some things," she said, slyly, her gray eyes the color of the sky outside. "Ha," she said. "You and Mom don't know me at all." Then she picked up an old toy army man and started batting it in the air. But as I said, she was thirteen and, I thought, dim-witted and there was no telling what things went around in her head. She was pretty, as my mother must have been years ago but in a different way. Both of them saw our move out of town as something important in the making. I knew different. I knew we were all wrong, that only tragedy and doom came from things like this, that we were all of us heading into something as crazy and untidy as the way we'd always lived. I was fifteen years old and I knew it.

Outside the wind had picked up. The moving men shuffled around the truck, finished with their part of things but reluctant to leave as long as my mother strode around with the notepad in her hands. When my sister and I came out of the house she paused, squinting her eyes, staring at us as if we were another room to be packed, some more things to be dealt with, more reasons to make the lives of the moving van men miserable. The men looked at us warily, squaring their shoulders, just as though they really might have to heave themselves up after us suddenly, catch us on the run. It was hot and humid and all of us sweated and panted like animals.

"I guess that's it," my mother said, looking at her note-pad. "I guess we're ready to go." She glanced at me, surprised, her eyes confused for the moment. A drop of sweat hung at the end of one of her loose hairs, hanging there forever, impossibly, and I thought for a minute we would not leave, we'd stay, it was all a joke, we would really live in Tennessee all our lives, had never planned to leave, had never done anything to change things. But the next moment that sweat fell, and then I knew we would leave, maybe already had, that things had changed already.

"Maybe somebody should call Dad," Ann said. "I mean, maybe just tell him a few things. I mean, keep it vague and all."

"No way, José," my mother said. "Not till we get to New York safe and sound."

We were in the car, a used '71 Volkswagen Bug with windows so small you felt like you were surrounded by portable television sets whenever you sat in it. My mother had bought it after the divorce, making a great show out of the fact that it had air conditioning and new tires and an AM radio that worked. I hated that car, that tiny, untrustworthy car. Although I'd learned to drive it—in fact, had driven no other car—I knew that it would kill me if the right moment came. You could get the thing to go sixty-five miles an hour if you wanted to, as my mother often did, but I believed it was dangerous and foolhardy to have so much power in such a small thing. It was the perfect car for our family.

"I don't know," said Ann. "I think we ought to at least tell him we sold the house. He used to live there, too, and everything."

We were all of us looking at the house. Ann was leaning up from the backseat, her yellow-white head propped on the dip in my mother's seat, her tongue clicking like a cricket for some reason. My mother had both hands on the steering wheel, though the car wasn't started. Around two that afternoon the moving van men had left, heaving sighs of relief, grinning covertly at each other. I'd been ashamed about it, that we were people strangers could grin and sigh over. After they left we had cleaned for a while and now we sat in the car, just looking things over, ready to leave but too overwhelmed to do anything about it. —But that's not true. I was overwhelmed and I believed my mother to be, a little, but Ann was not. For her the house was already "there," upstate New York already "here." The whole business of moving meant nothing more to her than an inconvenience in the way of getting home, home where there were friends waiting, new and better friends, prettier friends, larger bleachers in gymnasiums, a whole new America to date. I looked at our little old house, at the paint husking off around the frame, at the petunias my mother had planted in the front flower bed, wilting, already needing our help, and I began to hate something I could not name.

"God," I said. "This is no fun."

"Oh," said my mother, rousing herself, taking her hands off the steering wheel. "Just you wait. Both of you just wait. Pete has an aboveground swimming pool!" She looked at me, her eyes as bright and green as the water in Pete's pool probably was. I wondered, looking at her, what she saw in my own eyes, whether in the green of them she saw a reflection of herself, or of my father, or of someone else, someone nobody knew yet; I couldn't figure out very much when I was fifteen, though I knew at that particular moment, Pete's pool meant nothing, nothing at all to me.

"I'm going to give pool parties," Ann said. "You can come, Harriet. We'll have people of all ages and maybe you'll get Mom to make you a new swimsuit." She leaned over toward my seat, and though I thought her head was filled with boys and pool parties and bikinis, she fooled me, which she could do a lot of the time. She said, "Still. I think Dad ought to know about this. He *lived* here," she said, as though he were dead already.

"Forget it," my mother said and put the key in the ignition. "We're not saying shit till we get there. Two days won't kill anybody. Ignorance is bliss." She turned the key, and suddenly the radio came on, blaring, saying crazy things about cures or worries or burrs or something. My mother turned it off. "We'll tell him when the time comes, not before. Not a single minute before. I mean it."

We pulled out of the driveway so quickly the gravel spun out in an arc outside my window. What I felt leaving was guilt, not of course because of the gravel, or the leaving, or even the sight of our house getting smaller and more pathetic as we reversed up the drive, not because of all that but because I'd already talked to my father. The house was nothing compared to that talk; the house was where everything had already happened and we were leaving that and so nothing would happen there anymore. The talk I'd had was where everything would be, a worse place, a place I'd never seen before. It is no crime, at fifteen, or maybe any age, to want to hold on to a past place, however sad, when other places could be even sadder. I don't remember leaving my neighborhood and the town, never felt what I should have, seeing the houses I knew disappear, the clumps of trees and advertisements I recognized, everything disappearing backward, sucked back behind the Volkswagen like scraps of paper in the wind. I never saw all that because I was picturing my father. I was picturing him as he must have looked on the telephone when I'd talked to him the night before, some man in a lobby, some guy hunched over a phone—I don't know—somebody without a family.

"What would it hurt?" I asked finally. "Ann's right. What would it hurt?" We were already on Interstate 81, hurtling north in that car the size of a doghouse.

"I was wondering when you'd chime in. Ann's wrong. You're both wrong. Knowing what you know and you can still say that. I can't believe you two. Are you masochists or something? Honest to God."

"It's not like he could do anything about it," Ann said, irritated because she couldn't stand the thought of being wrong. She put her shoulders up between the seats. "Don't they have guards and stuff down there?"

"Damnit, Ann," my mother cried, "get away from the gears. You throw this thing into reverse and we're dead meat."

"They'd have to pick us out of here with forks," I said. "Tweezers."

"Three dead meats," Ann said. "I read that a really strong wind can pick up a Volkswagen and flip it over, just like a toy."

"Great, Ann."

"Bridges," she said. "Bridges are notarized for it."

"Notorious," said my mother.

"You have your wind going over and your wind going under and then—zap—off you go into the river. Notorious."

"The wind *is* picking up," I said and we all three looked out. Up ahead of us were the lights of cars heading south, their headlights on because the afternoon had grown dark under the coming storm. You could feel the car shudder when the wind moved through, bucking, then gathering itself up as though it had suffered a murmur in its heart. Along the pavement were wildflowers and leaves the wind had grabbed up, all of them scooting along at hunched, awkward angles, like the dying things they were. It was spring; life was still young and tender, susceptible to wind and storm, to violences of all kinds. Like I was, I thought, and Ann, and even my mother, who was thirty-five at the time, though that seemed old to me then. We were all three susceptible if we were anything.

"Notorious," Ann said, trying to sound spooky, hissing the word.

"This all really sucks," I said.

"Listen, ma'am," my mother said. She only said "ma'am" when she was angry or teasing, but she grew angry this time, her profile gray in the light, her eyelashes so long and dark I thought maybe they interfered with her sight, that maybe we were taking our lives into our hands letting her drive. "I'll only say this one more time."

"Uh-oh," said Ann.

"Uh-oh," I said, and we both laughed a little. Sometimes she was all right, my sister Ann, though when push came to shove, you couldn't count on her.

"Goddammit, I mean it. How many cardiologists are there for divorced women in my situation? Can you tell me that?"

"Married or unmarried cardiologists?" I asked, as though I had a book in my lap that could tell me the answer. I was trying to lighten the mood, keep my mother's mind on the road in front of her. When she got angry, she had a tendency to look right at you, which is dangerous and scary in a car, or anywhere else for that matter.

"Pete's a good man. I have found a good man. He could live in Ethiopia for all I care. I'd go there. He could be a fucking missionary in Ethiopia and I'd go there. Do you understand that? I'm not young, Harriet. I am no longer young. Can you just stop a minute and understand that?"

"Yes," I said, "yes, I can." But I couldn't really, or didn't want to, or else just wanted something else for her, for myself, for all of us. A cardiologist in upstate New York with an aboveground swimming pool was all wrong; that's what I could understand.

"Thank you," she said, very quietly, and it made me feel bad and start to hate things again.

"Storm's here," said Ann and she was right. Great hand-fuls of rain began to pop against the windshield, then there was a flash of lightning that seemed to illuminate all of Virginia ahead of us, our path through it tunneled out like something seen through a crystal ball, the vision of it fading slowly into darkness. Only the wiper on the driver's side worked, and it thumped so violently it might have been an arm trying to get inside with us. But what frightened me was being blind. I could see nothing but a rushing of water outside my part of the window, a view from a submarine turret.

"Let's pull over," I said. "We can't see."

"I can see. I'm driving OK. I can see all right."

"No, no." I had my hands on the dashboard, pushing it all away from me. "We'll die if we don't pull over. Pull over, pull over."

"My God, Harriet, it's just raining. I can see fine."

"Pull the goddamn car *over!*" I shouted in a way I never had before.

She did. She did it so quickly a semi behind us squealed around into the other lane, honking past us like a huge wild animal in the night. That we all might have died at that moment was nothing to the thought of carrying ourselves on, blindly, into that storm. All I could think of was stopping, braking, quitting it for a time. I think I was crying—I don't remember—but I do know that nobody said anything for a long while. And nobody mentioned it afterward. We all sat in the car, looking at the rain and the lightning, the head-lights of cars coming up from behind and streaking past, the lights so bright we had to squinch up our eyes until it was over. Though there was thunder everywhere, and the sound of water coming down, the inside of the car was incredibly quiet. It was so quiet I remember the sound of my sister's breath behind me, clicking a little as it came and went, a soft sound, the sound of spring winds through the twigs of trees— the quiet sound of the way things were supposed to be.

II

When I was around ten or eleven I used to watch ducks from the tops of trees. I'd liked ducks. They were beautiful to me. Back in the mountains, about a mile from my neighborhood, was a small, slow-moving river, the Holston, that ran through a valley called Poboy. It was all curving and wooded, the banks moss-covered and green as precious stones, the river more like a series of little ponds than anything that might have been trying very hard to get where it was going. In the fall ducks came there. They came in groups of ten or more, slashes of gold-fired green on their faces, and on their wings some of them, and the sound of all those ducks was like waking up from a nap in a peaceful mood. They'd come wheeling in over the water, dipping in unison, then changing speed and direction, all at the same time, not one of them left behind. They were like family.

I'd climb a tree and watch them eat things. The pleasures I got from my own dinners seemed pale, ridiculous even, compared to the pleasure I got from watching the ducks eat theirs, the families of ducks on the Holston. But hunters always came to that place, too, men who dressed like potbellied stoves, mostly in dark clothes, bringing with them stupid dogs that barked violently at each other and then sat down and scratched themselves, just like the men. I didn't know those men but they were all alike. They were dangerous, and bad at what they tried to do, which was kill the ducks and take them home. They never took the ducks home. They'd come shouting into the woods, beers in their hands, the dogs tripping all over themselves, the guns pointing in all sorts of directions, just as though it didn't matter what it was that got killed, and it didn't much. Once one of them accidentally shot somebody's dog and they all of them laughed, even the owner of it, I guess, because it really *didn't* much matter to them what got killed back in those woods. They were mostly drunk, was one answer. Another answer for it would be one I didn't know the question to, and still don't. They'd come in there and just start shooting. But the ducks—the ducks were different. As soon as one of those ducks got hit by some shot, it dove, dove straight down in the water, dove right into the middle of the Holston as though that was where its heaven lay. I'd pull back against the trunk of a tree and grimace and wonder over it all. They never came back up, those ducks, not until the hunters left. Then, after it was over, they'd rise up, dead, and float there on the water, as brown-colored and stiff and benevolent as the end of autumn. Teals. Green-winged teals. I'd looked them up. That was their family name and they'd come back for their dead and hover over the water, sometimes even poked around, nudging the dead one just to make sure. And I wondered why it was they were that way, after I buried them under the green moss on the banks of the Holston, under moss less green than the feathers on their heads. I wondered what it was that had made them dive down, had told them to grab hold of the weeds down there in the dark and danger at the bottom of the water; what it was that made them grab on and die and not release themselves till whatever badness around them was gone. I respected them. Green-winged teals, I remembered.

I remembered all that, sitting on the side of Interstate 81

in a thunderstorm, because I was remembering my father. When I was fifteen the relationships between the men and women in my life were a mystery, as they still are, but the ducks taught me some things early on. I'm not saying the ducks were women or the hunters were men, or that somehow diving deep into the shade of things and holding on to it is something that only men or only women do—I'm not saying that because I am not simple. I'm saying I remembered my father, and my mother, and our lives together, and somehow the ducks fit into it. We'd been a family in some sort of way.

"Harriet," my father had said, breathless somehow. I could hear the echoes of his voice hitting a tile floor, moving away from wherever he stood into something bigger and more spacious. "Honey," he said.

"Dad," I said, "Daddy, we're moving."

He didn't say anything for a minute and I heard laughter from somewhere around him, the sound of it flattening out over the telephone until it sounded like a lunatic's. "Well," he said, "I told her the house payments might be too much. You heard me. I told her not to take the second mortgage or she could kiss the house goodbye. I told her, Harriet, you heard me. Jesus."

"Daddy," I said.

"Listen, I've got some money hidden away, you know, a little account on the side, something the old lawyers and doctors and tax man don't know about. We'll use it, Harriet. Jesus, Harriet, Harry honey, that house means a lot to me. Don't let her sell it. Don't let her do it, Harry. Just knowing you kids are there, it means something. God. Jesus."

I held the phone on my chest while he cried. I stood in the pay phone booth on Douglas Drive, watching the cars go by, waving to all the people I knew, as though I were just calling my mother to come pick me up. In that town you were either a teenager using a pay phone to call your parents, or else you were an adult up to no good. As a consequence, only kids were dumb enough or helpless enough to use the pay phones in my hometown.

"Harriet, Harriet?" he was saying when I put the phone to my ear.

"I'm here."

"Sorry, baby, I'm really sorry. I'm all right, I'm OK. Really. It's just the house, you know. Only house I've ever owned, you know. *Did* own, I guess I mean. I just got excited, a little excited is all. I figured you and Ann would live there till you grew up, right there in the house and everything. It's OK, though. I can handle it. So what's going to happen? You going to rent a place or something, live in the projects, go down the tubes, or what?"

"It's not like that, Dad. It's something else."

"What's that?" he asked, then there was some confusion over the phone, somebody else's voice moving across the tile floor toward my father's, a happy voice of some kind. "Hold on a minute, Harriet."

I put the receiver on the little stand that held the phone book and went outside the booth and did a few windmills, the way they'd taught us to do them in grade-school gym class. It loosened my neck and shoulders a little, which helped some. I wasn't paying for the call, it was collect—the first collect call I'd made in my life. And it came to me, while I did the windmills, that for the rest of my life collect calls would be hateful, that they would always mean something uneven and unhappy was about to happen. When I got back in the booth I was puffing from the windmills.

"Dad?" I asked because I couldn't hear anything for the puffing.

"Yeah, hold on. Put him in right field, for God's sake," he said away from the phone. "That way he can start digging all the holes he wants. Nobody hits to right field anyway."

"Dad?"

"I'm here, Harriet. Sorry. Got a big softball game tomorrow morning." He mumbled something else, his hand over the phone, and I couldn't hear him. "OK, I'm back," he said.

"This is costing a lot," I said.

"Forget it. I'm solvent. I'm solvent as hell. I'm so solvent I'm almost the sanest person in this place. Softball, I swear to God. I'm captain of the team, Harry. Haven't lost a game yet. I'm pitching the old fuck-'em-up curve—remember when I taught you that? Damn, you learned it fast enough. Remember?"

"Yeah. Yeah, I remember."

"We've got a hell of a team here, considering. So, what's it all about? I can handle it. You moving into an apartment? You all moving across into Tip Jackson's top floor? That'd be all right. I mean, it always looked nice enough, all those trees in the front yard, good parking. What's the scoop, Harry?"

"We're moving to upstate New York, Daddy," I said. "Tomorrow." I looked through the glass of the booth and into the storefront across the street. Up in a second-story window I could see a geranium that needed watering, and down below there was a sign that said YOU NAME YOUR OWN PRICE. I remember thinking that was a strange thing to ask anybody to do.

"New York? Upstate New York? What's the fuck's in upstate New York? Are you kidding me? Harriet?"

"No, I'm not kidding. Everything's already in boxes and stuff. They come tomorrow. Ann's even got her cheerleading outfit in a box. I wasn't supposed to call, but I had to. I couldn't not."

"Oh," he said.

"Don't cry anymore, Dad. I don't think I want you to cry anymore."

He didn't say anything for a long while, and it seemed to me that I could hear the tiles whispering all around him in that place. I could see him on that softball field, too, pitching curves, winning, happy out there under the sun, grinning at everybody while his right fielder dug holes in the grass behind him, a guy with no glove, just digging, all for some crazy reason. My father's hair would be cut short, blond, glistening with sweat, and he'd be throwing way inside, to keep the batters away from that lunatic who was just digging holes in right field. And he would be happy in a way he deserved to be, ought always to have been, but couldn't.

"What's his name?" he asked calmly.

"Pete," I said.

"What's his last name?"

"I can't tell you that, Dad. You know I can't tell you that. It's all already happened and you can't stop it. I can't stop it. Ann can't either. We're moving. We're moving tomorrow and everything's packed and everything's already done and gone."

"I'll kill the son of a bitch, Harriet. I'll kill him."

"No," I said. "No, you won't do that. Dad, it's over. It's all over now. I don't like it when you say stuff like that so quiet. It's over. It's over."

"I'll take his fucking pumpkin head and smash it all over the place."

"No," I said. "You're getting better, Dad. Don't think like that. Think about the big game tomorrow. Think about your pitching." I stopped talking and waved to somebody going by in his car, a neighbor who'd slowed and pointed at the seat beside him, next to his wife, though I shook my head —no, I didn't need a ride with him right then. The neighbor, a Mr. Greene, shrugged his shoulders, then laughed a little, showing me he knew I was talking on the pay phone to a boy my mother didn't want me talking to. *Teenagers,* he was thinking. "Think about me like I'm thinking about you. Please try to do that, Dad."

"Tell me this," he said, his voice low and hard. "Is she already married?"

"No, it comes later. After we get there."

"Where is that exactly?"

"I can't tell you that. You know I can't tell you that. Dad, please don't make it hard for me. When we get there, I'll call you. I just wanted you to know. I felt bad. But don't worry. Please don't worry, don't get excited. Ann and me, we're OK. Really, we're OK. Things happen, you go with the flow and everything. It's not so bad." I heard him cough, the sound of it like a wrong note in the middle of a band concert, the kind of note the parents all try to ignore. "Don't cry again. I really don't want you to cry again."

"I'm not crying."

"Ann's excited," I said, trying to change the subject. "You know how she is. She thinks she'll be the best cheerleader they ever had up there. She thinks she'll be a superstar."

"She will, by God," he said. "She'll kick their goddamn asses."

"Don't get upset, Dad. It's OK."

"I know it's goddamn OK because she'll kick their god-damn asses."

"Dad . . ." I said, and then all of a sudden some feeling came over me. "Daddy, I'm not happy," I said.

"*I'll* kick their goddamn asses," he said.

"I've got to go," I said. "I just wanted to tell you."

"I'll kill all the sons-a-bitches for her."

"No, I've got to go. I've got to get home now."

"Wait," he said. "Listen, Harriet. Harry, honey. Listen. I'm going somewhere this afternoon. I'm going for a visit."

"What do you mean?" I wanted off the telephone. I didn't want any more people driving by and looking at me talk to my father, thinking the wrong thing. I was tired of the wrong thing. I was tired of just about everything by then, the whole rotten shebang.

"One of the guys here, I'm going to visit him at his place tonight. They let you out for that if you act right, you know. It's not a prison, for crying out loud. You know? Don't you know that, Harriet?"

"No," I said. "Yes. I don't know."

"Listen up here, now. I'm giving you the guy's number. I want you to call tomorrow night. Can you do that? Will you do that for me, Harry?"

"I don't know."

"Sure you will," he said, jovial all of a sudden. "You can be counted on. You're *my* kid, you can be counted on. Right?"

"I guess so," I said, though I didn't want to be—not counted on, that is. I didn't mind being his kid. He gave me a number with an area code I didn't recognize. "Where is this guy's place?" I asked. "I thought you had a big softball game tomorrow. I'm supposed to call?"

"Sure," he said. "No problem. Just give me a call there tomorrow night, OK? Honest to God, Harry, it'll make me feel better about things. It'll really put my mind at rest, having you call and all."

"I'll call."

"Great, honey. I'll be waiting."

"I'll call," I said, then I hung up the phone. Across the street a man with a bag of groceries was walking down the sidewalk, a carton of milk and some white bread sticking out of the top of the bag, and I watched how normal he was till he reached the intersection and turned down Maple Avenue, out of sight among the humid new leaves of trees.

I remember so many things about my father, I don't remember when all the bad things really began. Maybe they began long before I had the sense to know what badness was, before I knew that the people who could be so good to you could also be bad and wrong and not responsible for any of it, that the difference between childhood and adulthood is a matter of opinion. When you're a kid, everything is supposed to be the way it is because it already is that way. If your father acts crazy, that's normal. And that is what resilience means when you talk about children.

When Ann and I were very little, six and four, our father worked the graveyard shift at the TVA steam plant. The graveyard shift meant that you worked in the middle of the night and slept during the day, like a desert lizard, and when you finally got up, around five in the afternoon, you were disoriented and still tired and felt angry about the way the world must have gone on while you slept. Ann and I had to tiptoe around the house during the day, whispering to each other, scared to death we'd wake him—*"him,"* we called our father—and scared to death some kid in the neighborhood would yell out too loudly outside his window. Once during the summer a boy named George Greene, who was a well-fed, happy sort of guy, caught a baby rabbit with his bare hands and, ecstatic from the miracle of it, began to shout his pleasure at the top of his lungs. All of a sudden our father came bursting out of his bedroom, looking like a madman, which is what he was right then, bellowing and running till he got out in the front yard where he smacked George's face and yelled at him, his face puckered with sleep, pink, swollen like a drowning man's, and then the baby rabbit went running somewhere. Later Ann and I gave George a Ken doll from our Barbie collection, just to make him feel better about the whole matter. George never talked about it afterward. He was a good man.

But that happened before things got really bad. That happened while things were still handleable and straightforward, while I could still look at our house and see it the way it was—a house in the neighborhood, a place I lived in the way all the other kids lived in theirs—a homely, honest-looking white house in a homely neighborhood surrounded by mountains. Those were the good times.

Later, when I was ten or so, my father went through a bad spell and had to be hospitalized for a while. It came over him one night while he was working graveyard, though the details of it never got handed down to me. What I know is that they found him sitting and staring in some corner of the steam plant, stiff as a board, then they took him right on to the hospital, and then straight to Elmhaven, which is where he would return during that spring I turned fifteen. His first visit to Elmhaven lasted six months. When he finally came home, my sister and I were afraid of him, a thought that shames me. But we were young and he seemed changed, fundamentally changed, possessed by some demon like the zombie people we saw on *Theater X* on Saturday mornings. He spoke slowly, carefully, and he walked the same way, as though a quick word or action might be misinterpreted and land him back at Elmhaven. Ann and I would refuse to ride in the car alone with him, and although our mother begged us to straighten up, to act right by him, we wouldn't budge. We were afraid. And our father knew it, had to know it, but he never said a word, accepted it all as if it were his due, as if he now had to take full responsibility for not having been responsible for himself. Those were bad times and I began to see our house differently. I began to see it as a sad place, sad and mysterious and closed to the rest of the world, a house totally unlike any other house in the neighborhood, or in the town, or in the whole of East Tennessee.

He didn't go back to TVA. In fact, I think at that time both he and my mother believed the graveyard shift was the sole reason he'd gotten sick. For a while he worked as an Amway salesman, then he went into selling encyclopedias. I remember how the big boxes of them would be stacked in the living room, higher than my head, and how my father went through every one of them, cutting the tape with a pocket-knife, checking each one to make sure all the books were there. One time he found an extra volume in one of the boxes and he gave it to me: *X-Y-Z* is what it was. I read the entire thing. Every so often he'd ask me where I was and I'd say, "Xenophon," or "Yellow Fever," or "Zephyr." "The meaning of the whole world is in these books," he said, and I believed him. Xerxes, Xylophone, Yokohama, Zeitgeist—I was proud of him, that he spread such things all around town, and by the time I'd gotten to Zythum I was no longer afraid of him and loved him, though I'd never stopped that to begin with.

Eventually he ended up reading meters for the electric company. He worked outside, during the day, a job so unlike what he'd done at TVA it seemed to guarantee that he'd be safe and normal and happy till the end of his days. In the afternoons he'd go outside and throw a ball around, a baseball or a football or a basketball. That's when he taught me the fuck-'em-up curve, and how to spiral a football so that it soared in the air like a cannonball, and how to do a reverse lay-up that could score against the tallest of opponents. "Opponents" was his word. They were everywhere, whatever game we were playing, and they were alarmingly invisible. Your opponents were always stationed in the strongest positions, and though you couldn't see them, they could ruin you, like evil spirits in the wind. "Your opponent just intercepted that pass," my father might say, or else "That jump shot was rejected by your opponent and he scored on a lay-up at the other end in of the court. Higher, Harry, higher." I don't think all of it made me a better player; I'm sure it didn't. What it did was make me see the world the way my father saw it: a place full of danger you couldn't see, of forces at work like riptides against you, moving in to thwart you here, defeat you there, mess up the best-laid plans. An opponent was affliction, was trouble, and my father knew its face as intimately as anybody I've ever known.

Then things got bad again. I can't now say when exactly the change came, though I remember a night, when I was fourteen, that showed me the shape of what I would come to expect. Ours was only a two-bedroom house so Ann and I shared a bedroom, an arrangement that drove us both crazy because I liked to read late at night and she liked to sleep in pitch-darkness. We ended up stringing a blanket midway across the room, pretending we had our own bedrooms, and my side of the blanket happened to be nearest the door. During the summer—and it was summer, that night—we all of us kept the doors of our rooms open, to keep the air circulating, though it usually didn't. The house had been built by a Canadian firm for TVA and the architects must have known zip about hot summers. I was up late, reading. I remember it clearly. I was reading *War of the Worlds*, scaring myself half to death, imagining long-legged alien spaceships stepping darkly over the mountains toward my window. For some reason I gave the ships legs, like insects, so that instead of whooshing in the way they were supposed to, they invaded the mountains as stealthily and as quietly as cockroaches. After twelve, maybe after one, I don't know, I heard my father talking. They'd gone to bed at ten o'clock, so I figured he was having one of his nightmares, something I'd grown used to ever since he came back from Elmhaven. He'd start out by talking, then he'd begin to yell things, then he'd breathe hard, as though in his dream he'd been running for a long while and had finally had to stop to catch up with himself. But it wasn't a dream this time.

"Barb," he kept saying, "Barb, stop it. I can't stand that, Barb." He said it over and over, but my mother was a serious sleeper. If she'd had the job working the graveyard shift, George Greene would never have gotten his face smacked. She'd never have heard him. Of course, she'd never have smacked his face if she had. But she slept hard when she slept, and Ann and I called her The Mummy behind her back.

"Stop it," my father said. "I can't stand it, don't do this to me," he said, but I could tell my mother was out of it, asleep as she could be. Then she woke up—he must have shaken her—and then I listened hard for whatever might come next.

"I can't stand it, I can't stand it," he said. "You're playing with yourself. I saw it. It's sick. Playing with yourself, my God. What am I, another woman or something?"

"What?" said my mother. "What is it? What's happened?"

"You heard me," he said. "You heard me fine. Jesus, Barb."

"Playing what? Do what?"

"Just tell me. Was it Ted Jenkins? That little fucker. Or was it Bob? It was probably Bob. Here you are lying right beside me thinking about Bob fucking Taylor."

"I was sleeping," she said. "I was thinking about sleeping. I'm thinking about sleeping right now, for Christ's sake. What's the matter with you?"

"I'm telling you I can't stand it. I won't have it." Then I heard a slap, not a hard one, just a sort of quick tap.

My father would never strike a woman with his hands closed; I knew this because he'd told me so himself. He'd been called in to see the principal of my school after I got into a fight with a girl in the grade above me—an asshole, frankly, who'd said a few unkind words about my family on the school playground. I'd punched her face with my fist and she'd needed five stitches in her tongue, a turn of events I found appropriate and satisfying. When we left the principal's office my father explained to me that you didn't hit girls with your fist. You could hit boys with your fist, but not girls. I asked him why that was. And he said, "Because with your average man, you can gauge yourself—hit him hard enough to make him think a minute, or hit him hard enough to lay him out.

With your women, you can't do that, Harry. You might just kill 'em." And then he'd taken off his meter reader uniform top, there on the school playground where I'd had my altercation that afternoon, and he gave me some pointers in boxing, which was a sport he'd learned in the Air Force, in Korea, where, he said, "the sweet science came in handy."

"You frigging *lunatic*!" my mother shouted. I heard her come stumbling out of her bedroom into the bathroom, then in a minute she came into our bedroom, breathing fast. "Get up, girls. Come on."

"Barb," said my father, coming up behind her. He hovered in the doorway a second, swaying like a drunk man. Then he put his arms around her waist, his head down on her shoulder. "Honey," he said. They stood like that for a long while, framed by my bedroom door, the two of them so close together they might have been the shadow of one large man, an inhumanly large man, an alien maybe, who'd moved into our house as invisibly and quietly as the wind.

III

"I think we should stop at a place with a swimming pool," Ann said. "I think it should be a hotel, not a motel. Motels are for trash."

"We *are* trash," I said. "It's not like we have a home anymore or anything. I'd say we're pretty close to being white trash at this minute."

"You hush," said my mother. "Pete gave me over seven hundred dollars for this trip. Think about that for a second, why don't you."

"Yeah, but what happened to the money from the house?" I asked. "Where's that?"

"I'm the adult here. You two just sit back and act like children, which is what you're supposed to be. I swear, sometimes you-all make me crazy."

"All I'm saying is I want it to have a swimming pool. That's all I'm saying. Jeez, what's so crazy about that?"

We were in Virginia, between Harrisonburg and Winchester, and far enough away from East Tennessee that we had trouble understanding what people were saying when we stopped for gas. Ann interpreted for us, because she was surest around strangers and also watched the most television. She could even imitate Californians when the mood struck her, could get rid of the twang in her voice as easily as clearing her throat. At the gas stations she was the one who asked for directions for places to eat. She'd go up to some man in a grease-stained uniform—actually, usually two men, who always seemed to have nothing better to do—and the way she walked up to them, so enthusiastic and cheery, you'd have thought she was twirling a baton at the head of a parade. After maybe five seconds with her the men would begin to give my mother and me short, furtive glances, as if what they'd like to do was take Ann into a back room and discuss things with her in detail, over a few beers. And Ann knew it. She spent a long while getting the simplest of instructions, acting dumb, pretending to forget the street names or else deliberately confusing them with each other. Then they'd all laugh hard and long over God knows what—nothing, probably. It didn't seem to bother my mother at all, though it bothered me. I was afraid Ann was becoming someone she didn't need to be, someone she'd regret having become when the years had added up and she had a past to ponder. But I was fifteen, could barely speak coherently to strangers, made friends only with difficulty, and didn't understand the ways of men and women. And, of course, Ann knew that, too, which is probably why her flirtations bothered me. You could call it a rivalry, but you'd be wrong. Two people who have certain abilities for completely different things—even things like living their own lives—can't compete. They can make each other miserable, but they can't compete.

"There's a Holiday Inn. Mom, let's stay there." Ann had her face pressed up against the back of our mother's seat, whispering in her ear, begging really, her face flushed with the thought of swimming pools. "Please. I won't ask for anything else ever. Please, let's stay there."

"I just wish you wouldn't whine, Ann," she said, shrugging her shoulders irritably. "It's really unbecoming of you."

"I vote for it, too," I said. "It's almost ten and dark and you're tired. You might fall asleep at the wheel or something."

"I most certainly will not fall asleep at the wheel," she snapped, but she turned off at the exit for the Holiday Inn.

"Yippee!" Ann said. "I believe I'll take a dip in the pool before retiring," she said like someone from a movie, draping herself across the backseat in a pose. She was happy now.

"We're up and out of here by six A.M.," my mother said grimly. She was tired, and whenever she was tired she assumed the worst, that people would be late, schedules would not be met, things would fall apart. The fact of the matter was that she would sleep in, not us, and six o'clock really meant between ten and eleven. "No joke, six A.M. and this car goes, with or without you-all."

"God," Ann said, still lying on her back on the seat. "You really get tense sometimes. Tension is the number one cause of heart disease. I heard that on the radio."

"Then I should have dropped dead fifteen years ago." She pulled into the parking lot, then turned off the engine. "Ten minutes. You can swim for ten minutes but that's it. We've got to hit the road. Harriet, get my bag while I pay for the room."

Ann and I got the luggage out of the front trunk and set it on the pavement. The parking lot wasn't crowded and only a few rooms were lit here and there across the front of the building. To the left was the pool, blue and white under the utility lights. It looked pitiful and forlorn to me, like something you'd hoped would be good turning sour and bad. It looked like Pete's pool must is what it looked like to me, but Ann stood staring at it, transfixed, her mouth tight with pleasure.

"Too bad it has to be night," she said. "I bet in the afternoon it was crowded with people of all types." She looked at me. "You better get a new bathing suit, Harriet. Seriously. Yours is all brown from swimming in the river. People notice things like that."

"Nobody I know. Jesus, Ann, we're in Mount Olive, Virginia. From now on, anybody who notices things like that is somebody we don't know."

"Yeah, but for later is what I meant." She turned back to the pool, her hands on her hips. "I wish old Pete had a belowground pool. I mean, aren't aboveground pools tacky or something?"

"It's like dogs and their owners. The man and his pool start looking like each other."

Ann wheeled around and stared at me, her eyes dark gray in that unlit parking lot. "You don't like him, do you? Is that what you're saying?"

"Put it this way," I said. "Mom does and that's the big factor here. Mom likes him and we're moving up there to live in his house. What I think about him means zip."

"Well, I sort of like him. I mean, he bought me that cashmere sweater and everything. And those dinners out. Don't forget all those dinners out. I never had lobster before."

"You didn't like it."

"Well, I never had it before either."

"And I guess if we get shark meat and rosebuds every other week you'll start calling him Daddy."

"You know, Harriet, you act like being unhappy is fun or something. You're such a jerk. Really such a jerk. I can't believe you." Then she squared her shoulders, huffed out some air, and went walking toward the pool. I sat down on our mother's vanity case, stared at the pavement, wondering about myself, wondering whether I really was a jerk. It was possible. A real jerk would be the last person to know herself, I knew that much.

In March our mother had brought Pete home to visit for a week. She'd met him in February through some of her friends in Chattanooga, a fluke of circumstances that involved a cardiology convention and mutual acquaintances and maniacal matchmaking on the part of my mother's friends. I don't really know exactly how it all happened, though I do know my mother was ready—primed, so to speak —for something like that to happen. My father had been in Elmhaven two months by then; they'd been divorced three weeks. I hadn't turned fifteen, but was old enough to keep

Ann out of trouble, so we stayed by ourselves at home while our mother went to Chattanooga. The Greenes checked up on us every day. And so did Mr. Jackson across the street. We were all right. My mother was not irresponsible is what I guess I'm trying to make clear.

Whatever happened in Chattanooga must have been serious because within four weeks Pete was standing on our front porch, smoking a cigar and shaking our hands. My mother stood to one side, smiling so hard her lipstick came off on her back teeth. He was an older man—older than my mother, I mean—about forty-five, and he had tremendous thighs. That's all I could think about when I first met him, that his thighs were huge. His stomach was pretty flat, but those thighs were like a couple of tree stumps. I kept thinking about the pine poles they used at the electric company, where my father had worked. Right from the beginning he loved Ann. You could tell by the way he touched her hair, asking her whether she used hydrogen peroxide on it, whether she had a lot of boyfriends, whether she liked to swim. His was the perfect approach for winning Ann over, which was exactly what he was trying to do. With me he became circumspect and serious, as though I were a nun or something and he didn't know what to make of it.

"So," he said, "I hear you like to read."

"Yeah, I like it."

"And sports. You like sports, right?"

"Yeah."

"That's fine. Hell, that's swell."

That was it. He didn't touch my hair, possibly because I looked evil and might have bitten his finger off. My mother began to make shooing noises, smiling wildly all the while, then we went inside. I believe now that my mother must have told him I'd be the "difficult" one, because whenever we were alone during that week he'd run like a stuck pig out of the room. And it was true: I *was* difficult. I couldn't stand him. I couldn't stand his cigar, or his thighs, or the fact that he had his hands all over Ann half the time. I'm not saying he was a pervert or anything; I'm saying he was just what you'd expect a cardiologist from a small town in upstate New York with an aboveground swimming pool to be.

That first day with him felt like school was about to start, although it hadn't ended for the year yet. Everyone was jittery and nervous and smiling through it all like a bunch of salamanders. Pete turned out to be a proud man, at least in the sense of pride being a direct result of income. We all of us knew how much he made a year within the first couple of hours, though I'm sure my mother knew it already. Before he came to visit she'd spoken of his "numerous investments" and his "portfolios" as if she knew what she was talking about, which she didn't, frankly. Money and our family had always been opponents. At dinner that first night—the only night my mother cooked for us—Pete explained the difference between investments and tax shelters. In the end they seemed to be the same thing, though in one you gained a lot and paid a little for it, in the other you lost and gained something better from it. It was completely different from my father's view of life, of opponents and invisible forces at work against you, of good and bad luck at constant war with each other. It made no sense to me, or to Ann and my mother for that matter. The two of them just smiled and clicked their tongues encouragingly.

"So what I'm saying is," he said, putting down his fork, then lighting his cigar, "one thing I'm saying is you can give a couple a thousand bucks to the American Cancer Society and end up making a profit. That's all I'm saying."

"What if they find a cure for cancer?" I wanted to know.

"Then you go to the Heart Association or something," he said, blowing out some blue smoke. "That or the lung place or the muscular dystrophy or the Parkinson's. Hell, they got a million different things. Save the Children, for instance."

"I sold cookies for poor people in Bangladesh once," Ann said brightly.

"Thata girl," he said and reached over and put his hand on top of hers. "A girl after my own heart."

"Boy," I said, looking at my plate.

"Harriet, honey," my mother said, her voice high and brittle, "why don't you get us the ice cream. I got chocolate chip," she said in a different tone, looking at Pete knowingly. There was something irritating about my mother knowing Pete's particular flavor of ice cream; but there was something more irritating about her whole attitude, that the issue of ice cream could become an intimate and exclusive emotion between them, an issue that struck me right then as silly, even sinister in some way. I don't know, I lost my head.

"So," I said, loudly, still looking at my plate. "So, I guess chocolate chip ice cream could be a real investment. I guess you could make a few bucks on it, too, just as long as people stopped dying of cancer and heart attacks and, and mental illness or something. I guess it could be a real tax break." I was shaking when I finished and knew even then that I hadn't made a lick of sense. I looked up at my mother and she was angry, then I looked over at Pete and he was hurt. His cigar drooped like a flagpole with the wind gone. He'd taken his hand off Ann's and was studying it, opening his fingers one by one, slowly, as though he'd forgotten how many there were and had to count them.

"Hey," he said, "hey. I don't mean to say everything's money. I feel things, too. Hell, I've seen people die right in front of my eyes. I've seen some things. Look, I'm sorry about your dad. Really I am. But it's not my fault. It's not your mother's fault. Right? She deserves a good life, right? Am I wrong or am I right? Hell, I say I'm right. I'm sorry, but in my business you realize life has to go on. Life marches on and that's a fact. If you're lucky, that is, and I've seen enough of the old bad luck, too. Me and your mother, I think we're lucky. Am I wrong or what?"

"I think you're right," Ann said and grinned at him.

"Say you're sorry, Harriet," my mother said. "I think you owe Pete an apology about now. He's being a big man here and I think you ought to apologize." She picked a pea off her plate and held it between her fingers, showing me she meant to get pretty nasty if I didn't agree. And I did, I did agree. I thought Pete was at that moment being as big a man as he could be.

"Sorry," I said. I was looking at my plate again. "I'm sorry, Dr. Carlisle."

"That's OK," he said. "Hell, that's fine. This is great. I figure we've made a breakthrough here or something. What do you say? Huh? I say we all have us some ice cream and do something fun. Huh? What do you say?"

"I say we go shopping," Ann said. "I need some sweaters. Mom, didn't you say I needed sweaters? Please? I think it'd be fun. Please? Mom?"

"Don't whine like that, Ann. You sound just like a Labrador retriever when you do that."

"She sounds fine," said Pete. "Sweetie, I'll buy you every sweater this old town has. We'll do it up."

"Yippee," Ann said. "I know just exactly what I want."

"I'll bet you do," he said. "And Harriet, we'll buy Harriet some books. Sports books or something. The sky's the limit." After that everyone sat around the table, smiling, looking satisfied about things.

For the rest of the week Pete was as generous and kind as he could be, although some kindnesses are a burden and a torment. You'd think you'd always want to be on the receiving end of someone's generosity, but that's not true. When you receive you have to take responsibility for the other person as well as yourself, the way a victim has to account for himself and his attacker, too. "Dishing it out," my father had told me once, "is almost always easier than taking it. If you can manage to be on top, which you usually can't." It is difficult and morally complicated to remain passive and accept what's given you, good or bad, when you can't stand somebody. My sister didn't see it that way, of course. She accumulated sweaters and skirts, blouses and knee socks, even underwear, wearing as much of it at one time as she could reasonably coordinate. I ended up with seven books and a sweater, and I put them all in a box at the bottom of my closet. At all the restaurants I had hamburgers—no bun, no lettuce, just a plain hamburger—and a glass of water. Pete kept asking my mother to get me to order steak or prime rib or lobster, but I said no, I liked hamburger. I'll admit I was pretty close to being a reason why some people never have children, or else why some people never remarry a person with almost grown kids. I might have been a jerk, probably was, but I already knew that you had to be responsible for yourself in any given situation, whether you'd created that situation or not—and at that age I usually hadn't—that certain wrong-headed situations can include you in them without your consent and you have to know where you stand in the middle of it all. Pete, it seemed to me, had created such a situation in my family and the way I took responsibility for it, I suppose, was by becoming his opponent, an affliction to him—in his mind, I'm sure, a jerk kid. And in my own mind through it all I thought my father would be proud of me, because he still loved us, crazy as he was.

On a Saturday we took Pete to the airport. My sister and I rode in the back of the Volkswagen, the two of them up front. It was fifty miles to the nearest airport, a drive we had to make on 11W, a twisting, dangerous stretch of road that killed or maimed people at least once a week. My mother drove with one elbow out the window and I was itchy with the suspicion that something might happen. The two of them had slept together in my mother's bedroom the whole week, and although I hadn't heard anything in the night, still the anxiety I felt waiting to hear them do something was a lot like the feeling I had on 11W, waiting for disaster to come upon us. Every night I'd stayed awake till two, three in the morning, reading, waiting for that something. Even Ann had taken down the blanket in the middle of the room, though whether she stayed awake I can't guess. It was difficult to imagine Pete's big thighs resting on my father's side of the bed. It was impossible to imagine whatever else might have gone on. The entire house had begun to smell like cigar smoke, and the smell of it was thick in the Volkswagen on the way to the airport.

"You know . . ." my mother said, wistfully. Her dark hair blew straight behind her, just as though it had someplace else it wanted to go, if it only had the means to do it. "One thing I'll miss is these mountains."

It had already been decided between them—as they'd solemnly told Ann and me earlier in the week—that we'd be moving to Fulton, New York. That was established. I believe it might have been established in Chattanooga, the weekend they met. But it was no surprise to either of us; we knew our mother had wanted something different, hopefully better, fast.

"I don't mind leaving all this place's small-town nonsense and the hot summers and the—well, everything. But these mountains, I'll miss. I surely will."

"Barbara, let me tell you," said Pete. "You'll be exactly an hour's drive from the Adirondack Mountains and they make these things look like some old gum on the sidewalk. When you see the Adirondacks, you'll know you've seen some hellish mountains."

"But I'm saying I'll miss these mountains, Pete. That's all I'm saying."

"Yeah, but the Adirondacks are the queen of their kind. Everybody knows that."

"I don't know that, dear. I've never seen them." She pulled her elbow back into the car and began driving with both hands on the steering wheel, her joints stiff all of a sudden. "I'll miss *these* mountains is what I'm saying. I can't miss what I haven't seen, you know." She turned her neck, then smiled at Pete, looking very pretty and young when she did it. It struck me then that my mother was a beautiful woman, not regular pretty but beautiful, and that that was a piece of information I shouldn't forget.

"You won't think twice about these things once we get up there and see God's own choice of mountains. I'm telling you, they're a sight to see."

"I'm sure that's right," she said. "I'll give you that. But

you have to give me my mountains. OK? Don't you think you have to give me my own mountains?"

"Sweet thing, I'll give you your own mountains and raise you one. I'll give you the whole Appalachian range if that's what you want." He said "Appalachian" like somebody from somewhere else, as if he'd been drinking wine too long.

"But they're not yours to give," my mother said quietly.

"Hey," Ann muttered, batting her hand in the air the way you'd get rid of an insect. She was half asleep, her jaw resting against her collarbone, but even asleep she'd recognized the irritation in our mother's tone of voice. I had, too, though I was willing to see the situation percolate some.

"Hell," said Pete, "you can miss anything you want to. I'm looking to the future. Our future. That's what counts. Isn't that right? Our future together's what counts. At least in my book it is."

"Yes, yes it is. You know I agree with that. You know that. The only thing in the world I'm trying to say is I'll miss my mountains. That's OK, isn't it, Petey? I can miss that. My mountains."

"Yeah, you can miss them," he said, staring out of his side of the car with a mean look. I could see what he was thinking. All week it had been sweetness and nice, then this little thing had to happen right when he was leaving. He wasn't ready to say that a beautiful woman, with an opinion on something he couldn't change, was not the woman for him, but he was depressed by the turn of events. "You can miss anything you want. Shit, you could miss your demented husband and I'd still love you."

"You don't mean that, Pete. Pete, honey, don't say that kind of thing."

"What kind of thing? You're the one with the most wonderful mountains in the world. I'm just a regular guy telling you about some stuff I know."

"Well," my mother said, really irritated now, "well, maybe you don't know enough stuff."

"Listen, Barbara," he said and shoved his hand hard on her right thigh, "I know plenty."

"Get your hand off her," I said, poking my head up between the seats. "You just get your hand off of her."

"You shut up, Harriet," she said, glancing in the mirror, and I could tell by her eyes she regretted all that had happened. "You just please for once shut up. Pete, honey," she said, "get me the road map out of that basket there. We're getting close and I don't go to this airport much."

"You bet," he said, with obvious relief. "One road map coming up." He coughed. And then, the orange tip of his cigar moving around in the Volkswagen like an evil eye, Pete brought out the papers with a flourish, settled them down, then discovered in his big lap a way for us to get where we were going around the mountains.

IV

The motel room had two double beds with Magic Fingers. Ann put a quarter in one of them, then sat in the middle of the bed with her legs out in front of her, as if it were a pony ride. She already had on her bathing suit and was waiting for our mother to come out of the bathroom.

"Jeez, these things aren't so special," she said. "Only a catatonic could think this was relaxing. It makes your butt feel like it's sitting on top of a washing machine. Try it, Harriet. Put your hand down on the mattress. It'll be a real thrill."

"Where did you learn what 'catatonic' meant?"

"I don't know." She turned onto her stomach and put her arms in front of her. "Hey, I'm floating. I think I'm flying. The Legion of Superheroes. The Fantastic Four."

"I mean it, where did you learn it?"

"I don't know, radio or something. TV. Comic books. Somewhere."

"You read Dad's medical report, didn't you? Didn't you?"

"I did if you did," she said. "You know where Mom keeps things as much as I do. Anyway, what's the big deal? I have as much right to know what's going on with him as anybody else. I'm his daughter, you know." She began to roll back and forth on the bed, her yellow-white hair twitching from the effect of the Magic Fingers.

"So when's the last time you ever wrote him? When did you give him a call or something? I'd say you're being a daughter in name only, is what I'd say."

"Harriet, you're a big fuckwad. Daddy knows I care about him, I don't see why you don't. God." She flung herself over to the side of the bed and sat up, pounding her legs against the wooden frame. "If you don't loosen up on this, you're going to get cancer or something. Hives. Ulcers. Whatever it is you get when you're a fuckwad."

"Jerk. Fuckwad." I sat on the bed opposite her, my father's friend's phone number in my back pocket.

"Just because everything doesn't happen the way you want it to doesn't mean you have to get hateful to me. I think we're doing all right. Unless Pete turns out to be an ax murderer. Or out for Mom's money. Ooo," she said, making her face look evil. "Dr. Pete, famous gold miner. Notorious. We're in for it now."

"Gold digger," I said. "God, I just wish you'd be more serious about it all."

"I am," she said. "I am serious. I seriously want to go swimming right this very minute." She heaved herself off the bed, which hummed like mosquitoes when the weight lifted, then she went over to the bathroom and pounded on the door. "Mom, I'm going swimming, OK?"

"OK," she said, her voice muffled through the door. "But take Harriet with you. I don't want to find you belly up in the morning. And ten minutes is all. Fifteen tops. I mean it."

"I don't see why Harriet has to go. Mom? Why does Harriet have to go?"

"She goes. Fifteen minutes. And stop whining. When I get out of this bathtub I want you both back here."

"Jeez," Ann said. She looked at me. "Do you want to swim?" she asked unhappily.

"No. Have no fear. I won't embarrass you with my bathing suit in Mount Olive, Virginia. I'll just hang around, act like I don't know you."

"Let's go," she said, angry with the way things had turned out.

When we got to the pool nobody was around, another disappointment to Ann. She had on her light-blue bikini suit and looked good in it and knew it and wanted somebody else to recognize that fact. And I don't believe it was vanity; I think she simply liked the play of eyes on the surfaces of things. When she dove into the water and started swimming around, I told her I wanted to buy a magazine in the lobby. I'd seen three pay phones in the motel, one on our floor, but

I wanted to be in the lobby in case my mother wanted a Coke or something.

"All right. But just don't get back and find me belly up. Mom'll kill you." Her head bobbed on top of the water, dark, almost black in the strange shadows the utility lights cast, her smile an even darker scar in the shade. For a moment I thought maybe I really should stay around, watch out for her, make sure she didn't slip underneath those surfaces she loved so well.

"Just stay in the shallow end, OK? You might get cramps."

"Yeah, sure. I'll pretend I'm a baby. I'll pretend I can't have a good time or anything."

Lobbies are ugly everywhere. I don't know why that is, except maybe there are too many different people doing things for too many different reasons, which makes for a bad feeling in the air. This lobby had a green and maroon plaid carpet and big mirrors on the walls and you couldn't help but see yourself and everybody else coming and going across that ugly plaid carpet. Lobbies like that aren't supposed to remind you of anything personal, but this one did for some reason.

When my father had had his first sick spell and ended up in Elmhaven for six months, my mother decided to take night courses in shorthand and dictation, "to supplement our income," she said, "which is zero right now." One time I went with her to the night school, one night when Ann was sleeping over with friends. I was seven at the time. The school was in Kingsport, Tennessee, about forty miles away, a formidable distance it seemed to me then. Before that night I don't believe I'd gone so far in a car; my grandparents all lived within a thirty-minute drive, and then, too, we'd always made the trip during the day. Maybe the darkness increased my feeling of great distances being traveled. At any rate, I remember thinking the two of us were on an incredible adventure.

The night class was in the basement of an elementary school, the kindergarten section, I guess, because there were mirrors all over the walls. It seems like kindergartners are always at the mercy of mirrors when they go to school, as though the burden of self-consciousness is something they need to practice a lot before adulthood. But there were blocks and tricycles and funny drawings, too. And in one section of the room were ten desks, each with a typewriter and notepad and some other things I can't now recall. The teacher was a harried-looking man with a pointed face and eyeglasses that made his eyes look very far away, so far away you felt he might not really be there. He kept saying, "Ladies, prepare to begin," then he'd put a tape on his tape player and all the women, even my mother, began to type for all they were worth, their tongues showing a little at the sides of their mouths. Because of the mirrors there seemed to be dozens of them, typing hell-for-leather, and there seemed to be three harried men, not just the one, controlling the tape recorder.

I sat in a corner near some fingerpainting materials, staring at the front of myself and the back of myself and at all the women who came between. "There are fifteen different species of fish in these waters," the tape recorder would say, then the women typed it down as fast as they could. "And so we recommend you sell the stock at this time," it said, then they typed that down, too. The voice boomed out like a football coach with a loudspeaker in his hand, except it was tinny and strange and didn't sound like what normal people would say. I never understood what the men were talking about, although I wasn't typing. When it was over, when the women had covered their typewriters with plastic and had gathered their coats, the man in the glasses came over to my mother.

"How about a cup of coffee?" he said, fiddling with a tape cassette in his hand, not looking at her. "I don't know, what about a beer or something?" My mother had a bunch of papers in her hand, all the work she'd done while the voice had told her things.

"Can't," she said. "Got to get home." She was trying to get her coat on, but the papers kept falling down. He stepped over, and though he still kept looking at the tape, somehow he managed to help her with the coat—what my father would have called a blind assist in basketball, and not the best of strategies, since an opponent might come from nowhere and ruin everything.

"But I'm talking thirty minutes. Thirty minutes won't kill anybody. It's just that we could discuss the course, Barbara. I really think you're doing well. You're probably the best I've ever taught."

"Thanks," my mother said, smiling brightly. "I know I try hard enough."

"I can see that," he said enthusiastically. "I can really see that."

"Harriet?" she said. "Harriet, where are you?" I came out from the fingerpaints. "Are you bored to death? I'm sorry it took so long."

"Oh," said the harried guy with eyeglasses, drifting back toward the front of the room, and I could see that disappointment had made his eyes look even smaller, more distant. "Well, see you."

"See you," my mother cried gayly, then the two of us went outside to the car.

When we got there I asked, "What did that man want you to drink coffee and beer for?"

"Because I think he liked me."

"So why didn't you?"

"Because," she said, "because I think he probably wanted more than I could give. At least he wanted more than I could give yet." Then she smiled in a tired way, put her papers in the backseat of the car, and we went home on a dark drive that seemed to take forever.

That "yet" is what I remembered in the lobby of the Mount Olive Holiday Inn, surrounded by all those mirrors. "Yet" is a word that means there are always possibilities, which is true; there are always possibilities, good and bad, depending on which way the wind blows in a given situation. But the way my mother said it when I was seven—and of course my memory of it in that crazy plaid hotel lobby—meant one thing to me: trouble. And I was right, though I'd been only seven and hadn't understood it at the time, because most of the scary, wrongheaded things hadn't yet begun. At fifteen, during that spring of storms, I knew trouble a little better.

I got the phone number out of my back pocket, leaning into the open telephone booth as furtively as a spy. When I was punching the number, I had a little shock, because it came to me that the area code number on the pay phone was the same area code I was trying to get. I kept looking from the piece of paper to the white circle pasted on the phone, then back again, my finger stuck on one of the buttons for the numbers. For a few seconds I felt all dreamy, standing there in that lobby full of reflections; I felt as though any minute I'd get a tap on my shoulder and I'd turn around and then I'd see myself with an identical piece of paper that had an identical phone number, and the two of us would just stare at each other in confusion, wondering what was next. But of course that didn't happen. I punched in the rest of the numbers and waited for my father.

The connection wasn't very good. The buzz of other people's private conversations blended with the buzz of the phone ringing, and it seemed to me there was a hurricane of talk going on in Virginia right then—a busy, rushing confusion of words that hummed in my ears like a garbled dream. Then a man answered the phone, not my father, his voice crippled by all the talking people.

"Yeah?" he said in an unfriendly way, though I could hardly hear him. "Is this Russell?"

"No," I said, "no. This is Harriet. My father said I should call him here. I mean, he said I should call him. I'm Harriet."

"Harry, right?"

"Right. Harriet. Is my father there?"

"Harriet," he said and laughed, his laughter fizzling out over the hum of the crowded phone lines. "I thought you was a boy. Harry, he kept saying. I thought you was his son or something. Harriet," he said and laughed again.

"Is he there? Can I talk to him, please?"

"Yeah, he's around here somewhere. I'll get him in a minute. Say, where are you? Sounds like you're calling from Alaska."

"I'm not there," I said. "Look, I'm calling from a pay phone. Could you just get him? I don't have much time. I don't think I have enough quarters."

"I bet you don't," he said in a loud voice that seemed mean, though I couldn't tell for all the buzzing. "I'll just bet you don't. Don't have enough time. Do you know what that man's gone through? Do you have any idea what these past few days have been like for him? Well, do you?"

I said I thought I knew some things.

"Sure you do, you with your not enough quarters. Well, I been with him through the hard times. You don't know shit. I seen the guy cry his eyes out because he couldn't be home. You ever seen that? You ever seen a grown man do a damn thing like that? Well, I have. I've seen it and I've done it myself. You don't know shit, Harry."

I said no, no, I probably didn't, and where was my father?

"Listen up here," he said, "this is important. You kids out there, you should know this shit. I have a kid myself, twenty-one and the idiot doesn't know bullshit from shinola. Name's Russell. He's a flaming idiot. Listen here. Are you a flaming idiot, Harry? Don't answer too quick. Think about it."

"I just want to talk to him. Is he there or not? All I want to do is talk to him. My father."

"He's around here, you can talk to him. But listen here. I've got a story for you there, Harry. Harry, Harriet. Whoever. You kids, you don't hear enough stories. You haven't seen things like the way we seen them. You think old crazy is something you push under the rug, you know, just push it under the rug. Can you imagine what it's like, being under some sort of rug? Think about it. I mean it, just think about it, being there under the old rug. Here's what it was. Here's what it was that happened. All on earth I wanted to do was make things right between us, me and Mary Alice and Russell. That's all on earth I wanted to do."

"Mister," I said, "mister. I don't know what you're talking about. I'm calling my father. I'm Harriet. Calling my father."

"Yeah, sure. I know who you are. This is all on earth that happened. Maybe it was my own fault, I don't know. I'm the one that took the damn thing, that damn dog. If you ever saw a sucker born in a minute, that's who I was, when I took the dog. It was in a bar in Waynesboro, Virginia, and it seemed the thing to do, and it was. I swear to God it was the thing to do. You don't have to be crazy to do a crazy thing and that's a fact. It was a German shepherd that was supposed to be put to sleep, but how could I know that? Tell me, how could I have known? Everything looked good to me. Would you blame me? I mean, would you hold me—"

The operator came on and wanted some quarters for five more minutes. I put everything I had left into the machine, maybe six or seven quarters, trying to listen to whoever it was talk through the operator and on through the conversations of all the people in Virginia. I stood in the phone booth and listened, which turned out to be harder than the thought of talking to my father, though not much.

"—but not that you could notice on his face. So the upshot is, they'll put you away for anything. That's what I want you to know. One mistake and they'll pull the rug and have you playing softball every goddamn day. That's what I want you kids to know. You tell Russell if you see him. Tell him it can all be a big mistake and not your fault. Tell him that. You just tell that story to anybody that looks like he doesn't know shit. You just do that."

"I will," I said. "I'll tell it. I'll tell my father right now if you'll just put him on the phone. I'm trying to call my father. I'm Harriet."

"He's right here," he said, his voice normal all of a sudden. "Hey," I heard him yell out, "your kid's on the phone. Hey," he said, "old Harry-Harriet's calling you. What a surprise."

"Harry?" my father finally asked, his breath coming hard, his voice a good thing to hear. "Is it Harriet?"

"Dad, Dad," I said. "Daddy, where've you been? I've been trying to get you, I've been trying to talk to you."

"I'm right here. It's OK. I've been right here, just in the backyard is all."

"Where are you?"

"I'm at Bob's, guy from Elmhaven. He got out a couple weeks ago, I figured I'd visit him."

"He doesn't sound too good, Dad, that guy." After that there was silence for so long I thought maybe the connection had gone bad.

"Maybe," he said at last, "maybe he doesn't sound good because he's been sitting by this phone for two and a half weeks, waiting for his son to call, which he won't. Christ, Harriet, maybe it's because his wife's been the town poontang for the past six months while he's been sitting in a hospital bed waiting for his mind to get right so he can come back and find out he might as well have cut his fucking throat. Maybe that's why he doesn't sound good, for Christ's sake."

I stood very still in the phone booth; I think I held my breath. An older couple passed behind me, arguing about something, and I watched their backs in the mirrors till they turned into the bar. You didn't have to be a genius to see that he wasn't just talking about Bob, that he was talking for himself and maybe most of the people he knew at Elmhaven. And there was a meanness in his tone I didn't like, the same tone his friend Bob had had, a tone that meant he wasn't getting better, was getting worse, and there was nothing on earth I could do to stop it.

"I wish you wouldn't talk like that," I said. "You were getting better. I could tell. You sounded happy."

"Shit, Harriet. I mean, honey—I don't mean that." He cleared his throat. "What I mean to say is, I'd like to come visit you-all. You know, see Ann and you, take you out to eat or something."

"You can't do that yet. We haven't even got there. We've just been driving one day. We won't even be there till day after tomorrow." I said it all so quickly my tongue felt tough in my mouth, like a wad of bubble gum. "Why do you want to do that?"

"Because I'm your father," he said, quietly, so quietly I barely caught it over the noise of the phone line. "And I have a right to see you."

"But Dad," I said, "we're not *there* yet. There's no place to visit us till we get there."

"I'm going to kill the son of a bitch, Harry. I swear to God, I am."

"No," I said.

"I'd like to strangle her. I'd like to take my hands and put them around her neck and just choke the ever living fucking life out of her."

"No."

"I'm coming, Harry. I'm coming up there. I know where she's going."

"No, you don't. Please, Dad, don't act this way. It's crazy."

"Crazy," he said and snorted. "Crazy, my ass. I talked to the real-estate guy. I can figure things out, I'm no dummy. I know where she's going. I know where *he* is. I'll strangle both of them, by God. There's a limit, Harry, there's a limit. Fulton, New York. I'm coming up."

"Dad," I said.

"There's nothing else to do, Harry. I know that, you know that. You can call me, though, tomorrow night. I know where I'll be tomorrow night. You get put in the loony bin, you meet a lot of people. I could stay in fucking Arizona if I wanted to. Florida, Minnesota, you name it. You could call me, if you wanted to. Here's the number. You want to call, you can call, but I'm coming. I have some rights. I've got some damned rights."

"That's not good. You know that's not right. You're being crazy. It's too much." I was crying a little, and some guy in a blue suit stopped in the middle of the lobby and looked at me, his face very white against the green and maroon plaid all around him. I turned the other way. "It's just too much," I said. "I don't even know what I'm supposed to do."

Then he gave me a number. He said it twice, his voice so precise and clear it seemed like somebody on the radio, trying to sell something.

"If you come up there," I said, "you'll never get better. Something bad'll happen, Daddy. Don't do it. Go back and get better."

"I am better. I'm better enough."

"No."

"You don't know anything, Harriet. Nothing."

"Don't do it. Daddy, don't do it."

"I'm coming," he said loudly, "and I have every right, every right—" But then whatever else he might have said was gone, because the phone suddenly went dead, hushing all the sounds of all the people talking in Virginia.

V

When I was thirteen my mother began to get obscene phone calls. At supper the whole family would talk about it, even Ann, who was only eleven. We conjectured about who it could be, why he was doing it, what could happen from it. It became a topic of discussion around the table, the way the Vietnam War was a topic of discussion. It was nothing that really seemed to touch us—something that happened to other people somewhere else—and so Ann and I talked it over as though it were the plot of a television show. But none of this is to say my mother was not concerned; she was. I think now that she was trying to spare Ann and me something she felt we didn't need to know by making a game out of it, a sort of connect-the-dots adventure that meant little in our lives— and that was a gesture she would find more and more difficult to make later, impossible really, when the whirlwind of bad times came down fast and hard on our family.

"He's probably real ugly," Ann said one night at supper. "Probably a hundred years old. That's why he calls."

"It could be anybody," said my father. "Nothing to do with appearance. It's all in their mind." He was spreading gravy onto his meatloaf with a big spoon, making sure none of it fell over the side onto the plate. If the obscene phone caller bothered him, you couldn't tell it. "It could be Cary Grant for all we know."

"Who's Cary Grant?" Ann wanted to know.

"Famous movie star," said my mother. "Ann, either eat that meat or leave it alone. Ugh, it's like you're dissecting it or something."

"I wish it *was* Cary Grant then," she said and put a little piece of meat onto her fork. "I'd get on the phone and ask for his autograph."

"It could be a teenager or something," I said. "A kid who doesn't know you're an older woman."

"I'm not an older woman." She looked over at my father, who grinned at her. "For heaven's sake. And anyway, I know the difference between a kid's voice and an adult's. This guy's between twenty-five and forty, you can bet on it."

"So what's he say?" I asked. "What exactly does he say when you answer the phone?"

"Yeah," Ann said. "What does an obscene phone call mean? What's 'obscene' mean anyway?"

" 'Obscene' means something a stranger isn't supposed to say to a married woman."

"Baloney."

"Don't say 'baloney' to your mother, Ann." My father reached over and got the bowl of corn. "Technically, she's right. Technically speaking, she's right on the money. You could call it a generalization, but you can't call it baloney."

"So what's a generalization?" she asked.

"I had this dream last night," I said. "There was this guy all dressed in black and he had a white circle on his chest, like Superman or somebody, or else like a telephone, only it was a man. And he kept creeping around outside the house, sniffing the windows. Then he turned into a cat and something else started happening, I can't remember. But could this guy find out where we live? I mean, could he find out where you are and, and I don't know, *look* for you or anything?" I glanced up from my plate, taking in the two of them warily, trying to see in their faces whether there was a dangerous heart of the matter.

"Most certainly not," my mother said immediately. "That's ridiculous."

"Yuck, Harriet," Ann said. "You've got creepy dreams. You are what you dream," she said solemnly. "I read that in a comic book ad. They say you can change all that if you put your mind to it. They say if you try to dream about lots of people all the time, you'll be popular."

"I don't care if I'm popular."

"Yeah, and that's why you just dream about one creepy man."

"Girls, now," said my father, a warning, his fork pointing between us, upside down. "Harriet," he said finally, pointing his fork at me, "statistics show that these guys don't want to get involved. They just call. They get their kicks just calling people. That man in your dream doesn't bear out the statistics."

"But he was *there*, outside the windows."

"It was a dream, honey. Dreams don't count. We're talking reality here. Statistics in reality."

"Then statistics don't know what they're talking about. Dreams are real. They are, they're real, too."

"Can't really argue with that," he said, smiling at me. "Ah, Harriet," he said and sighed and smiled again, pulling his fork back toward himself.

"So what does he say, Mom?" Ann asked, putting her chin in her hand, staring at her as avidly as if our mother had some great sixth-grade gossip. "Tell me some of his obscene stuff."

"Well," she said. "Well, hmm."

"Barb," said my father, drawing the word out.

"I *know*," she said and looked at him, then back at us. "He says, he says he wants to date me."

"God, is that all? Why don't you just say no? Tell him to jump in the river. Tell him to get lost. God."

"Ann," she said, "don't be so irritable. If I could get rid of him that easily, he wouldn't be an obscene caller."

"Well, it all sounds so boring. I mean, it'd be different if he said he'd kill you or something. It'd be a better story."

"Don't be silly. This is a little more important than that. Lord. You tell any of your friends about this, and *I'll* kill *you*, Ann. This is strictly a family affair. You understand? I mean it, tell no one."

"Sure," she said. "It's too boring to tell anybody." She began to eat little pieces of her meat and corn. "I just wish something really exciting would happen every once in a while."

"I don't," I said.

"Me either," said my father.

"Me three," my mother said.

We all went back to eating. The light from the late-afternoon sun shone down through the windows, the orange and yellow of it muted over the table, all of our forks poised in midair at the same moment, and shining a little, like we were eating the sunshine. It was a good moment, whole and clean and full of radiance, the kind of moment that made us a family, that made things calm, kept things in place. In the distance I heard the 6:15 Southern coming down the tracks, clicking. And it seemed to me just then, all of a sudden, that I was hearing it for the first time in my life—the old Southern on its tracks, making a wise sound, its hushed, soothing movement a voice that kept saying: *be still, be still, be still.*

For seven more weeks the calls kept coming. Whenever Ann or I answered the phone, he'd hang up after a long pause, a pause that scared me to death with the thought that he might say something to me, something obscene, even though I wasn't married. He never talked to the two of us, though, and never called when my father was at home. After a while it seemed he'd become a part of our mother's week, like grocery shopping or *Upstairs, Downstairs,* a show she watched every Sunday for a while. He wasn't consistent in his calls, except for the fact that my father was never home from work when he did it, and the fact that he did it every week. My mother got so she simply hung up as soon as she'd figured out who it was. That was that. We had an obscene phone caller the way other people had mice. Even my own strange dreams about him stopped coming. He'd been scary to me only when he'd been an unknown; now that he was regular, I relaxed myself, because I understood that no real opponent was regular. Real opponents came from nowhere. My father had taught me that.

What happened, finally, was a little unusual. One day it so happened my father came home early from work, about two in the afternoon, just a half day off was all. He did that sometimes, whenever he got through with his route early and there wasn't much going on at the company. So when the obscene phone caller called that day, he was home, sitting in the living room, in fact, where the phone was. I was there, too. My mother answered it. She stood there for a few seconds, listening, then she made a little motioning gesture with her hand, as though she wanted my father to come over and take the phone. Instead of that she put her hand over the mouthpiece and whispered, "It's a pay phone."

As I've said before, adults almost never used the pay phones in my hometown. It was foolish, and especially foolish for the obscene phone caller, because there were only four of them, spread around town within a two-minute drive of each other, which is exactly what my father was thinking when he said to my mother, "Keep talking to him." He ran into the kitchen, grabbed the car keys, then went running outside with me right behind him. I was elated, frenzied really, and hadn't even tied my sneakers. When I got in the car my father looked at me in confusion, as if I'd appeared out of thin air.

"You stay."

"I'm going," I said.

"Don't argue, Harriet. Get out."

"I'm going."

I went. I believe he let me go because he couldn't bear the thought of my mother listening to obscenities while he argued with me in the driveway—or at least that's what I counted on in refusing to stay. We whirled gravel getting out of the driveway, did sixty down the residential streets, the houses blurring by like things in a movie. I held my head out the window, lapped at the wind. No one was using the first pay phone, but at the second one, as my father said, bingo.

"Get a pencil and paper out of the glove compartment, Harriet. Take down the license plate."

"Do you know him? Dad, do you know who this guy is?" He was a dark-headed, burly man, and even though his back was to us, you could tell he probably had a big stomach. The car was a dark green Pontiac, an old one that had primer painted on it in different places.

"Nope. Just take down the number," he said and I did. After that we raced by the other pay phones, just to make sure —nobody was in them—and then went home, my father driving like a maniac. All he wanted to do was get home and let my mother off the phone. I could see that.

"So what are you going to do?" I asked on that mad dash

home. "Will you call the police? Will you find out who the license belongs to? What'll happen now?"

"I'm going to get your mother to read him his license plate and tell him not to call anymore. That ought to do it."

"Oh," I said, because it seemed anticlimactic somehow, or too simple. But when we got home my mother, looking drugged and worn out, hung up as soon as she saw us come in the living room.

"God," she said. "If you all hadn't come when you did, I was just about to have to make a date with the old bastard. He was in seventh heaven, talking so long. God. So who is it?"

"Next time," said my father and handed her the piece of paper, "just read this to him. It's his license plate."

"But who is it?"

"I don't know, don't want to. Some guy. I didn't recognize him."

"I just wish I knew who it was. It gives me the creeps, him out there like that."

"Forget it, Barb. Ignorance is bliss."

"Yeah, but only when you don't know you're ignorant."

"Just read him the number, honey," he said, then he went over and hugged her, held her close, patting around on her, and I noticed the phone then for some reason, hanging on the wall above them like a distorted face.

The unusual thing is that I found the green Pontiac the next day. I was just walking around the neighborhood, doing nothing as hard as I could, which was what I mostly did right after school. I had my bookbag across my shoulder, letting it thump between my shoulder blades at every step. I was on the street down from my own, walking along, and then I looked up and saw the Pontiac turn into the drive right in front of me. The man was inside, the same man. It struck me as incredible good luck that after all that time, here he was, right in my own neighborhood. He could even see the back windows of our house from his own back windows, if he could get an angle on the trees in between. As soon as that thought came to me I felt a chill, then moved behind a tree so he couldn't see me when he got out of his car. At first, seeing the Pontiac, my only thought had been to run fast to my house and, after I'd caught my breath, nonchalantly tell my mother the exact whereabouts of the obscene phone caller. That he could see us, had been watching us, watching my mother, soured my enthusiasm. My mother didn't need to know that; *I* didn't need to know that.

From behind the tree I watched him get out of the car. I'd been right—he had a big belly—but he was not an ugly man, just normal-looking. After he stood up from the car, he turned and held out his hand and a little blond boy took it, climbing over the seat on his knees. The two of them walked with their hands together up the sidewalk and stood on the front porch while the man fiddled one-handed with his keys. Everything was normal-looking. It reminded me of the way I'd seen my own home not long before, a place where bad things happened in the middle of everything looking nice as pie. Everything looked so normal I couldn't find my breath, started panting hard, my cheek against the tree trunk. That's when I decided once and for all that I wouldn't tell my mother or my father or anybody else. I decided I'd handle the situation myself, would leave him a note, so he would never have to call my mother again, for whatever sad reason he was calling her. And what he'd been doing seemed to me at the time to be the saddest thing in the world. I got a pencil and paper out of my bookbag and wrote a note. I said, "Dear Sir: Do not call my mother anymore. It scares her. She is a married woman. She will never date you." Then I signed my name. I folded it in two, left it on his porch, rang the bell, then ran home, feeling the bookbag pound against my back, feeling the new secret grow inside me like a fist.

I believe there is a fist inside everybody. I don't mean anger or violence, although everybody has those, too. The fist I'm thinking about is more like honor or integrity—honesty about yourself, maybe—except those are words whose meanings can change from one moment to the next and what I'm thinking about does not. Or else it isn't as grand as all that. It has to do with knowing how much or how little you're willing to do in a given situation, knowing where you stand. The fist is a sort of knowledge you accumulate about yourself, how far you'll go and why, how good or bad you can be, a kind of internal map, something you get from living your life, not thinking about living it. You could spend all your life getting different glimpses of your fist and still have to discover it all over again in a brand-new situation. I glimpsed mine the year my father first went to Elmhaven, and with the obscene caller, and again that year I turned fifteen. When you are young you constantly surprise yourself, like somebody charting new territory without a map, the fist just a vague, pushy feeling you have about things. When you are older, if you're sane, you tend to avoid those surprising new circumstances, to avoid encounters with the fist, though possibilities are everywhere, and unpredictable. Frankly, it's no fun, understanding that fist.

When I left the phone booth after talking to my father I felt the fist, like a new organ, heavy above my stomach. It had come to me, while I was talking to him, that the first thing

I should do was tell my mother everything, have her call Pete, advise him, warn him, whatever. My father was acting crazy, as crazy as he had right before he ended up back at Elmhaven, not catatonic but active, moving-around crazy. It was only fair to involve my mother and Ann and Pete, sound the alarms, admit I'd made a mistake in calling him at all. That was what I should have done and I knew it. I knew that. But I couldn't. I saw my father surrounded by grim sheriff's deputies beside Pete's pool, the way he'd been taken in not six months before from our own front yard, red lights flashing, neighbors looking from windows, my father's face as gray and taut as clay, and I felt the fist and I couldn't do it. And I was thinking, too, that between wherever he was and wherever we were going, he might get better. There were always possibilities. Maybe the next friend he stayed with would talk him out of it, calm him down, bring him back to a place he couldn't get to by himself. Maybe he'd see for himself the wrongheaded direction he was taking and quit it. Maybe his car would break down, the storms would hold him up, the stars would shift, the wind would change. Or else maybe I wanted Pete and my mother and Ann and me to have to face him in upstate New York, and I just didn't know it.

Outside the lobby, the heat of the night felt like a comforter laid down over the world, hot and stifling and all wrong for the middle of May. I squinted my eyes past the parking lot, past the interstate, trying to see mountains in the distance. The interstate was full of headlights going in both directions, people going somewhere all unknown to me and doing it at eleven o'clock at night, a tired time of the night. Down in a little depression past the interstate I could see the lights of Mount Olive, yellow and glimmering as if from exhaustion, but beyond that was nothing—a blackness that

could as easily have been mountains or desert or the edge of
the world. It depressed me, that there wasn't a thing to see
but a parking lot and interstate and a little town I would never
know anybody in, or even look at up close. The world seemed
small and bound up and unpromising, which I knew even
then is not a thing you're supposed to feel when you're young.
I knew Ann didn't feel that way, or my mother, or Pete—but
my father did. My father did, absolutely.

I walked across the parking lot toward the pool, noticing
how the utility lights reflected off the pool and made strange,
flickering white designs on the side of the Holiday Inn. For
a minute I stared at the side of the building, almost expecting
the designs to form into words, a secret message that would
say, *Don't do it,* or *Do it,* or *Wait see.* After that I looked at
the pool. Ann wasn't in it, which was a shock. I went up to
the very edge and looked down, but she wasn't down there
either.

"Ann?" I called out, staring around the pool area. I saw
some movement in the shadows around there, and it was
Ann, standing up from something.

"Harriet," she said, giggling a little, her hair slick and
wet. "I didn't see you come back." Behind her was a lawn
chair with some older guy in it, wearing shorts. It didn't take
much to figure out there was only one lawn chair, and if Ann
had been sitting down, there was just one place she could
have done it.

"Who's that?" I asked.

"Oh," she said, "just some guy named Alan." Then,
whispering, she said, "He's in *college,*" as if that were a palace
somewhere. She still had the bathing suit on, I was glad to see,
although her bathing suit was about as much as nothing at all.

"Alan," she said, turning back to the guy in the shorts, "this is my sister, Harriet. Say something, Harriet."

"Let's go. It's already been more than forty-five minutes. Mom won't like it."

"See," she said and kept looking at the guy named Alan. "I told you she doesn't like to have fun. Old Harriet. She's backward."

"Come on, Ann. Let's go."

"Wait a minute," said Alan. He didn't stand up, just stretched his legs further out from the lawn chair, then clasped his hands behind his neck like some sort of big shot. "It's only eleven. Early. What's the rush?"

"Yeah," Ann said, smiling back at him. "What's the rush, Harriet?"

"I got a joint. Why don't we hang out and smoke a joint?"

"But she's thirteen," I said stupidly. "Ann's thirteen."

"Shit, man, I was eleven when I did it first. Relax there, Harriet. You look old enough, anyway."

"She's fifteen," Ann said, as though that might settle the matter then and there. "Please, Harriet. Just this once. No-body'll know. Please?" I looked from Ann's pleading, child-adult face over to Alan, whose face, it seemed to me, showed what a complete idiot he was. He had a dark tan and light hair, even on his legs. He had wispy blond sideburns, a few wispy blond hairs on his chin, and even in the shadows, I saw eyes as washed out and vacant as mineral water.

"Where do you go to college?" I asked for no good reason.

"James Madison," he said, looking happy about it and crossing his feet. "Third-oldest college in America."

"You're a complete idiot," I said, because I felt bad and felt like telling the truth for a change. "Let's go, Ann."

"Harriet!" she said.

"Hey," he said. "Who the fuck are you anyway?" He sat up in his chair.

"I'll never forget this," said Ann, pulling her arms across herself. "I'll never forget this for the rest of my life. You jerk, Harriet. You backward fuckwad *asshole!*" She kept looking from Alan to me and back again, hoping her anger would change things, would get her what she wanted, but I already knew she'd resigned herself. Whenever Ann cursed, it meant she'd given up all hope of getting what she wanted, or changing anybody's mind.

"Let's get going," I told her. "You know this is all wrong, Ann. I know you do."

"Huh!" She let her arms go loose, then went marching toward the Holiday Inn in a huff. I followed her. Behind us I heard Alan making noises in his washed-out way, muttering and cursing like a fool, which of course is what I thought he was.

Outside the door of our room she turned around with a serious face and asked me whether I'd tell our mother. Would I tell on her? Over her wet head, down the corridor, I could see a man trying to get into his room, but he was drunk, kept getting the key in the hole all wrong, staggering around in front of his door with the key held out in front of him. The carpet outside the rooms was green and maroon plaid, too, just like the lobby. It was a confusion of color that made you drunk just looking at it, and I felt sorry for the guy, staggering around in that crazy place.

"So," Ann said. "So are you going to tell her or what?"

"I ought to. I ought to tell her. You're a maniac, that's what you are."

"But will you? Will you? Harriet, I'm not kidding. Don't tell her."

"God, Ann. Why do you do these things? The guy was really a jerk. I'm serious, really a total jerk."

"He was OK. He didn't mean anything. Are you going to tell?"

"No," I said. "No, I won't tell." She already knew I wouldn't, because her expression never changed. She knew me; I'd never told on her before. "But you are a maniac," I said. "You've got to stop that, Ann. It's bad news."

"Oh, grow up, Harriet," she said and smiled, meaning she liked me again. "*You're* the one who's a maniac. It runs in the family or something." Then she put the key into the door and we went inside, where our mother was still in the bathtub, where all was forgiven and happy and just right, and all of that true mostly because everything was still a secret.

VI

It was eleven in the morning and about 95 degrees in the parking lot before the three of us finally got out to the Volkswagen with our bags. We'd eaten lavishly in the Holiday Inn restaurant—what our mother kept calling brunch but looked like breakfast to me—and we were all stuffed and sweating and irritable before we even got into the car. Ann kept begging to go swimming, our mother kept saying no, both of them going at it through breakfast and while we packed and even until we were sitting in the car ready to go. I didn't see

Alan around; he probably lived near the motel and hung around its pool at night, aiming to get exactly what he might have gotten last night, but thankfully hadn't. When we pulled out of the parking lot, Ann couldn't contain herself anymore.

"Did you see him, Harriet? Was he around the pool? Oh, I wish I could have gone swimming just one more time."

"Who's he?" my mother asked, putting the car into second. Ann sat in the front seat, twisting her neck at weird angles, trying to see the swimming pool from her window one last time.

"Some guy," she said absently.

"Nobody said anything about guys last night. What is this, Harriet?"

"We met this guy last night," I said. "At the swimming pool."

"So why didn't anybody tell me? I thought you two were gone a long time. What about this *some guy*?"

"He goes to college," Ann said reverently. "James Madison. A very old college."

"That's a good school," my mother said and surprised me. She hadn't gone to college and until that moment I hadn't thought she knew anything about it. "He's probably an intelligent boy."

"He was a jerk," I said.

"Harriet was the jerk, Mom. We were just sitting around talking and everything, and then all of a sudden she says it's time to go in. Just like that. I was having a very good time."

"You're a maniac, Ann, and he was a jerk."

"Now, Harriet. A boy like that, I don't mind so much. You could have come in and told me you wanted to stay a while and talk. I want you-all to have fun on this trip. I might even have come out and talked a while with you myself. I'm interested in young people's views."

"Boy," I said, looking between their seats at the interstate hoving in upon us like a streaming gray sea, cars whizzing toward us and away on the other side of the divider. "Boy oh boy."

"He said he liked my bathing suit. Mom, could you make me another for New York? I want a green and white one next time. This one keeps turning too dark when it gets wet."

"I dunno. Maybe Pete'll buy you a new one. Wouldn't you like that better, a store bathing suit?"

"I guess so. And Harriet, too, Harriet needs a new suit," she said, turning in her seat, smiling, a reward for keeping my mouth shut about Alan. She hadn't meant it about my being a jerk. That had been for effect, to keep the secret secret.

"I like the one I've got," I said.

"You would. Jeez, Harriet, it's got brown spots everywhere, like you wet your pants all over it."

"Uggh. I wish you wouldn't say things like that, Ann," my mother said. "It's disgusting." She pulled her visor down, as if to shut out the image of my bathing suit.

"Mom?" I said, because a thought came to me. "Seriously, what did happen to the money from the house? I just wondered."

"Not that it's any of your business," she said and looked at me in the rearview mirror.

"Well, well it is, sort of. I mean, what with all this talk of Pete buying store bathing suits and everything. I just wondered." I tried to make my voice indifferent, tried to imply that she could answer or not, that it wasn't a big deal. Except it was.

"Pete invested it," Ann said.

"How do you know that?"

"How do you know that?" my mother repeated.

"He told me he was going to," Ann said and shrugged. "On the phone one night when he was calling you. I talked to him for a while before I went and got you. I was telling him about how much cheerleading outfits cost—you know, how you always complained and said we didn't have the money and blah blah blah—and he said I didn't have to worry, I could have a dozen outfits, and I asked why, and he said because we'd all make a tidy profit when he invested the money from our house. That's all."

"Mom, is that true? Did he take all the money and invest it? Jesus, does he know what he's doing? He in*vested* it?"

"Pete knows what he's doing, Harriet. He's a very successful man. He's a cardiologist, for heaven's sake."

"But how do you know? God, what if he's lying? What if he's not what you think he is?"

"Because I know, that's why," she said through her teeth. "And one damn thing's for sure, he shouldn't have told Ann. I knew you'd go crazy about it. I even talked it over with him—'Don't tell Harriet,' I told him—because you can be one big pain in the ass. You're very willful, if you want to know the truth. I'm not saying that's bad, I'm just saying it can be a pain in the ass. You're just, just . . ." She paused, passing a car at seventy miles an hour, thinking it over. "You're just too *old*, Harriet. Though how you wouldn't be after this family, I don't know. Sometimes I wish we'd been more normal for you, honey. I really do." She turned around a little in her seat, giving me a sad smile.

"I didn't want anything different," I said. "You better look at the road." She turned back around. "Dad could use some money. It just seems like some of that money is Dad's.

All of it, really, except for the divorce happening and every-thing. He paid for the house and all."

"Bull*shit*," she said.

"Hey," Ann said and bobbed her head. "Hey now."

"That's bullshit," she said, angrily. "That's complete and total bullshit. I earned every bit of that house. I earned it." She turned around in her seat again, the car veering, her face distorted by so many bad thoughts and anger—ugly anger—I pushed my spine hard against the backseat. I was afraid of her, looking like that. "I goddamned *earned* it!" she yelled.

You might think from what I've already told that I sided with my father through the divorce, or that somehow I was on his side more than on my mother's. That is not true. It's just that the person he'd been those months before he was taken back to Elmhaven wasn't my father; no connection between the two is how I saw it, although my mother didn't, couldn't, for which I didn't blame her. She had had the worst of it those long weeks he'd walked around the house a lunatic.

As I've said before, I started paying attention to him after the night he slapped my mother's face. That night the two of them had simply gone back to bed. "A nightmare," my father kept saying, "I must of been dreaming and didn't know what I was doing," and though I believed that, I paid attention from then on. At first it was little things. He'd joke around with her, say stuff like "That Matt Powell has a nice ass for a man, Barb, don't you think?" And my mother would snort and say, "Yeah, Matt's a real tight-ass," and then that would satisfy him for a while. Later he'd do it again, always some man around town, something about the way he looked and how did my mother like it. Just joking was all, it seemed. At some point it got more serious. Nights were the worst— which made sense when you consider that that was the time of day he figured had ruined him to begin with—and at night he quit pretending to joke around.

"What do you think of Boyd?" he asked her in their bed one night when I was listening as hard as I could. I had taken to half-crouching in my bed, listening. But my mother groaned, told him just go to sleep.

"Do you think Boyd's a good-looking man?"

"No," she said.

"Do you, though? Think he's good-looking?"

"Damn it," she said, irritably, sleepily. "To tell you the truth, I can't right now remember what Boyd looks like."

"You do," he said. "I can tell you do."

"OK, I do."

"Remember what he looks like or think he's good-looking?"

"Oh shit, both, all of the above. Can we sleep or not?"

"God, have you slept with him? Is it him then? Fucking Boyd. I'll kill the lousy bastard."

"Are you out of your mind? I never thought twice about him. Boyd? I can't believe you. He's got a *boyfriend*, for heaven's sake. Everybody in town knows that."

"Oh," he said, and I could tell by the silence he was calming himself down. "Oh."

"What are you looking at me like that for? No, come on. I don't want to do that right now. Stop. Stop now. I don't want—" After that I put a pillow over my head and didn't hear any more.

It went on like that for a while, nothing really crazy but

nothing good either. One night my mother got fed up with it, grabbed her pillow, and slept on the couch in the living room. She slept there a couple of nights, then they had a fight and then they made up and then she slept in the bedroom for a while. Nothing too upsetting, just regular family life it seemed to me, although I was worried. I saw signs everywhere, the way my father looked, the circles under his eyes, the squint, the way he'd make his hand into a fist just watching TV or sitting at dinner. He even began to start in with it in front of Ann and me—not joking, but serious, or else starting out joking around and then getting serious.

"Girls," he said at lunch one Sunday, "I believe your mother's dating the obscene phone caller." He looked at us and winked.

Ann laughed. "Sure. Mom and Mr. Pervert. The perfect couple. Whatever happened about that guy anyway?"

"He just quit calling," my mother said. "Strange, too, because I never read him his license plate number."

"Probably got hold of another hot number," Ann said and snickered. "He's probably calling married grandmothers now."

"I'm not sure I like your tone. Harriet, I wish you'd eat the skins. I don't know why I go to all the trouble of frying it when you turn right around and pick all the skins off like that."

"I just like the chicken part."

"Girls," my father said, interrupting in a strange voice, "I believe your mother is having an affair. What are we going to do about that?" He looked over at us expectantly, as though he'd proposed we all go for a walk by the river.

"Ha," Ann said. "Who'd have an affair with Mom?"

"No, she's not," I said quickly, because I knew he was serious.

"No, I'm not," she said and looked at my father, shocked. She put her fork down.

"Oh yes, I think so," he said, smiling at Ann and me, not looking at her.

"That's crazy, Dad," Ann said, her face puckered with concentration. She was considering the point. "No way," she said finally. "She never goes anywhere."

"Of all the sick ideas," said my mother. "Of all the sick, mean things to say." She stood up in front of her plate. "And in front of the kids, too. You've lost it. You've completely and totally lost it." There was water in her eyes, a film of it, like plastic. She went around the table and headed down the hall, toward the bathroom.

"What do you think, Harriet?" my father asked me pleasantly. "What do you think of your mother having an affair?"

"You're wrong, Dad. It's wrong, what you're doing. It's just really no good. It's all wrong."

"Yeah," Ann said. "It's embarrassing."

"What do you two know?" he asked, not pleasant any longer, but bitter and resigned. "You're just children. You don't know anything." Then he stared out the window into the trees, his hands in fists.

The next week after that, on a Sunday, everything happened. "Escalated" is the word for it, though we weren't going up or down, just haywire. The week before my father had taken to stopping by the house in his meter reader's truck —a bright red truck that had an insignia on its side, a picture of an eagle with electrical wires in its claws, which of course would kill a bird if it were real and that was a thought that made me dislike the thing—the truck with my father in it stopping by in the morning, or the early afternoon, or both, before Ann and I got back from school. It drove my mother crazy; I heard her complain on the phone to her sister. My aunt wanted him committed again, but my mother kept saying no, it wasn't that bad yet, he wasn't harming her, he wasn't harming himself, the kids would go to pieces, though I wouldn't have and would have been glad to avoid what came next.

On that Sunday something snapped like a wire in my father. Whatever bad dream he was creating out of his life suddenly became unbearable to him. He was fixing a window in the living room with a hammer he'd gotten out of the toolbox in the back of his truck. My mother was roaming around the house, dusting things, picking things up, doing what she always did on Sundays. Ann was in the backyard, practicing frantic cartwheels and backflips, and I was leaning against an armrest of the living room couch, reading a book, my feet pushed underneath one of the cushions. I heard my father make a noise, like a sob, which sounded strange and awful after all the pounding he'd been doing against the windowframe. I don't know, it frightened me, that sound of something terribly human coming after the sound of metal against wood.

"I can't *stand* it," he said, gasping, the hammer hanging by his side. Then he looked right at me on the couch, his eyes squinted up, dissatisfied, as though I were a picture that needed straightening.

"Dad?" I took my feet out from under the cushions. "Daddy?"

"Fuck it," he said. "Just fuck it." He patted the hammer against his palm a couple of times and then, as if he'd remember something, he walked out of the living room. I followed him, kept saying, "Dad? Dad? Dad?" First he poked his head into his bedroom, then into the bathroom, all the time patting the hammer into his palm. Eventually I followed him to the kitchen, where my mother was finishing up some dishes. With the hammer still patting away he walked up to within a foot of her back and stood there, not saying a word, and I could see his elbows moving from the weight of the hammer. From the back his hair was very short and in the kitchen sunlight almost white, as short and white as the ends of fingernails, like a criminal's haircut.

It may seem odd, what my mother did next, although you have to experience a crazy situation yourself to know whether an action like that is odd or not. Trouble has a tendency to suck the oddness out of things, when you're in the middle of it. What my mother did was nothing at all. Absolutely nothing. She acted like he wasn't behind her, wasn't doing anything with the hammer, wasn't in the room period. She finished the dishes, wiping her hands on a dish towel, taking her time, the way she did everything on Sundays. After a while she draped the dish towel over the counter to dry. Everything normal, like always. She turned and stepped across the kitchen into the den and my father followed her, both their expressions distracted, lost in their own thoughts, my mother because she always looked that way doing housework, which she hated (though there was more to it this time), and my father because he was being a lunatic, which he couldn't help. I had to squeeze against a wall to let them go by, the sound of the hammer like a drumbeat syncopating their steps. In the den my mother started picking up things, newspapers, sneakers, plates, the flotsam of a family room. He stayed right behind her, about a foot away. Nobody said anything, unless the sound of the hammer was somebody saying something. We walked around the whole house like that, my mother in front, my father following, and me keeping my distance, watching the whole thing like a show on the TV. Finally my mother picked up a throw rug from the bathroom, took it outside onto the back porch, the two of us behind her one after the other, and she began to shake it over the railing with all her strength. Dust floated everywhere over the yard, the wind grabbing it up and taking it like a dark swarm of insects over the grass. We all watched it. Every time my mother cracked the rug, my father hit the hammer onto his hand. After the third or fourth time he was hitting his palm so hard I thought maybe he'd break something, one of the little bones in your hand he had told me would break so easily if you hit somebody in the head. "Hit them in the chest," he'd said, "if you know what's good for you." Then all of a sudden my mother wasn't cracking the rug anymore. She was looking at him, her face pulled together, the skin stretched tight, so that what you noticed most on her face was her nose, her aristocratic nose. She said, and she said it just as if she wanted him to mow the yard or trim the bushes, she said, "I want a divorce from you." And it was a terribly wrong, frightening time for her to say something like that. It seemed to me at that moment they had both of them gone insane.

"Hey, everybody," Ann shouted, twenty yards away from us. "Watch this." She did a somersault that turned into a cartwheel and a backflip. "What about that?" she shouted, her long hair twisted around her sweaty, smiling face. "Hey, what about that? Am I amazing or what?"

"I'll kill you," my father said, his teeth gritted so hard together it sounded weirdly like "Ah kee-yoo-oo," the exact sound of the mourning doves we had in one of our back trees. "I'll kill you." He raised the hammer and brought it down heavily, all his dreamy certainty of the bad things around him smashing with a thud onto the porch railing, which shuddered and then fell over with a sigh, all in one piece, one second there, the next down in the grass three feet below our shoes. "You bitch!" he yelled, bringing his teeth loose from each other now. "You fucking-fuck of a bitch!"

I remember this: I watched the hammer. If he had raised it then turned toward my mother, I would have grabbed his arm and put all the weight of my left knee into the back of his right kidney, a technique my father had taught me, among other things. The truth is, the man before me at that moment was not my father; he was somebody my father had prepared me for, an opponent, somebody all the boxing and fighting lessons, somebody all the throwing of balls, and jumping higher and higher, all the reading of books and sprinting around like a maniac, somebody all of that had prepared me to restrain: an opponent. I watched the hammer. It did not occur to me then, as it does now, that what he'd been preparing me for was himself, himself in some sort of deranged state, violent and implacable. But I don't believe that. I don't believe it for a minute, frankly. What he'd been preparing me for, when he was the father I recognized, was me, myself, me finding myself in a position of trouble and having to know where I stood, who my opponents were and where they stood, what I was capable of, how far I would be willing to go and for what good reasons—in the end, the fist within us all, the thing you don't find out until you actually might have to do it. I watched the hammer. I realized right then, the three of us standing on our back porch together, the dust settling on the grass like a shadow, like a rug—I realized with no feelings at all that I would try to kill that man, the man with the hammer, if he raised it the wrong way toward my mother.

He didn't, though; didn't raise it again, I mean. I watched, kept watching, but he didn't raise it. I was grateful, the way anybody in trouble is grateful when sheer luck lets them slide by the worse possibilities that there are. I was grateful but I don't think I was feeling a thing else. He went down the porch steps and over to his truck, which was parked by the side of the house, then he leaned against the back of it, the hammer pressing flat onto the toolbox in the bed. For a while he didn't move or say anything; it looked like he was ready for the police to come right then, and check him for weapons.

"Harriet," my mother whispered to me while we watched him, "run over to the neighbors and have them call the sheriff. I don't want you going inside. He might come inside. If you can, motion for Ann to come away from the yard. But have them call first. Go on." She said it all so calmly it came to me that she wasn't feeling anything either, not a thing, that the only person feeling anything at that moment was my father.

I ran immediately to Mrs. Nelson's house. She was a widow who lived across the street and every summer gave all the kids in the neighborhood Kool-Aid ices and for whom I felt a certain affection, because she was decent and nice to us all. I didn't go to Mr. Jackson or Mr. Greene because I didn't want them to discover any heroism in themselves, which might result in hurting going on in the backyard. I pounded on her door. She answered it holding a plucked chicken by the legs.

"Mrs. Nelson," I said, and was breathless. I stood for a few seconds, panting, looking at the yellow skin of the chicken. "Would you please call the sheriff and tell him to come to my house? Would you do it right now, please?"

"Burglars?" she asked, alarmed. She looked ready to

slam and bolt the door, her brown eyes pushing out of their sockets. Her greatest fear in life was that somebody with a gun would come to her house and steal her grandmother's china, the only objects of worth she owned, and she kept a derringer under her pillow, a thing she showed us sometimes while we sucked on the Kool-Aid ices.

"No, it's Daddy," I told her. "It's just Dad and Mom having a fight. Mom told me I ought to get help. Please would you call?"

"All right." She turned away, relief softening the lines of her face, the chicken's yellow neck sticking like a finger to the side of her dress. I ran back down to the house. My mother was still standing on the back porch, though now she held Ann by the shoulders, the two of them staring up into the big poplar in the backyard. My father was climbing it.

If you are familiar with poplar trees, at least the common ones in East Tennessee, you know they are mostly worthless things, grow fast, die young, and in between they are susceptible to a hundred different diseases. They aren't climbing trees, the branches too small, the purchases too skinny. But here was my father climbing ours. It swayed from his weight. He was about fifteen feet up, the hammer still in one hand, using his arms around the trunk to heave himself up. It must have hurt because his arms were bare, though I don't think that was a thing anywhere near on his mind.

"He's very athletic," Ann said and there was admiration in her tone. My mother and I looked at her. "Well, he *is*," she said.

"Is he coming?" my mother asked me finally.

"Yes," I said. "Yes, he is."

"Doesn't look like it to me," said Ann. "Looks to me like he's going all the way to the top."

"The sheriff, I meant," my mother said, looking worried. "I meant the sheriff, is he coming?"

"Yes," I said.

"What's wrong with climbing a tree?" Ann wanted to know.

We watched until he was as high as he could get without having the top snap down on him, about forty or forty-five feet. Behind him the mountains lay seductively against the sky, an undulating green darkness that seemed amazingly solid compared to the white-dotted light blue above it, my father swaying a little in front of everything. In the end it was a sight as lovely as it was unlikely and scary—a grown man doing an almost impossible thing, a dangerous, insane thing, with a view impossibly beautiful behind him. There was something exhilarating about the extremeness involved in it all. And I thought, *What* is *wrong with climbing a tree, after all?* But then I remembered that the man with the hammer was not my father, not right then anyway, and the vision soured and went bad in front of my eyes.

"Barbara," he yelled out, his voice high and thin from the top of the poplar. "Barb!" He'd gripped the trunk of the tree with his legs, and was holding the hammer above his head with one hand, the other hand palm out. "You rotten—" he cried out, and had to grab the tree trunk with his free hand to right himself. "You rotten filthy rotten cunt of a *bitch*!"

"Wow," Ann said and my mother said, "Hush." She still had Ann by the shoulders, threading her fingers through her hair, pulling them through the cartwheeled tangles like a comb. "You two just hush for a while now."

"Barbara," my father yelled, his voice muffled, "Baw-bawah!" He had his mouth around a finger on his left hand, the ring finger as it turned out, his other hand, the one with the hammer, gripping the tree now. Finally he got the ring off, held it in his teeth till his fingers could pull it out and he could hold it up over his head like the hammer—a plain gold band, nothing fancy, the kind of wedding ring men who don't like jewelry but like being married wear. I'd never paid attention to it before then. "Here it is, Barbara." He held it out to her like fishbait, leaning away from the poplar, farther into the greening silhouette of the mountains. The ring didn't glint in the sun or anything, didn't flash gold or shine out against the limbs of the tree or reflect the light of something meaningful, the way you'd hope it would in that situation; I just knew it was there because he'd so clearly taken it off. "Here it is, you bitch, you, you bitch of a cheating bitch. Barbara!" he cried, and I think he was crying. "Barbara!"

"Oh," my mother said, and she was definitely crying. She was feeling something then, that's a fact. "Oh, when will they get here?"

"Don't cry, Mom," Ann said, rubbing her shoulders. "They'll come get him down. They've got trucks with machines and everything. They'll get him down. Don't worry. I saw them get a cat out of a taller tree than this. It'll be OK. He won't be stuck up there forever."

"Oh," said my mother and cried harder, her shoulders rattling under Ann's arm.

"Jeez," Ann said, looking at me, rolling her eyes, although I could tell she was scared. "You'd think it was the end of the world. They will get him down, won't they, Harriet? I mean, is he stuck up there or what? What's going on?"

I didn't say anything. And what was there to say? That he, our father, was out of his mind. That when he came down, if he didn't jump and kill himself, the sheriff and the deputies would take him away. That our lives would be changed forever when he came down, already had been, and that the beautiful sight of our athletic father against the mountains was only the beginning of an ugly, wretched mess. I didn't say anything, just looked at my father high in the poplar. He'd pressed his wedding ring against the trunk of the tree and had begun hammering it in. He kept hammering madly until it was, I guess, a small gold circle embedded in the wood, like an eye, the eye of whatever storm was going on in his mind.

They came when he was on his way down, two patrol cars, the sheriff himself in one of them, two deputies in the other. They all knew my father and were as polite and wary as they could be. After they got out of their cars they all walked over to the tree, the handcuffs and keys and things attached to their belts clicking against each other. But the meanness seemed to have gone out of my father. He went with them without doing or saying anything. There were cuts up and down his arms, bleeding, and he held himself in a way I'd never seen before, a loose, bent-over way, as though his spine had aged as soon as he got down from the tree. He looked like a very old man, or else like a man used to being a prisoner in custody, none of which is what he was. My mother talked with the sheriff for a few minutes while the two deputies hung around my father, looking intensely embarrassed, embarrassed and alert, too. The sheriff kept nodding toward my mother and looking out of the corner of his eye at the hammer my father still held in his hand. He was taking notes on a spiral pad.

"Daddy?" Ann said, coming down from the porch. She went down into the space of yard in front of the deputies and our father. "Daddy, watch." Then, from a standing position, she did a backflip, landed upright, and then did a cartwheel and a front flip, all of them perfect. Our father watched without any expression at all, unless having no expression at all is itself an expression, and it is. "Daddy?" Ann asked, anxiety making her out of breath.

"That's *good,*" one of the deputies said vehemently, a guy with freckles all over him and red hair that showed on his arms and under his hat. He was a young guy. "Did you see her do that, Buddy?" he asked the other deputy. Right then the sheriff snapped his notebook shut, nodded to the deputies, then all four of them quickly headed toward the patrol cars.

"I'll kill her," my father told one of the deputies quietly, the one named Buddy, though my father didn't look like he would or could, and the deputy took the hammer out of his hand. "I'll break her fucking head in two."

"Aw," said Buddy, who was another young guy; he had a black mustache. The freckled one stood behind him, staring at Ann with admiration. "You wouldn't want to do that." He opened the car door and put my father into the backseat, behind a sort of cage. "You just need some rest is all." He said it kindly, shutting the door, and it struck me that he probably played softball in the city league with my father, though I didn't know who he was then, and now never will.

"I'll call you about the, the—" The sheriff stood beside his car, staring at my mother, stumped by something, scratching the hair under his hat with his fingers. I noticed he had a ring on his hand. "The arrangements," he said at last, seeming grim about everything. Then he got into his car.

The last I saw of my father, he was staring intently into his lap behind the squares of a cage, looking doomed and ruined and altogether changed. I saw him then in profile, a man—my father—who'd always taught me that opponents are invisible and incredibly strong and who'd turned out to be right in the end, because there's no defense or preparation possible when a crucial part of yourself goes wrong and out of control in your life. Around the neighborhood I saw people standing still on their porch steps, wondering what the fuss was. Across the street and up the hill I saw Mrs. Nelson standing at her door, her face behind the screen as yellow as the chicken she'd have for supper, her eyes watching the patrol cars leave, the derringer probably in her hand at that moment. I thought about the ring my father had hammered into the poplar, about what it might mean, though at the time I couldn't guess. It was a ring, just a ring in the wrong place. And so far as I know it's still there, a lump in the smooth line of the trunk, buried golden and deep where the tree has healed itself of the damage—nothing more than a knot in a sickly tree, in a normal East Tennessee neighborhood, swaying whenever the wind blows.

VII

We drove all that day, mostly in silence. Ann had the college boy from James Madison on her mind, my mother had God knows what on her mind, and I was thinking about my father, which made me tired, sick and tired of everything. We drove with the windows down because the air conditioning had suddenly begun to smell like gasoline, but the day became so hot the breeze through the windows seemed to whisk the air from our lungs, as if we were bellows over a fire. It was like that through Virginia and West Virginia and Maryland and into Pennsylvania, where finally we parked at a rest stop to put water on our heads. My mother believed in the curative powers of water against heat. When Ann and I had been younger, she'd line us up in the front yard on a hot day and water us down with the garden hose, spraying it back and forth mechanically, as though we were a driveway. She'd read somewhere that children are more likely to suffer heat stroke than adults, and from then on she'd hosed us down regularly in the summer, whether we felt hot or not.

"I'm not getting my hair wet," Ann said when she got out of the car. "You-all can do what you want, but I'm not going to look like a bluegill for the rest of the day."

"If you get heat stroke," said my mother, "your eyes'll bug out and your face'll turn red and it won't be a pretty sight. I'd take wet hair myself."

" 'I'm NRA and I vote,' " Ann said, reading a bumper sticker.

"It's clouding up fast," I said, because it was. Over the interstate a big whirl of black clouds was moving in from the west, the little silver clouds in front of it scuttling along quickly, like salmon up a river. It was about five in the afternoon, time for the storms. "Where are we exactly?" I asked my mother.

" 'If you can read this you're too damn close,' " Ann said, reading another bumper sticker. "Jeez," she said, "who are these people?"

"Just south of Harrisburg, wherever that is." My mother was standing at the drinking fountain, cupping her hands and pouring the water onto the back of her neck. Most of it went down behind the collar of her T-shirt and turned her spine a dark blue, so that she looked healthy and vigorous, like someone who'd been running a long distance. Ann and I stood behind her, staring across her at the parking lot.

"I think we should stop here for a while," I told her. "This storm, it looks like a bad one. Look at those clouds. Killer clouds is what they look like."

"Yeah," Ann said. "Wow. They look like the clouds they show before *Shock Theatre*—horror, nightmare, evil lurks in the night. Notorious." She lost interest and stared out at the parking lot. " 'I'm a virgin,' " she said, reading, " 'But this is a very old bumper sticker.' " She looked at me. "Jeez, who thinks these things up?"

"Who buys them is the question. Like you said."

"No kidding," she told me, rolling her eyes up. "I bet obscene phone callers do," she said and laughed a little, then watched a big, earnest woman herd two kids into a station wagon, smacking their butts as they went along. The station wagon had a pasteboard CAUTION: CHILDREN sign in the back window, a tired-looking man behind the wheel. "Bumper sticker zombies, vampires, the walking dead. *Theatre X* on wheels. We're talking *Shock Theatre* here. Frankenstein."

"Maybe we could make it to Harrisburg," said our mother, patting water onto her face. "I don't want to hang around here for hours. What do you think, Harriet? I'm not that tired."

"We *can't* stay here." Ann turned toward our mother, began rubbing her hands together frantically. "We've got to get to a hotel. I mean, this is a stupid place to hang out in. There's nobody here. And I'm hungry. Mom? Don't stop here. It's stupid. Mom? It's, it's an *eyesore.* Mom?"

"Oh, Ann," she said and wiped her face with the back of her hand.

"But Mom, Ann, just look at them," I said, pointing my arm in the direction of the clouds. The three of us looked at them. Ann had been right, they looked horrifying, monstrous, black at the heart of them all, brown at the edges, white on the very tip, moving in fast across half the sky. The wind had picked up, but it wasn't a cool breeze, just hot and

217

stifling and risky feeling. Even the color of the air had turned as yellow as a yield sign over the parking lot and the interstate and all the rest of the world that we could see.

"Lord," my mother said. Some people came out of the rest rooms and stood beside us, looking, then some other people at picnic tables came over, and we all stood there like a bunch of cattle, huddling together underneath the eaves of the rest stop, wondering what would come next. There was a middle-aged man with a fat stomach beside us, and his middle-aged wife. His wife had on a hat that had fruit sticking out of it, grapes, tiny apples, even a miniature banana. Next to those people were two young couples, one of them with a five-year-old wearing thick glasses who had a fake machine gun he kept pointing at everybody, the other one with a baby in a faded pink bassinet, the mother holding it awkwardly in her arms. At the other end of the rest stop was another group, but I couldn't see what they looked like; I was busy looking where everybody else was looking.

"God Almighty," said the baby's father. "Would you get a load of that."

"Russ, Russ," his wife said in a whiny voice, a voice that sounded like she'd had some practice sounding that way. She had a pointed nose and hair the color of pondwater and her front teeth stuck out a little, as if she'd been working her tongue against them for most of her life. "Russ, honey, is it safe?"

"Safe where?" he asked absently, staring at the storm in front of him.

"Let's go, Mom," Ann said and pulled on our mother's arm. "Let's get out of here."

"I wouldn't do that, young lady," said the man with the fat stomach, his face stern, and you couldn't tell whether he meant pull on a mother's arm or leave a rest stop before a storm.

"If you can read this you're too damn close," Ann muttered, cutting her eyes at him irritably. He looked startled and the fruit shook on his wife's hat. "Mom, please, we can't stay here. If we wait for the storm, we'll be here *forever*. Please?"

But it was too late for that. The storm came within seconds, first the wind and then the rain. There were tiny maple trees planted around the rest stop, scattered here and there like posts in a crazy fence, and they bent sideways, pointing toward Philadelphia, toward England even; the wind seemed that strong. The woman with the hat put her hand on top of it; two of the trash cans along the parking lot fell over, broke their chains, and went spinning off across the blacktop, making a racket, garbage flying out everywhere. All of us moved back a few yards, into the shelter of the gray concrete blocks of the rest rooms.

"Russ!" cried the woman with the baby, her voice high and piercing against the dull bawl of the wind. "Russ!"

"God Almighty," he said and didn't look at her. I glanced at him, then. He was a good-looking guy, skinny with a face like a rough woman's, and I could tell he'd bolt and leave everybody if he got scared enough, and right then he looked scared to death. His wife knew that, too, kept calling his name and shoving the baby toward him. Then the rain came, drops as big and fast as fists, wetting everything in sight in a matter of seconds. It sounded like hail, it hit things so hard, except I could tell that nothing was shattering, which is what you'd expect from hail.

"Maybe we should look for a ditch," I said to my mother.

"Oh, Harriet," she said, but before she could tell me not to be silly, not to panic, whatever it was she was going to say, the rain stopped abruptly and the tornado appeared on the horizon. What I remember is that everything was still yellow. Beyond Ann's yellow head was air the same color, almost like summer squash. The tornado bounced around in that yellow air, huge beyond all understanding, tree trunks twisting around inside it, and other things, too—I thought I saw a vehicle, a red one, flash by thirty yards high, half a mile away, rotating inside the tornado—dust heaving up in great waves whenever it touched down, the interstate full of kiddie cars compared to the immensity of the thing, the whole world pivoting and focusing around that incredible piece of wind.

Things happen. Anything can happen. Couples divorce, grown men go crazy for no reason, children carry pretend automatic weapons, people get murdered for no good reason, a person loves somebody who can't in a million years love the same way back, and tornadoes touch down in full view of rest stops in Pennsylvania. These things happen. The lucky turn of events is that they don't usually happen to you, and that is what keeps all of us halfway sane. But sometimes these things do happen to you, a couple of them at once sometimes. And then you have to make do as well as you're able. The tornado sucked around the Pennsylvania soil like an anteater, pausing in midair, then pouncing down, biting into the earth with a vengeance. Every time it hit the ground a lot of multicolored stuff went up into the air, flickering in the middle of that yellow landscape, churning and flickering and hurtling all over the place. I don't know what to say about it. It happened.

Unlike animals, people can be smart or they can also be very stupid. We were huddled together against the cinder blocks of the rest stop, out of the wind, watching the tornado come down and go up and then come down again, all of us a bunch of dumb clucks waiting for the worst to happen and not going anywhere, just happy to be surrounded by other people in trouble, hypnotized by the tornado lunging imposs-ibly into our lives, too fascinated to be afraid, or else too afraid to be smart. We were idiots. We didn't move. Then it was over: The tornado skipped across the interstate two hun-dred yards from the rest stop and headed away from us, bouncing away so quickly it was soon the size of a hornet's nest, and then finally it just wasn't there anymore.

"Wait till Pete hears about this!" Ann cried. She was ecstatic from the excitement of it all, her cheeks pink with the feeling; maybe it was shock, but I think it was ecstasy, as though she'd witnessed the best football game of her cheer-leading life. "I bet nobody up there in their whole junior high has seen anything like this."

The woman with the fruit on her head had an arm around the woman with the bassinet, the two of them looking at the baby's pink head and weeping sadly over it, like some tragedy had killed it, except it was only asleep, had slept through the whole thing. Their husbands were so gray-faced and rigid they looked close to being cardiac cases. They didn't make a sound, kept staring at the place on the horizon where the tornado had disappeared, as if it might come back any minute. The only sound was the rat-tat-tatting from the kid's machine gun—he'd been shooting at the tornado ever since it came into sight, his face as grim as a mercenary's.

"Mom," I said. "Mom, are you all right?"

She wasn't, that was clear enough. She'd leaned herself against the concrete blocks and her face was flattened out, squashed somehow, the way people in hospital beds look. "Ann, go get a Coke can from the car and put some water in it. It's all over, Mom. It's OK now." When Ann came back with the water, my mother took the can and held it in both hands, sipping. She didn't look young and beautiful anymore. She looked old. One sure way of looking older is to drink with both hands, that and see a tornado come straight at you. "Maybe you should lie down or something," I told her, but she just smiled at me, a smiley smile that didn't mean anything.

"I was thinking of Aunt Lois, you know?" she said. "I was thinking about what she said to me one time. You remember Aunt Lois?"

"Yes," I said. Aunt Lois was my mother's aunt, my great-aunt, and she was dead and gone and, so far as I knew, had never seen a tornado.

"About three years before she died, I was thinking about. She got this lump on her neck and for a long time she wouldn't go to the doctor. She hated doctors. Said they'd as soon kill you as look at you. But this lump kept growing real fast. It was unbelievable how fast it grew. It was the size of a softball by the time we got her to go to the doctor. She went finally, of course, because she got scared enough. It was an ugly, ugly thing, flopping around on her neck. Uggh. The doctor didn't know what to make of it, sent her right to the hospital and that was the last place she wanted to go. She didn't want to die in a hospital."

"Me neither," Ann said. "I don't want to die, period."

"Shut up, Ann," I said, leaning against the blocks beside my mother, afraid she might faint or run crazy across the parking lot of the rest stop. It seemed like silly talk, shock talk, what she was talking. "Just be quiet for a minute, Ann."

"I'll talk if I want to. I can talk if I want to. I don't see why everybody has to be so grouchy with *me* all of a sudden." She turned to the kid with the machine gun. "Stop shooting that thing, you," she told him. "You're making me crazy." The kid stared at her for a second, then pointed his gun and shot her, his brown eyes the size of figs behind his glasses.

"Harriet, though," my mother said, "this is the thing. They took her to the hospital and operated and you know what it was? It's unbelievable. You'd think it was a tumor. We all thought it was a tumor, the whole family. You know what it was? God. It was maggots. Even the surgeon looked shocked. A fly had laid eggs in the side of her neck and her neck was full of maggots. Can you believe that? Maggots. The size of a softball. The surgeon said all he did was put the scalpel against her neck and then it all came out. Uggh. But the thing is, I visited her in the hospital afterward and she said, all she said was 'Barbara, a fly almost killed me. I'll be goddamned if something the size of a fly will kill me.' Then she got cancer and died."

"What do you mean?" I asked. "What is it you mean?"

"I mean," she said, smiling that nothing smile, "I mean that a tornado wouldn't be a bad way to go. At least it's bigger than a fly. At least it's not cancer."

"Yuck, Mom," said Ann. "Gross City. Morbid City."

"Let's get out of here," I said. "Let's find a place to stay. I'll drive."

"I can drive," my mother said.

"I'll drive," I said and, for once, I wanted to. The Volkswagen didn't seem dangerous to me right then, didn't seem like as big a deathtrap as the rest of the world had suddenly become. My mother shrugged, the corners of her lips still tucked up at the edges, then she turned to me with that strange look on her face, an expression not smiling so much as puzzled, as though she couldn't at that moment recognize me to be somebody she'd always known.

"Harriet," she said and she said it just as if she were naming me for the first time. "Harriet," she repeated vaguely, "you take the keys."

We were near Carlisle, on the way to Harrisburg, and I wanted to find a motel as soon as I could. The first place we saw off the interstate, a Best Western two miles up from the rest stop, had a lot of ambulances in front, the roof of it gone somewhere, swallowed up inside the tornado. One bedroom on the upper floor didn't have a wall anymore, but inside it the furniture and lamps stood untouched, perfectly normal, ready for somebody to come in and lie down and watch TV. It wasn't a view you see every day. Just north of Carlisle we found a Holiday Inn, a replica of the one in Virginia, and it looked all right, no ambulances, a roof, everything you'd expect. I pulled in there. The whole time my mother had sat in the seat beside me with her eyes closed, napping I guessed, getting the shock out of her system. I could see the tiny network of veins on her temple, delicate and blue under skin as fragile as tissue paper. Seeing that made me think about how quickly and easily people die, how easy it is to kill somebody or be killed or get in a situation where one or the other is possible. A tornado, I thought, is a big thing and a hammer is a small thing and both can kill you. Things happen, like I said.

When we parked I got out with my mother's purse and went in to get our room so she wouldn't have to worry with it. The guy behind the desk was beside himself with a self-importance sprung from having survived a catastrophe while never being in real danger himself. He'd do the best he could for us, he said, though every car on the interstate had come

to that motel for a room after the storm hit. Had I heard?—
the town had been declared a national disaster area. He just
didn't know whether there was anything left, but he'd personally do his damnedest to find a room. He knew we must be
exhausted. We were very lucky, because if the *other* guy had
been behind the desk—and he wouldn't name names—we'd
be out on the street right now. Ah, yes, he said, here's one,
the last room, the very last room in the place, just one double
bed but, what the hey, it's a room. Then he charged us
twenty-five dollars more than the room in Virginia had cost.

"Thanks," I said when he gave me the key, and I meant
it. When I went out to the parking lot, Ann came around the
side of the building and met me at the car.

"There's all this crap floating in the pool," she said, a
disgusted look on her face. "It's like you can't even see the
water."

"What?" I asked, but I wasn't really listening to her. Our
mother was still slumped in the front seat, her mouth open
a little, her bottom teeth showing white and even in the
shadows of the car.

"Crap," Ann said. "Floating crap. All over the swimming pool. Dirt and leaves and oil and stuff. Crap."

Her window was open so I went over, shook her arm.
"Mom, wake up. We're at the motel." She opened her eyes,
squinting down on my hand. I realized I was still shaking her
and quit it.

"All right," she said, blinking.

"Mom," said Ann. "You can't swim in the pool here.
What are we going to do?"

"Well," she said and grimaced sleepily. "We survived, I
reckon."

"Ann would survive anything," I said. "I've got the key

to the room. Let's go inside. You could lie down on the bed in there. We'll get you something to eat, if you're hungry. I know I am."

"I don't feel very well. I've got to call Pete. I've got to— We've got to— Something."

"Let's just go inside," I told her and after Ann and I got the bags, we did. Inside the lobby, though, my mother insisted on calling Pete. I wanted her to wait until she'd had something to eat, but she said no, he'd be worried, you-all go on up to the room, so Ann and I took the bags to the room.

"We've come down in the world," Ann said once we got inside. "Somebody's going to have to sleep on the floor," she said, meaning it certainly wasn't going to be her.

"I'll sleep on the floor. I'd rather sleep on the floor anyway."

"How come you didn't get two beds?"

"We got the last room in the place, the guy said."

"Then how come I saw two people check in when we came into the lobby?"

"I don't know. God, I don't know." All of a sudden I felt dizzy, as if the world had begun to spin too quickly and I could see it happening. I sat down on the bed, lay back, my feet dangling over the carpet.

"Rip-off artists," Ann said, trying to be nice. "And their pool's a toilet bowl. At least we don't live here, Harriet. At least this isn't where we live."

"We don't even know where we live," I said. "We don't even know that."

"Yes, we do. Upstate New York. Fulton, New York. That's where we live." She sat down on the end of the bed, started brushing her hair, the ends crackling with electricity and standing out from her neck, fluffy and yellow-white, like thick corn silk, the color of the air around a tornado. "Dr. Peter Carlisle's house in New York is where we live."

"Yeah. Wherever."

"Pete'll be all excited. Maybe he'll be worried, maybe he'll insist on driving down to bring us home. Wouldn't that be something? It'll be romantic and everything."

"Nothing happened, though. Nobody worries all that much when nothing actually happens to you."

"Oh, you don't know people. You don't know lovers." Ann put the brush down beside her, ran her fingers through her hair until it had stopped crackling, lifting it away from her neck, patting it. "I bet you they talk for an hour at least. I bet you."

"OK," I said. Ten minutes later Ann was in the shower with a cap on and my mother came into the room, tired out, pale, shivering a little, although the air conditioning of the Holiday Inn barely made the heat outside feel normal enough to live in anyway. It was too hot outside even for air conditioning to beat back the bad feelings, too hot for a tornado to do it for that matter. My mother was shivering.

Ever since she'd met Pete my mother had been well, as well as could be expected given her life and our lives, but right after my father left with the deputies—and until she met Pete, about two or three months later—she had not been well. Nothing serious, just not well. I'd wake up in the night and hear her gasping for air. It was like asthma or something, except the doctor said it was anxiety that made her do it, made her sit up in the bed and not be able to breathe. All you had to do was make sure she drank some water, the doctor said, and that's what I did. As soon as she sipped some water from the cup, everything turned out all right; she could breathe again. It got to be routine. I'd wake up at night, hear her gasping and snorting at the air above her bed, her night-gown heaving under the covers, and then I'd come in and give her some water. Sometimes she didn't even know I'd been in there with the cup, didn't know until I told her the next day at breakfast. After a while I didn't tell her anymore. I could tell it made her more anxious, to know about all that. I didn't sleep well for those months. I didn't like Pete, but I liked my mother being well again, which is what she was by then because of him. The good and the bad mixed up is what it was, or at least that's what I felt at the time. But when she came into the motel room she looked ill again, the same way —anxiety made her breath come out in fast, short puffs. As I've said, nothing serious, but nothing good either.

"Did you get hold of Pete?" I asked her. "Why don't you lie down? Why don't I get you some supper?"

"Uggh," she said and fell down on the bed like a statue. I was standing up by this time.

"Do you want anything? What do you want?"

"You know what I want?" she said, not asking a question. She lay where she'd fallen, staring up at me. I was over by the dresser, next to the bathroom door, and behind me was a mirror that made the room seem bigger than it really was. "I'll tell you what I want. I want to be your age again. I want to be fifteen. That's what I want."

"I wouldn't. It's not that great. It sucks."

"Oh, Harriet. It's a terrible thing. Isn't it? A terrible thing. What do *you* want? Tell me the truth. At this moment what do you want?"

I watched her face, thinking. I could tell her about my father, about how he was following us up the coast, as disturbed as a dust devil, how he wanted to kill her or Pete or somebody, anybody, and how I didn't want him to. I could tell her that I wanted her to look better, to look well, not old but beautiful, the way she ought to look, could look, but didn't, lying there on the Holiday Inn bed. I could tell her that I wanted Ann to stop being a half-wit and get serious about a few things, to stop looking at swimming pools with crap on top and recognize the awfulness of a tornado when she saw one. I could have told her I loved her. But I didn't. I did not. I said, "I want to be your age. I want to be your age and as far away from all of this as I can get. That's what *I* want."

"It's terrible," she said and I said, "It sure is." We just looked around the room after that. In a while she sat up on the bed.

"Pete couldn't talk. He had to go to the hospital. Some kind of bypass surgery or something." She snorted. "Some kind of bypass is right. He was all caught up in his own world. I say 'tornado' and he says 'heart.' I don't know, he was in a hurry. I don't know."

"He's probably saving a life," I said.

"Yes, he probably is." She sighed, then leaned back on the bed, stretching her arms out behind her, looking sick and anxious and as if it were her own life that needed saving, which I think now was just exactly the truth.

VIII

Around six that night we went down to the motel restaurant to eat something and to be around people, instead of ordering through room service. For once both my mother and Ann agreed on the need to socialize, my mother because she was scared and felt better around other people, Ann because the more, the merrier. There were plenty of people in the restaurant, looking haggard and about as merry as pallbearers, milling around a buffet set up in the middle of the room. Some kind of manager was going around from table to table, looking concerned and sensitive, and saying, "Eat up now, folks, all you can eat. All you can eat. All you can eat." He wasn't the guy from behind the desk in the lobby, but he was the same type of guy—happy as a clam about the disaster and making the most of it. They charged everybody ten bucks for the buffet and it was leftovers from the day before: pasta shells in tomato sauce, the pasta hard and brown at the edges; wilted lettuce and spinach salad; macaroni and cheese that had a skin on top as thick as a lizard's back; brown fruit salad, brown avocados and cheese, brown everything.

"Yuck," Ann said when we sat down at a table. "They must think people come out of tornadoes changed into morons. I can't eat this. Harriet, can you eat this? Mom, can you? I'd rather eat the stuff on top of the pool." She leaned back in her chair, sulking, staring around the room with a hateful look.

"I could eat anything right now," I said and ate some avocado.

"Well, that's what this is," she said. "Anything. They're probably laughing like crazy back in the kitchen, eating lobster and ice cream."

The manager-type guy finally made his way to our table and said, "Eat up, ladies, all you can eat." He had a tiny mustache below his nose that looked like he'd watercolored it on and he was acting like a Red Cross volunteer. "All you can eat," he repeated, beaming down on us.

"This is all crap," Ann said, "and you're a jerk."

"Ann," I said and smiled a little.

"Ann," said my mother and she didn't smile.

"Eat as much as you want," the man said as though he hadn't heard, then he went beaming off to the next table.

"I don't want to hear you say anything like that again," my mother whispered fiercely across the table. "Things are bad enough without you being rude and ill-mannered and, and *shitty*." She had her fork poised over some salad and she stuck it so hard onto a pile of lettuce, the plate rang out like a bell. Ann sat up in her seat.

"I'm sorry," she said and looked surprised. "God, Mom, I'm sorry." Ann glanced at me, but I shrugged. Our mother was on edge, upset, and there was nothing I could do about it. She'd just told me she wanted to be fifteen, which, it seemed to me, was an upset thing to want to be. I finished my plate of food. Our mother went to get some fruit.

"Is she all right? I mean, she's acting funny or something."

"She's scared," I said. "The tornado scared her. Everything's all up in the air and then this happens. You'd be scared, too, if you were her. Think about it, Ann, for heaven's sake."

"I really am sorry." She meant she was sorry our mother was upset, not that she was sorry about what she'd said, I could tell that.

"I know," I said, "forget it. I know you are." She looked unhappy, a look I suddenly realized I didn't like on Ann. "Caution: children," I told her, holding my dinner knife out and making a machine gun sound, and she laughed.

"I could've strangled that little sucker," she said. "Kids. Guns. Kids and guns and tornadoes. It was unbelievable."

A man and woman were talking with my mother up at the buffet table, just nervous chitchat, then when they turned away they headed for our table. They were about my mother's age, thirties somewhere, dressed like people on vacation, jeans, open-necked shirts, though their faces didn't match with the relaxed appearance of everything. They'd seen the tornado somewhere, had been in it or had almost been in it like us, or else they'd just picked up on the atmosphere it left behind.

"Hey, there," the man said. "Your mother said we should come sit with you." He said it in a jolly way, a way I could see he was used to being, except all the excitement of the tornado had him forcing it a little. All I can say is he seemed to have led a jolly life. "Joe Merrimac," he said loudly, "and this is my wife, Anna." He pointed toward his wife as though we might not know who he was talking about. She had short brown hair and a kind face, a kind face that appeared to have been strained silly by her husband's jolliness. She was either going to leave her husband soon, I figured, or she was going to quit having a kind face. "You can call us Joe and Anna. Hey, no need to be formal after something like this."

"You can say that again," Ann said.

"We were in a gully during the whole thing. Passed right over us. Right, Anna? Sounded like a train or something. Right over us, it passed right over us." He stared at Ann, smiling a jolly smile.

"Close enough," Anna said and looked at the ceiling. The way she said it, she seemed to be contradicting him.

"Right over us," he said, a little uncertainly. Then he gave Ann a big grin, his face shining like an apple. "You don't look the worse for wear."

"Well," Ann said, "you know. It didn't kill me or any-thing."

"Ha!" he said. "Did you hear that, Anna? It didn't kill her. I like that. I like that attitude."

"It could've," I said, but nobody was listening. My mother came back with some sorry-looking cantaloupe and watermelon and grapes on her plate. "Mom," I said, "can I go buy a magazine in the lobby?"

"OK, we'll be here for a while." She sliced into some cantaloupe, squinted at it warily. "Do you need money?"

"Some change is all. I could use some change."

"Look in my purse."

Her purse was on the floor, next to Anna's feet, and when I got up and bent down, she bent down, too, her brown hair tufting all around her face. "We were nowhere near the tornado," Anna whispered in my ear. "We weren't even in a gully." She smiled at me and I smiled back, wondering what on earth possessed her to tell me a thing like that.

"Thanks," I said for some reason—maybe because a complete stranger simply telling the truth was a pleasant surprise, a good omen—then I got all the quarters out of my mother's change purse and stood up. "I'll be right back, Mom."

I'd been thinking. I'd decided I would call my father. The next day my mother and sister and I would be in New York, at Pete's house, where whatever was bound to happen would happen. If I could convince my father to go back to Elmhaven, I would; if I couldn't, that was that. I'd decided to leave the rest to the adults, let them sort it out, handle the situation, make fools of themselves if that was what adult thinking led to. My father would be going to upstate New York at that moment whether I knew about it or not, whether I liked it or not. I was fifteen, just one of their children and, really, no one special in the scheme of all that was happening, except I knew a few things I didn't want to know. My mother was feeling very weak, my father was being very weak and didn't know it, and Pete Carlisle, it seemed to me, had always been weak. I didn't want to feel responsible for them anymore, or figure out what the right thing to do would be, or try to make things work out when they would not and could not and maybe even should not. They'd just have to face each other, I thought, if events put them together. And in the end, what could I do? What could I have done? I could tell my mother about my father's mad dash up the east coast. She'd panic and call Pete, who would be too busy to worry about it, too busy with infirm hearts palpitating underneath his fingers like budding red roses. Then she'd simply have to go up there anyway, anxious as a cat, because where else was there for us to go? Nowhere. Who else would care about us? Nobody. There was nobody else and nowhere else but my family closing in on Fulton, New York. If there was a fist within us all, and I knew there was, mine had drawn back so far I couldn't feel it any longer. Something important had gone away from me. I felt tired to death of everything, as tired and overused and squeezed dry as a kitchen sponge, and what I'd been thinking for most of that afternoon after the tornado was: *Fuck it.*

The phone booth had a door in that Holiday Inn, one of those doors that accordion shut. I had trouble with it, couldn't get it to do the right thing, which was push out, then slide back in. Finally I kicked the bottom of it as hard as I could and all of a sudden it slid into place easily, like going to bed. After it shut so quickly, I kicked it again, just because I felt like it. I was feeling halfway crazy is the truth of the matter. I dialed the number my father had given me the night before, although this time the area code I called from was different from the area code I was calling to; I didn't know whether that was a good sign or a bad. I just listened to the phone ring, wherever it was, wishing I could bite into the receiver like a piece of licorice. I was still hungry from the ten-dollar buffet, for one thing; for another thing, there was the rest of it all.

A man with a liquidy voice answered it. He said, "What is it you want?" sounding suspicious and reluctant, sort of hiccuping in the middle of his words, as if he expected me to be a blackmailer, or an FBI agent, somebody no one wants to talk to on the phone.

"Hello?" I said. "Hello?"

"Oh," he said. "Sorry. Who's this?"

"My name's Harriet. My father said I should call here, he said he'd be there. Is he still there?"

"Harriet," he said. "Are you his daughter?"

"Yeah," I said.

"Listen, don't get me wrong. I don't want you to get me wrong."

"OK," I said. Frankly, the sound of his voice made you want to get him wrong. It was like tomatoes, soft and juicy.

"He's not here," he said. "He's at a motel."

"OK."

"Listen there, he's got a knife. He came over here and showed me it, a great big long one. He says he's going to use it. He says he's going to kill somebody" For a while he didn't say anything. I heard the wires crackling around next to my ear inside the phone booth. "He's not right," the man finally said, his fluid voice melting the words together. "He's just not right."

"Where are you?" I asked.

"I've got a wife and a baby to take care of. I can't handle

this. I'm not a well man. Did you hear that? I'm not a well man."

"OK."

"I had to tell him to go. He scared Priscilla out of her wits, coming in here with that knife. I don't know what he plans to do, but he's going to hurt somebody. He wasn't this bad at the hospital. He was an all right guy. But he can't stay here, not the way he is, not with my wife and baby."

"What motel?"

"I don't know, he just said he'd find a motel. He looked wild, like he'd been drinking all day. I'm not well enough to take in somebody like that."

"OK. What town is this?"

"Why, Allentown. Allentown, Pennsylvania. Hey, is your father a criminal? I didn't ask him much personal stuff in the hospital, but did he commit some crime?"

I hung up the phone, thinking, *So this is what it has come to.* Carrying knives, drinking, looking wild. He was a criminal in the eyes of the world. And all because he loved a woman in a crazy way. He'd go up to New York, something would happen, and he would be lost forever. I tried to picture him in some dingy motel, a place criminals went to and got caught in, but I could not picture it. Whatever place he was in, whatever madness gripped him was invisible to me, though I supposed I'd see it all the next day in New York. Tonight he was free, but the next day he probably wouldn't be, and it struck me for the first time that freedom could be an opponent like anything else, that even free, my father was a prisoner. He could no more move out of the place he was in than we could have moved out of the way of the tornado. I began to feel sorry for him, which scared me, because feeling sorry, I thought, was the beginning of not caring about him at all.

I went back to the restaurant and sat down at my place, staring at a rusty piece of avocado. The Merrimacs were still there. Joe Merrimac had edged his seat around closer to Ann.

"You didn't get a magazine," Ann said.

"All they had were those romance things."

"I'll bet *you* like those romance magazines," said Joe Merrimac, winking at Ann. He had a tuft of hair curling out over the top button of his shirt, and it moved whenever he said something.

"Sometimes," she said. "I don't like to read."

"You're a doer," he said. "I could tell it the minute I saw you. A doer."

"I'm a cheerleader." Ann scooted her chair sideways a little, as if being a cheerleader had suddenly made her irritated with him.

"Ha! A cheerleader. I knew it." He bobbed his head up and down. "Anna was a cheerleader in college, weren't you Anna?" He didn't look at his wife.

"I went to an all-girls school," Anna said. "We didn't have cheerleaders."

"There you go," Joe said. "Here in our very midst we have one of those rarest of breeds, a cheerleader." He lifted his glass of milk toward Ann. "Cheers."

"Quit it!" Ann yelled out, then she scooted her chair again, then all of a sudden Joe Merrimac stood up.

"Time to go," he said, pulling his wife's chair back. She wasn't prepared for it and nearly went sprawling on the floor.

"Joe!" she said, her hands holding on to the table.

"No harm, no foul," he told her. "Gotta get moving. Listen here, ladies. If you'd care to join us for a drink later tonight, I've got some Kentucky bourbon. Only cure in the world for tornadoes. We're in room forty-four. Come see us." He looked at Ann, then at my mother. "I don't know about you kids, but your mother could use a drink."

Everybody looked at my mother, and she looked awful.

"It's true," Anna said. "Barbara, come to our room. You could talk it out or something. Maybe it'll make you feel better, talking it out. And you really do look like you need a drink." She said it so kindly, and her face seemed so big-hearted and good, I could tell it made my mother feel better already.

"All right," she said. "Thank you. The truth is, I don't much feel like being alone tonight."

"Swell," Joe said, smacking his hands together, back to Mr. Jolly again. "Bring the kids. We'll get some soft drinks. Have a party. Dance until the wee hours."

"We'll talk," Anna said, then she got up, went around the table, touched my mother on the arm, and then the two Merrimacs left the restaurant.

"She's nice," my mother said. "They're a nice couple."

"Humph," Ann said, slumping low in her seat, which by now was so close to my mother's they seemed to be sitting on a bench together. "*She's* nice enough."

"I hope you girls don't mind. I just feel like being around adults right now. I don't think I could face that room by myself tonight. I really don't." Ann and I looked at each other. Our mother wasn't much given to crying, although she'd had plenty of opportunity, all things considered, but right then she was as close to it as we'd seen in a long time, at least since the divorce. "I wish Pete was here," she said.

"I don't mind going over," I said, and Ann made a hateful face at me. "Well, I don't," I told her.

"You wouldn't," Ann said. "Mom, you really need to sleep. I don't see how partying all night's going to help."

"I am not staying in that room tonight alone," my mother said fiercely, and that was that.

Around nine o'clock, after my mother showered and changed clothes, we went over to the Merrimacs' room. It was just like ours, except that Joe Merrimac was drunk in it. He hadn't gotten to the stumbling-around stage, was just jollier than ever, bustling around fixing drinks, talking nonstop. He'd put on a jacket of some kind, the kind suave people in movies wear. He looked like a bartender. I wondered whether he was jolly all the time because he was drunk all the time. There was no way of knowing. Anna Merrimac looked the same as she had in the restaurant, harried and kind, her hair soft all around her face. Pretty soon my mother and she were whispering together on the bed, and every once in a while Anna put an arm on my mother's shoulder. It was an odd sight, as though Anna were the mother in the room. For a while Joe tried to show us magic tricks, making a coin disappear and reappear behind Ann's ear or behind his own ear, but that was the only trick he knew, and besides, you could tell the coin was stuck between his fingers on the back of his hand. Maybe it was the drinking that spoiled it. We got bored with him, and it was clear that Ann didn't like him. After a time he got restless and dissatisfied and roamed out of the room. Anna made pallets for us around midnight. My mother wasn't through talking and Joe was still gone, so Ann and I went to sleep on the floor. It was like a slumber party, except it wasn't.

I woke up late that night, I don't know how late, just late. The room was dark but I turned my head to the left and could see my mother and Anna asleep on the bed. When I turned my head the other way, there was Joe. He was crouched on his knees beside Ann and had his hand up the back of her T-shirt, stroking her spine. The lump his hand made moved up and down her back like a shark in water. I sat up.

"What are you doing?" I asked. He jumped in the dark, pulled his hand back.

"She couldn't sleep," he said and his tongue lolled the words around. Then I smelled the bourbon come right after his voice. "She wanted me to rub her back."

I stared at Ann. She was fast asleep, her mouth open a little, her tongue resting against her teeth. She'd been asleep for a long time and she was like a puppy, sprawled on her stomach, her fingers twitching in the middle of a dream, her face as free of anxiety as a spaniel's.

"My father will kill you," I said. And I meant it at the time. Maybe it was sleepiness, or the shock of it all, but I meant it. It passed through my mind that my father had a knife. He was a criminal in the eyes of the world. He would kill him. "He'll slit your fucking throat," I said.

"Hey," said Joe. He put his hands in the air and reeled backward off his knees, squatting and swaying beside Ann. "I was trying to be nice. I'm a nice guy." He shook his head sadly, as if the world had never understood him.

"Get away," I said. "Get out of the room or I'll scream."

"Hey," he said, batting his hands. He stood up and stumbled toward the door. "I'm a nice guy." He opened the door, holding on to the doorknob. "I'm a nice guy. *Every* body knows that." Then he went out and was gone.

I stayed awake for the rest of the night, watching the

door. I fantasized for a while about my father killing Joe Merrimac, though I got tired of thinking along those lines. Every time I got to the part where my father lifted the knife, Joe Merrimac turned into somebody I'd never seen before, a stranger, somebody who might or might not deserve to be at the business end of a knife. At any rate, the fantasy gave me no pleasure. The world seemed too full of knives and craziness and tornadoes without having to pretend in your mind about it. I wondered who made pretend automatic weapons, whether they let their own kids use them, whether they were good or bad. You never knew, pretend could be a good thing, get it out of your system early. I pretended I was my mother's age, taking two kids to New York. I wore jeans and looked like I was fifteen, except I had two kids. We drove a solid, purring Mercedes-Benz, and whenever the two kids got irritable, I said, "Be calm, be calm, be calm." I said it like a priest, my hands raised up over the steering wheel: "Be calm," and then they were. On that trip, with my pretend kids and my pretend Mercedes-Benz, it wasn't spring, it was autumn, the air was cool, the leaves were colored—hushed and unmoving on their stems—and everything and everybody was calm.

IX

I slept in the backseat of the car most of the next day, didn't even get out of the car for lunch. My face sweated where it lay against the plastic upholstery. Occasionally I'd open my eyes and outside the side windows I'd see a blur of green, or a wash of gray concrete. Once I woke up in complete darkness, though when I lurched upright on the seat, it turned out to be the tunnel underneath some mountain, the end of it a small, white semicircle wavering like a spotlight between my mother's head and my sister's head. And I dreamed. They were complicated dreams; you had to be on your toes to remember them, and although I was always waking up and going back to sleep, the dreams kept connecting up, blending together into one long story:

I'm in the attic of a big house, a dim, musty-smelling place that has old books and old clothes and old magazines. Everything's old. I'm not safe, but I don't know why yet, so I decide to look out the window, find out where I am. Outside the glass a monstrous tornado bears down on the house as black and fast as a locomotive—pure evil it seems, pure, rotating evil. I find a door out of the attic where there wasn't one before, which seems like a lucky break. Through that door and down the stairs that come after it is a bedroom with my mother and father in it. I try to explain about the tornado, but I'm so scared what I say is gibberish. My voice sounds like a monkey's. They stare at me, puzzled looks on their faces. Finally I sound like myself again: *Run, run, run to the basement, it's a tornado!* I shout. They don't move at all, just stand there, side by side, puzzled. But I am no fool, even if they intend to be, so I run down the next flight of stairs. Somehow my mother beats me down there (I figure another door, another set of stairs have appeared for her when I wasn't looking), because now she stands in a different bedroom, with Pete this time, and he's standing by her side in exactly the way my father was standing, his big thighs separated by only a tiny chink of air. *Run*, I tell them, *it's coming!* They smile fake smiles, humoring me. It's obvious they don't plan to go anywhere. I get angry, so angry I want to shake them by the throats, then I forget to be angry because I'm going down a staircase. *There's a tornado coming, no time to waste,* is my thinking. *Fuck it,* I think. The next floor has another bedroom. This house has only ugly bedrooms everywhere; it's a house of bedrooms and whoever built it must have been crazy. This time my sister and Joe Merrimac are lying on a bed, my sister's hair splayed out on a pillow as if the wind had hold of it, which strikes me as funny, because of the tornado. I even laugh. The two of them look over at me and frown, their faces disapproving, as if I'd insulted them or something. I stop laughing, get incredibly embarrassed, even though the wind might kill us all any minute. *I'll get my wife to slit your fucking throat,* Joe Merrimac tells me, his hand in a fist on top of Ann's bare leg. Something happens then, I'm not sure what, except, abruptly, I'm not embarrassed anymore; I'm not even in the same place I was before. I'm on another staircase, a very clean, tidy staircase, no dust anywhere, a brand-new set of stairs. It's so different from the old attic and the other grubby staircases, I start to wonder about this place, I wonder about who built it, wonder why they built it this way. I wonder about myself. That's when I understand that there is no basement to run to in this crazy house. There are bedrooms and staircases forever. If I finally get to the safety of the basement, I'll be as dead as a doornail. Dead is at the bottom of it all. *Tornado,* I hear Ann say.

"Next thing you know," Ann said, "it'll be locusts and boils. God, Mom, it'll be floods and famine. Disease. The many faces of chaos."

"Have you been reading the Bible or what?" my mother asked. "I don't know where you get these things. Harriet reads. I can see her saying that stuff. Where do you get that stuff?"

"TV," she said. "That and comic books."

"You should improve yourself more. Read good books. I don't know, think about things. Frankly, you've got a very la-de-da attitude on everything."

"Well, I'm happy," Ann said, clicking the words like a threat. "I'm la-de-da happy."

"A good point," said my mother. She popped her hands against the top of the steering wheel. "A very good point."

"Where are we now?" I asked and sat up in the backseat. I put my hand to one cheek and felt a lot of little bumps all over it, from the upholstery. Half of me probably looked like it had the measles, and I felt sleepy and feverish from the heat, and it seemed to me as though I might as well really be sick, the way I felt. "Are we in New York?"

"The voice from the grave," Ann said, peering around the side of her seat. "Jeez, Harriet, you look like shit."

"I couldn't sleep last night. I feel like shit."

"I wish you all wouldn't say 'shit' all the time," my mother said. "You sound like white trash."

"*You* say it all the time," Ann said.

"But I'm not white trash."

"Neither am I, then," she said.

"Me neither," I said, wiping my face off. "I just feel like shit."

"Oh, Harriet," my mother said. She turned on the radio and some country and western music came over, sounding festive. "Yes, ma'am," she said happily, rippling her fingers on the steering wheel in time to the music. "We're in New York. We'll be at Pete's by six o'clock. I hope nobody has a heart attack between then and now."

"It must be disgusting," Ann said. "All those hearts and blood and guts laid open in front of you. It'd make me sick. I'd throw up right in their heart."

"It's like a car engine for them," I told her. "Like they're mechanics. You just substitute oil and carburetors for blood and guts. Mechanics."

"Probably they come home with blood under their fingers, instead of oil. It's disgusting." Ann leaned around the seat again, grinning, not disgusted at all. "Pete'll probably have Lava soap in the bathroom."

"Commercials," I said. "We'll do commercials."

"Yeah, the doctor's family at home. Dr. Carlisle, would you tell us what soap your family uses? Well Bill, we only use Lava—it really gets the guts out."

"That's enough, ladies," said our mother, pulling her lips down to keep from smiling. It made her face go stiff. "Until we get to Pete's, for the next two hours, I don't want to hear a word from you-all. I mean it, not another word."

For the rest of the trip we listened to country and western music.

Pete's neighborhood was brand new, and he lived in a one-story ranch house that looked like it had been built sometime the day before. The brick was as pink and fresh as a baby's cheek. All the trees around there were about four feet high; the yards had hay with yellow-green new grass shooting up between the brown stalks. The general impression you got was that any minute you could blink your eyes and the whole thing would turn into a vacant lot. I couldn't even see any birds around—no birds, no trees, and no mountains. It was the kind of place where nature had been uprooted and some people like Pete had to call it home. And, of course, I didn't like it. There were no rivers, no ducks, no huge maple trees to climb up and hide in, no brown water to stain your bathing suit, none of that, just an aboveground pool in back of the house with green water and a pump to keep it moving around. I wondered whether Pete ever fooled around with the pump the way he fooled around with hearts. You couldn't tell, I couldn't tell, looking at everything from the backseat of a Volkswagen on the left side of the house. All of it looked temporary. I didn't like that place one bit.

"It's ugly," I said. "It's like a science fiction movie or something."

"If you say that to Pete," my mother said, "I'll smack your face."

"Well," said Ann, "there really is a swimming pool. At least that turned out to be right. Seriously, Harriet, there are probably millions of kids of all ages around here. We'll meet a lot of people before we have to go to school."

"I don't want to meet a lot of people," I said.

"That's because you're backward," she said. She had her window rolled all the way down, staring out at the neighborhood, squinting her eyes to see as far as she could. "You're the one in a science fiction movie, not me."

"We're none of us in a science fiction movie," my mother said and opened the door of the car. "Where we are is *home.*"

Pete came out on the front porch right then. My mother's face—I can't forget it, not now, and I knew even then I wouldn't ever—my mother's face went haywire seeing him. Everything a face is capable of went crawling over my mother's features. She gave a whoop and set off running up toward him. Her jeans stretched, stretched to the ground, like pistons they seemed, and when she got up to him she threw herself into his shoulder. Pete staggered backward a few steps, smiling, patting her arms, looking dumbfounded. He'd been living in his brand-new ranch house, living life as usual all along. My mother hadn't. That was the difference right there.

"Isn't that nice?" Ann murmured, glancing at the two of them on the porch for a few seconds before the neighborhood lured her back to staring at it. "There must be thirty houses around here. And look, Harriet, almost all of them have swimming pools."

Pete and my mother walked down to the car, my mother's face wild and happy and turned toward Pete as though he might dissolve in the air before her eyes.

Pete hung his head in the window and said, "I hear you had quite a trip. But here you are, safe and sound." He gestured broadly, including the house and the pool and some of the neighborhood in the sweep of his arm. "Worst spring for storms ever on the east coast. Heard it on the TV news. But don't you two worry. Old Miss Lake Ontario takes care of us up here. She don't let the storms bother us. Until the winter, that is. Hold your breath in the winter."

"It was the size of a mountain," my mother said. "It came within a half mile of us."

"My oh my," he said and gave her shoulder a squeeze. "You lead a charmed life, honey, that's what it is. The charming leading a charmed life."

"I'm not that charmed. Charmed would be just watching it all on the TV news."

"Hey," he said, looking hurt. "I'd of come down and helped you drive. You know I would. How did I know it would turn out so bad? Right, girls?" he asked and turned to us. "Old Pete couldn't have known, could he?"

"Not unless you were God or somebody," Ann told him. It pleased him no end.

"And I'm not that, I'm most certainly not that. Hey, come look at the pool, Ann. You'll love it. You can swim any time you want to. It's *your* pool, baby." Ann got out of the car, stretching her arms, the down on her arms glinting yellow in the afternoon light. I watched the three of them walk around the side of the house toward the pool, but I stood by the car. I felt miles away from anything. Ann said something, then Pete laughed, throwing back his head, and then he put his arm around Ann and my mother. They looked like a happy family at home. I felt lost and adrift in that new neighborhood. Soon there would be people to meet, directions to get used to, Pete to talk to every day, a new school to go to, everything brand new the way the whole trip had been; it seemed to me that when my father finally came, whatever he did, I would be relieved.

He came at eight o'clock that night. Nobody had wanted to cook so we were eating TV dinners in the kitchen. Pete had a Hungry Man; the rest of us had regular. The inside of the house was as new as the outside. Some of the furniture even had plastic still on it, the price tags still attached, like a showroom. Ann and I had our own bedrooms, exactly alike in every detail, except hers was painted pink and mine was plum-colored. Even with the lights on in broad daylight, that room seemed to be in the middle of the night. And it was a huge house, bigger than it looked from the outside—there was a den, a family room, a library that didn't have any books in it, a study for Pete, an extra bedroom, four bathrooms, a living room the size of our house back in Tennessee. All in all, it cost a lot of money and couldn't have been any uglier, though it was obvious Pete had worked hard to get it ready.

It wasn't ugly in intention, I mean, just appearance. The kitchen had all the newest appliances, things I'd never seen before, all of it done up in red and white. Red and white tiles, checkered curtains, a red plastic table, white plastic chairs, red counters, white cabinets. You felt dizzy in there.

I sat at the table beside my mother, facing Ann and Pete, while we ate our TV dinners. My mother had explained that Ann had let the cat out of the bag about the money from the house—"Though why you told her, I can't imagine," my mother said, flirting—and Pete was telling me what a good deal it was. He told me how investments were the only way to go with money. Then he went into the details and began to make no sense. I thought about how my father had gone crazy working for the money to buy the house, and now here was Pete, doing something incomprehensible with it. His big fingers worked the fork quickly around his Hungry Man turkey, speeded up by his investment enthusiasm. The whole situation in that red and white kitchen seemed like some sort of lunatic dream.

Then all of a sudden Ann looked up and said, "Daddy." She didn't say it in a scared or happy or shocked way, just neutral, as if somebody had asked her, Who's that? and she was simply answering: "Daddy."

"Oh, my *God!*" my mother said loudly. "What the hell is *this?*"

"Hey, buddy," said Pete, putting his fork down. "What are you doing in here?"

I turned around in my seat to see him. Nobody had heard him come into the house, which was a miracle, because the way he looked was loud, was a shout. If he wasn't drunk, he might as well have been. There was no control around him anywhere, not even around the air that touched him, it seemed. And he looked so awful I wasn't sure, for a moment, whether it really was him. I remembered his hair cut short in bristles, almost orange, but now it was so long it covered his ears and it had darkened. I didn't remember what color his eyes had been, except right then they were brown, the color of water in puddles on streets. He had the knife, too. But it wasn't the knife I had pictured him killing Joe Merrimac with. That one had been long and sharp and so silver it hurt your eyes. The one he had was a rusty butcher knife, the kind of knife people keep in the back of their kitchen drawer and never use. There were food stains crusted on the front of his shirt. He looked like a criminal, but not like a very good one; even in that, being crazy had robbed him of something.

"I said," Pete said, "just what the hell are you doing in here?"

"It's all right, Pete," said my mother. She stood up and went to the middle of the room, squaring herself up between Pete and my father.

"What do you mean, it's all right? What's going on?"

"Who are you?" my father asked. "Barbara, what's this man doing here?"

"I live here," he said. "I *own* this place, for God's sake. Barbara? Barbara?" Pete had stood up, but he kept staring indiscriminately around the room, as though he were a guest in that house and wasn't sure any longer how to act.

"I'm going to have to kill you, Barb," my father said, squinting and glaring at her. He was out of his mind and that's a fact, except the strange thing was he looked young when he said it, like a little boy who'd been whipped.

"Right here in front of God and the kids and everybody? You don't want to do that." She looked at us, then at my father. "You don't want to do that."

"Yes, I do," he said quickly and lifted the knife up. "I really do."

"I'm calling the police, goddamn it!" Pete cried out.

"Don't leave me here, Pete," said my mother. "Honey, sweetie, don't leave me here with him."

"Shit if I'm staying," he said. "I'm calling the police right now," and he left the kitchen through the door behind him, his big legs pumping up and down as fast as they could go.

"Daddy," Ann said. Her face was the color of her hair. "Daddy."

"I have every right, every right." He was standing in the doorway between the kitchen and dining room, his eyes dark and casting around, his hips swaying a little against the jamb. "I'm going to stab you in the heart and I have every fucking right in the world."

All that happened next couldn't have been predicted, not if it happened to a hundred people a hundred times, which it wouldn't have. My mother stepped over to the stove, picked up a pan of water, then threw all of the water in it at my father as hard as she could. It hit him smack in the face and went over the front of his shirt, down his pants, across his knees, and onto his shoes. It wasn't hot water, just room temperature, but it changed everything then and there. Abruptly my father looked like just exactly what he was: a sick, ruined, helpless man, crouched awkwardly in a crazy red and white room, getting older and lonelier by the minute. He dropped the knife. Then he dropped himself down on the floor. He lay flat on his back and started crying—it sounded like "Hoo! Hoo! Hoo!" and he lay there, all weak, just crying like that.

"Dad," I said. I got out of my chair, went over to him. "Daddy," I said, bending myself down to him.

"Get away from him, Harriet," said my mother. She still stood with the pan in her hand, although now she was swaying, too. "Don't go near him."

"Shoot me, Harry," my father said and sobbed, and it was a grisly sound. "Shoot me in the head." I looked down at his rusty knife, wondering whether he thought it was a gun, whether he even knew where he was. There was water all over his face, all over his hair, and his face was so puckered, so gray, it seemed as though he were underwater.

"I told you not to come up here. Jesus, Daddy. Daddy, I told you not to come."

He clutched the front of my shirt like a drowning man. "Shoot me," he said. "Harry, honey. Harry, shoot me, shoot me." For some reason it reminded me of the ducks down home, the ones that dove into the water and held on to the weeds till the bad things around them had gone. I thought of my father as one of those ducks, someone who had been beautiful and powerful and part of a family and who was now helpless, half-dead, drowning through no real fault of his own. He couldn't help himself and neither, I realized for good and all, could I.

"Hold on, Dad," I told him and touched his hand, although that was the last thing in the world I wanted to do. "You just be calm," I said.

I never saw my father again. After the New York police came to take him away, I never saw him again. My mother divorced Pete within two years. Whatever it was he'd invested the money from our house in fell through, collapsed, went bad, whatever you want to call it. He wasn't a crook, though, just a dumb cluck and, in my opinion, a coward, which is why my mother divorced him and not because of the money. She just couldn't stand him anymore. But I had left home by the time all that happened.

In the end my mother married a car salesman in Long Beach, California, who made her happy and still does. My sister married a lawyer from New York City when she was seventeen, a cheerleader right out of high school; they have three kids. One of them, I happen to know, is not the lawyer's. I am not married. One night eight years ago I got a call from a man whose name I can't now recall. He said my father had died of a heart attack in Columbia, South Carolina. He went peacefully, the man said. I remember being relieved when I hung up the phone. He was safe. He was peaceful and had gotten there peacefully. I don't know what else there is you can ask for.

There are more storms at night than in daylight where I live, something to do with the Gulf Stream and temperatures. I lie in bed and listen to the wind howl, the shutters creak, the aluminum siding give under the gusting pressure. For some reason, when I think of the wind I think of my father. While the storm heaves itself against everything, I lie there and think about my father and my mother and my sister, but mostly about my father. My father, Dad, Daddy, whatever. A man. Those nights I can almost bring myself to the point that I am grateful, at peace with the way things have turned out, as at peace as he now is. Things happen. Anything can happen. Everything *can* happen.

When the storms come, when the winds rush in, I can almost bring myself to say his name.

ABOUT THE AUTHOR

Born in East Tennessee in 1957, Leigh Allison Wilson graduated from Williams College with a degree in English, and did graduate work in fiction writing at the University of Virginia under a Henry Hoyns Fellowship. She received an M.F.A. from the University of Iowa Writers' Workshop, where she was awarded a James Michener Fellowship. Her first collection of stories, *From the Bottom Up*, was the winner of the Flannery O'Connor Award for short fiction, and was published by the University of Georgia Press in 1983. Her stories have appeared in *Harper's*, *Grand Street*, and *The Southern Review*, among others. She lives in Oswego, New York, where she teaches and is Writer-in-Residence at the State University of New York.